OUTLAW

OUTLAW

Roy Glenn

URBAN BOOKS
www.urbanbooks.net

Urban Books
10 Brennan Place
Deer Park, NY 11729

ISBN-13: 978-1-893196-76-6
ISBN-10: 1-893196-76-3

First Printing February 2007
Printed in the United States of America

10 9 8 7 6 5 4 3 2 1

Submit Wholesale Orders to:
Kensington Publishing Corp.
C/O Penguin Group (USA) Inc.
Attention: Order Processing
405 Murray Hill Parkway
East Rutherford, NJ 07073-2316
Phone: 1-800-526-0275
Fax: 1-800-227-9604

CHAPTER 1

Mike Black

I ran out of a bar on White Plains Road with two armed men right on my ass. I took out my guns, stopped, and turned around quickly. I fired a couple of shots at them as they came through the door. The shots ricocheted off the door and the men tried to return fire, but it was too late. It gave me enough time to make it to my car. I emptied the clip in one gun and got in.

I cursed André and started up the car. Back in those days, I worked for André. He controlled most of the drug activity uptown. I was his collector, enforcer, personal bodyguard. I cursed André because he was the one who sent me into this mess. He sent me to see a man named Dudley Roberts, but everybody called him D.R. He was a dealer of some note, but his downfall was that he was a shooter and liked to get high on his own supply. D.R. owed André fifty grand and he sent me to collect. A simple pickup, is what André told me it would be. No trouble, no resistance, and definitely no shooting!

As I drove off I looked in the rearview mirror and I saw those muthafuckas make it to their car. The question was, who the fuck were they and why the fuck did they just open up on me as soon as I came through the door?

I would have to take the time to consider all that later, right now the only thing I had to concern myself with was gettin' the fuck away from there. I reloaded my gun; I only had one clip left. It didn't take long for them to catch up with me as I weaved my way through traffic on the avenue. Once they got close enough to me they started shooting.

One of their shots took out my back window; I tried to stay low as I kept on driving. I fired a few shots blindly at them and they continued blasting at me. My car went into a spin when a shot hit my back tire. I gripped the steering wheel tight and cut the wheel into the spin. I slammed into a parked car and hit my head hard against the steering wheel.

My head hurt like hell and I felt the blood begin to trickle down my face. I tried to shake it off and start the car, but that wasn't happening. I got out of the car just as they rolled up on me. As soon as they got out of the car, I let go with both guns. When they both dropped to the ground I took off running. They got up and ran after me, bustin' shots all the way.

I wheeled and fired.

They took cover behind a car and shot back, but I was gone. I ran down the street trying, but couldn't remember the last time that I had to run away like a little bitch. When I reached the next corner I dropped down behind a car. I knew that I didn't have a lot of bullets left. I stayed still and quiet, waiting for them to come tearing around that corner, and then I'd have them.

Damn they were good.

I watched through the car window as they stopped at the corner. They stood and talked for a second or two before they seemed to look dead at me and split up. They knew where I was hiding and were gonna try and surround me. I stood up, spread my arms, and fired at both of them.

I didn't wait around to see if I hit either one of them and ran down the street. The sound of shots being fired from behind me answered that question.

I ran up the steps of an apartment building, took aim, and fired one of my guns until it was empty before running inside. As I ran up the steps, I saw that there was only one man following me now. Maybe I had gotten lucky and hit one of them. What was more likely was that they had split up again and the other would be waiting for me when I came out.

I would worry about him later. Right now I had his partner on my ass. He came bustin' through the door and fired a few shots at me as I ran up the steps. When I reached the top of the stairs, I shot back. Now, I was out of bullets. I ran down the hall hoping that there was a window to a fire escape, or back staircase, but there wasn't. Just more apartments.

I was trapped.

With nowhere else to go, I picked a door and kicked it. I closed the door behind me and made my way into the apartment. There was an old lady watching TV; she screamed when she saw me. "I'm not going to hurt you," I said and lowered my empty weapon. "Where's the fire escape?"

"In the bedroom," she said quietly and pointed.

I apologized for disturbing her and ran in the direction she pointed, through her bedroom and out the window. I made my way down the fire escape as quickly as I could. Once I reached the ground I looked around, I tried to decide which way to go. I looked up and saw my relentless pursuer. He fired at me and I started running down the alley. I could hear his footsteps coming up behind me as I ran toward the sound of traffic.

That's when I saw the other one standing there. "Hold it!" he yelled as his partner caught up with me.

They had me. I put my gun on the ground, *why not, it was empty anyway*, and put up my hands. I was about to die and I had no idea who these guys were or why they were about to kill me.

"Black."

"Huh."

"Black," Nick said and shook my arm. "Wake up, Black."

"What?" I said and opened my eyes.

"Were getting ready to land. You gotta fasten your seat belt."

CHAPTER 2

As requested, Mike returned his seat to its upright and locked position and fastened his seat belt, as the captain told him about weather conditions at New York's JFK Airport.

"How long was I asleep?" Mike asked, looking at Nick.

"Not long, half hour, maybe." Nick shrugged.

Mike and Nick had just flown in from Miami, after traveling to Todos Santos, an island located at the Tropic of Cancer in the southern portion of the Baja Peninsula, off the coast of Mexico. While they were on the island Mike closed the door on some unfinished business.

He had gone to Todos Santos to kill Diego Estabon. A year before, Diego had been the mastermind behind the kidnapping of Mike's wife, Shy.

For that he had to die.

After an attempt on her life, Mike had moved Shy to the islands to get her out of the game and insure that nothing would ever happen that would put her life in jeopardy. He thought that she would be safe in their quiet island paradise, but that wasn't the case.

Mike out found that Diego maintained a bungalow on that island. So he waited; waited for just the right opportunity to kill Diego.

Mike had Nick, who had served in an army special forces unit, wire the bungalow with C-4, and a remote detonator. Once it was set, Mike called Diego on the phone and Diego, who had been waiting on his associates to call, answered, "It's about time you called. Where are you?"

"I'm right outside, Diego," Mike said.

Diego rushed to the window and saw Mike standing off in the distance.

"What do you want, Black?" Diego asked and quickly armed himself.

"As soon as Sal told you that he had kidnapped my wife, you should have told Sal to let her out the car and apologize for taking her," Mike had said and hung up the phone.

Diego watched as Mike turned to walk away. He wondered what that was all about. Then he thought it would probably be a good idea if he got outta there. But before Diego could make it to the door, the bungalow exploded.

However, there was more to it than just a simple kidnapping. Diego was attempting to set Mike up to take the fall for conspiracy to distribute charges. Diego had set things in motion with the help a corrupt DEA agent named DeFrancisco. That plan failed, too. Now Diego was dead, and DeFrancisco was in jail as a result of the investigation of him running an unauthorized operation. That exposed all of DeFrancisco's illegal activities. Now, Mike could relax and enjoy the new joy in his life.

It had been a good year for Mike. Shy never really liked living in the Bahamas, so Mike decided in order to make her happy, they would stay in New York. Naturally Wanda thought that the two of them staying in New York was a bad idea. "There are just too many things that could happen," she said to Mike when he told her his plan.

Wanda was the lawyer for the operation. At her best, Wanda was smart, careful, just a bit ruthless and over the years, she managed the money and made a small fortune for her partners. She had played around in the game for a while, but Wanda always wanted to be a lawyer. So Mike paid for her to go to law school. After briefly working for the district attorney as a prosecutor, Wanda went into private practice, with one major client. One of the first things Wanda insisted was that we start a business to run the money through. The name of their company was Invulnerable Security, specializing in private security and personal bodyguards. Mike chose a security company because it would afford them a license to carry guns.

Since Mike insisted on staying, Wanda made a simple request. On the heels of the DEA investigation, Wanda suggested that he begin to insulate himself from the day-to-day operation of their illegal enterprises. Wanda suggested and Mike agreed that he would only give orders to one person. "You need a buffer, Mike. It's just that simple," Wanda advised.

Normally that responsibility would have fallen to Bobby. However, Bobby had been out of the city. After finding out that Bobby was having an affair, Pam moved to eliminate her competition. The stress of that traumatic experience caused Pam to suffer a nervous breakdown. Bobby had spent the last year trying to nurse his wife back to good health. He had checked her into a hospital upstate, and then Bobby bought a house in the area. Bobby moved out of the city, along with their four children, so they could be close to her.

With Bobby unavailable, the next logical choice would have been Freeze; however, Wanda had something else in mind. She recommended that Mike only talk to Shy. At first, Mike absolutely refused. His entire reason for moving her to the Bahamas was to get her out of the game and keep her safe. But as always, Wanda's impeccable logic wore him down and he reluctantly agreed. Naturally Freeze wasn't happy about this new arrangement, but when Mike explained to him that he would still run the day-to-day operations, being the good soldier that he was, Freeze agreed. There had been a great deal of tension between Shy and Freeze, though. Freeze simply didn't like taking orders from a woman.

The bigger challenge for Shy was her dealings with Birdie. After D-Train Washington met his untimely demise, Birdie, along with his partner Albert, had consolidated power and were trying to get things back to the way Chilly had it. Since it was established, Chilly had respected the so-called dead zone, where Black wouldn't allow anybody to sell drugs for years. He understood that respecting the dead zone had the advantage of allowing everybody to do business. That's how Birdie wanted it, because to him it was all about business. But Shy couldn't stand him. To her, Birdie was arrogant and conceited and it annoyed Shy just to be in his presence. When he got her to the city, Mike had made up his mind to intervene and see to it that Birdie and Shy worked out their differences, no matter what Wanda said about him getting involved.

As the plane prepared to land, Mike looked over at Nick. In Bobby's absence, Nick had taken over as general manager of Impressions; at Bobby's request. However, unknown to Nick, or anybody else for that matter, Mike had asked Bobby to put Nick in that spot, "'Cause I want Nick to feel like he's a part of this family again," Mike told Bobby. "And besides, it will show Nick and everybody else that Camille shit is behind y'all."

Nick and Bobby fell out over a woman named Camille Augustus. At the time Camille was with Bobby, until Nick saw her. From that moment on, Camille had Nick under her spell. It all came to a head the night Bobby found out about it and tried to kill Nick. After that, Nick joined the army and stayed away for ten years.

As for Nick and Wanda, they continue to sniff around each other and deny that there is anything going on between them. If you ask Wanda about it, she'll say, "Nick? Please, we are just two *old* friends that like to hang out." If you ask Nick about him and Wanda, he'll tell you. "Wanda? Come on. Be for real," he once told Freeze, who insists that something is going on. "Ain't nothin' up with that. Hangin' out with her is like old times, you know, when we all used to hang together." The truth, however, was somewhat different, and both Nick and Wanda are both still in denial. Neither would break down and admit the obvious, that there was something going on between them. Not even to themselves.

There is one more thing that happened that year. The new joy of Mike and Shy's life. Five months ago, Shy gave birth to a baby girl. Mike had bragged that he would produce a man-child, a son to carry on the family name. But she was a beautiful baby girl, and she instantly took her father's heart. They named her Michelle after her father— actually he insisted—but she looked just like her mother.

Once the plane had arrived at the gate, they got off quickly, made their way through the busy terminal, and went to the parking lot. They piled into Nick's new Cadillac XLR and headed back to the Bronx. On the way, Mike called Shy. "Hello, Cassandra." Even though everyone called her Shy, he always called her by her government name.

"Hi, baby. You back in the city?"

"Just got off the plane. What you doin'?"

"Same place you left me, on the couch watching TV."

"How's my baby?"

"I just told you, your baby is fine. I'm sitting on the couch watching TV. However, if you're asking about *our* baby, Michelle is fine; she's at Pam's sister's house. I called to check on her a little while ago."

"Tryin' to get me alone, huh?"

"You figured that one out all by yourself."

"I missed you, baby. I can't wait to see you."

"Well, hurry up, I'm here waiting for you," Shy said.

"You talk to Freeze today?"

"Yeah, he said he was coming by later tonight to drop something for me."

"If he gets there before I do, tell him to wait for me."

"Okay."

"So I'll see you in about an hour, baby."

"I love you," Shy said. "So much."

As Nick made his way to the Bronx, Mike asked about the new car. "What kind of engine does this heap got?"

Nick looked over at him. "Heap, huh? Well this heap got a three-hundred-and-thirty-horse power North Star V-eight engine."

"You know when I first saw these, I thought it was a new Corvette."

"No, this is definitely not a Corvette."

"I know that. I just said I thought it was," Mike said.

"Don't get me wrong, there are some similarities. The XLR is built in the same plant that builds Corvettes. It has

essentially the same electronics, suspen͘
ture, braking, and all that shit."

"So what you're tellin' me is that it's a
new body style?"

"It's a luxury car with a performance-car engine,
explained as he drove. "It's aimed at Mercedes-Benz's SL
five hundred, Jaguar's XKR, and Lexus's SC four-thirty."

As he pulled up in front of the house, Mike looked at him
and said, "Why don't you come by in the morning and pick
me up."

"What time?" Nick asked.

"I don't know, but not too early."

Nick laughed. "I'll call you."

"Yeah, but like I said, not too early, Cassandra hates it
when the phone rings early in the morning," Mike said as
he got out of the car.

"You don't have to worry about that. I'm goin' by the
club," Nick said. "I'll probably end up being there all
night."

"Call me when you're on your way," Mike said and
watched as Nick drove off before finally turning and heading to the house. Mike unlocked the front door, turned off
the alarm, and stepped inside.

"Cassandra," he called out to his wife. But there was no
answer. Mike went into the living room, and noticed the
television was tuned to the local news on CBS. "Cassandra," he called to her again, but still there was no answer.

The remote was on the couch, so he picked it up and
turned off the TV. *Where the hell is she?* he thought before
dropping the remote on the couch and heading upstairs,
thinking that it was funny that she would have gone out
just that fast.

Maybe she's hidin'.

Mike took his time, carefully looking into each of the up-

s rooms, but Shy was nowhere to be found. *Somethin'*
n't right, he thought and went back downstairs.

For the life of him, he had no idea where she could be.
Mike went back in the living room and called out to her
once again, "Cassandra, where are you?" but once again he
got no response. He sat down on the couch and picked up
the phone to dial her cell phone number. When he heard
the phone ringing, he followed the sound.

The sound of Shy's cell ringing led him to the kitchen.
"Figures she'd be hiding in the kitchen. She knows it's the
last place I'd look for her," Mike said aloud, as he walked
toward the kitchen. "What are you doin' in here, Cassandra?" He opened the kitchen door and immediately dropped
to his knees.

There on the kitchen floor, he found her, lying with her
arms out in front of her and her face turned to the side. Both
eyes were blackened, nearly purple; there were blotches of
blood on her cheek. Her face was swollen so much he
nearly couldn't believe he was looking at his wife.

There was so much blood, and there were bullet wounds
in her back. One just below her left shoulder blade, another
a little below it and the two near her lower back. He
reached out and took her tattered body into his arms. He
looked around the room. Everything that was on the counter
was on the floor. He wondered if somebody had broken in
and did this to her, but that was impossible since the alarm
was still on when he got there. Mike pulled her closer.
"Baby, I'm so sorry." A single tear fell from his eye. "I should
have been here to protect you." He grabbed her blood-
drenched body, holding her tighter. "Who could have done
this to you, baby."

Just then, he heard what sounded like banging on the
front door, but he couldn't move. He sat there rocking his

dead wife's body in his arms, cradling her, silently apologizing for not being there to protect her.

Mike held Shy's lifeless body in his arms, willing it to come back to life. Suddenly, the kitchen door flew open and four cops rushed in with their guns drawn.

"Police!" one yelled.

"Nice and slow, put your hands up and move away from the body," another cop said.

Mike looked at each one as they spoke, but didn't move.

"I said, put your hands up. Now!"

He looked down into his wife's eyes, and then back at the barrel of the gun pointed directly at his head. It was as if he had suddenly realized the gravity of the situation. He moved painstakingly slow. He eased Shy's body back to the floor, his hand shook as he closed her eyes and then he sighed and put his hands up.

"Now," one cop said. "Lace your fingers behind your head." He holstered his weapon and took out his handcuffs. The cop approached Mike very carefully and placed the cuffs on him. It was the first time Mike had ever been handcuffed. He didn't like the feeling of cold steel clamped around his wrists. He felt caged already, despite the fact that they hadn't even left his kitchen.

Mike took one last look at Shy. "I love you, baby, and I'm gonna kill whoever did this to you," Mike vowed softly as the cop stood him up and ushered him out to the patrol car.

"You have the right to remain silent. If you give up that right, anything you say can and will be used against you in a court of law. You have the right to an attorney and to have an attorney present during questioning. If you cannot afford an attorney, one will be provided to you at no cost. Do you understand the rights I have just read to you? With these rights in mind, do you wish to speak to me?" the officer recited.

Black didn't respond.

As he sat handcuffed in the backseat, Mike closed his eyes and could see her face, not the beaten bloody mass that he had just held in his arms. He saw her as she was the last time he saw her. Mike wondered who would have a reason to do something like that to her. Considering the life they both had led, the list of suspects would be long. He felt the cold steel around his wrist and wondered how the cops could have gotten there so quickly. Had somebody in the neighborhood took the time to call the police? That wasn't very likely; people around there minded their own business.

The biggest question was who? Who would viciously beat Shy and then shoot her four times in the back? And more importantly, why?

CHAPTER 3

When Detectives Goodson and Harris arrived at yet another murder in the hood, it was no big deal. A few patrol cars, ambulance, a small crowd had formed; it was just another crime scene. "I see the crime-scene guy beat us here again," Harris mentioned as they got out of their car.

"I like to think of it as the natural order of things," Goodson said and the two of them headed for the house. "Let's hope the nigger in the backseat is the perp."

"Wouldn't that be a switch?" Harris glanced in the backseat of the police car and then waved at Officer Hardaway as they passed. Mike looked at the detectives as they went in the house.

Not these two assholes.

The detectives entered the house and were told that the body was in the kitchen. Goodson came through the door first. The uniformed officers that arrived on the scene first, Officers Rodney, Zachary, and Persons were in the kitchen along with the crime-scene investigation team. Goodson looked at the body. "What do we have here?" he asked and kneeled down next to the body. "Damn, somebody fucked her up pretty bad."

"From the looks of it after he beat her, she maybe tried to get away and he shot her in the back," Reyes told him. Reyes was the head of the crime-scene investigators.

"Guy in the car; he the perp?" Harris asked.

"When we got here, he was on his knees holding the body," Officer Rodney said.

"You ID him?" Goodson asked and the uniform officers started looking at one another and smiling.

"Yeah, we ID'ed him," Officer Zachary said.

"Well, what's his name?"

"The suspect in custody is Mike Black."

"What?" Goodson asked.

"What the fuck did you say?" Harris spit out.

"I said the suspect in custody is Mike Black," Officer Persons repeated proudly.

"That was Black in the back of that car?" Goodson wanted to confirm. "And he was on his knees holdin' the body?"

"Yes, sir." Officer Rodney smiled.

"Get the fuck outta here," Harris laughed. "So who the fuck is this?"

"We think it's his wife,"

"You got a weapon?" Goodson asked eagerly.

"Forty-five caliber automatic," Reyes told the detective. "It was on the ground by the door." Reyes stood up and walked to the area where the gun was found. "My guess, he was standing here when he shot her, then he dropped the gun." Reyes went back to examining the items on the floor for fingerprints and Goodson turned to Harris and smiled. He knew from past experience with Black that a forty-five automatic was his weapon of choice. "Where is the weapon?"

he asked the young officers, who all seemed excited to be a part of the event.

"Reyes tagged and bagged it," Officer Zachary said to the detectives.

"He say anything?" Harris asked.

"Not a word," Officer Persons replied.

"He resist?"

"Just laid her down, closed her eyes and put up his hands," Officer Rodney said. "I cuffed him and took him out to the car," he added proudly.

At that point, Goodson had heard enough. He turned and left the kitchen, with Harris and the uniform officers in tow.

Officer Hardaway sat in the front seat of his police car, while keeping a sharp eye on the rearview mirror at his prisoner. He smiled when he saw the detectives rushing out the house after the way they casually walked by on their way in. Hardaway got out the car. "You can slow down, he ain't goin' nowhere," Hardaway laughed.

"Look, guys, it's your collar, but we gonna get him in the box," Goodson said.

"You know Kirk is gonna shit bricks when he finds out about this," Harris stated.

"I'm surprised him and Richards aren't here." Goodson bent down and looked in the car. "Finally got your arrogant ass, huh, muthafucka?"

Black didn't look in his direction.

"You think he killed her?" Harris asked his partner.

"Husbands kill wives everyday. Why can't this asshole," Goodson responded. "Book him."

"Yes, sir."

Officers Hardaway and Persons got in their car and headed toward the precinct. Black sat still and quiet in the backseat with his head hanging low. Along the way, Officer Hardaway, who was the only rookie in the group, had questions for his partner. He was attending law school and joined the force so he could learn the law firsthand. "So what's the big deal with this guy?"

"This guy's been doin' business in this area for years. Drugs, gambling, prostitution, murder, anything with fast money attached to it, this guy is into it. But he's smart, never been arrested. So catchin' his ass at the scene of a crime, some of the guys that have been around a while think it's a big time."

"What about you? You think it's a big deal?"

"Nope. To me he's just another asshole killer. After a while they all get caught," Persons announced.

"Yeah, well, I don't think he did it."

"Is that what your extensive experience on the job tells you?" Persons laughed.

"No," Hardaway spit out quickly. "But look at him."

Persons glanced back at Black and then quickly back to Hardaway. "So what, just another asshole perp to me."

"You gotta look beyond that shit. Yeah, he's just another asshole perp, but look at him. The way he laid her down gently and closed her eyes. He loved that woman, and that shit is eatin' his ass up," Hardaway observed.

"Is that what they teach you in that law school?"

"Why does it always gotta be about that?" Hardaway asked angrily.

"Calm down, it ain't all that," Persons said as they arrived at the precinct.

Mike Black was taken to the interrogation room, but only after he was photographed and fingerprinted. When Detectives Goodson and Harris entered the room, Black was cuffed to the table, but he still had his head hanging low.

"You wanna tell us why you killed her, Black?" Goodson

pulled out a chair and sat down at the table next to Black. "What happened—you caught her cheatin' on you?"

Harris sat down across from Black. "Naah, he caught her stealin'," he threw out.

Black raised his head and looked at the two detectives. "Lawyer."

For the next thirty minutes, Goodson and Harris laid out several scenarios of how the gruesome crime had been committed and Black's motive for killing her. Black's answer was always the same: "Lawyer."

CHAPTER 4

"Wanda."

"Hi, Mike. It's about time you called me back. I've been calling you—"

"Wanda!"

"What!"

"I'm in jail, Wanda," Mike said, and now he had her undivided attention.

Wanda sat straight up in her bed. "What'd you say?" she asked quickly. "You're where?"

"I'm in jail."

"Where are you?"

"Forty-seventh precinct."

"Okay, Mike, I'm on my way. What are you charged with?" Wanda asked as she rolled out of bed and began grabbing clothes to put on.

"Murder."

"Oh my God. I'll be there in fifteen minutes. Do you want me to call Shy?" Wanda asked as she hurried to get dressed.

"That's who they say I killed," Mike said and hung up the phone. He knew Wanda would have a million and one questions and that would just keep them on the phone longer. The sooner Wanda got there; the sooner he would be out and after the muthafucka that killed Shy.

Wanda stood holding the phone in total disbelief of what she had just heard. Shy was dead and Mike was being held for her murder. The first person she called was Bobby, but she got his voice mail on both his home and cell phone. "Bobby, it's Wanda. I need you to call me as soon as you get this message. It's important." Wanda grabbed her cell phone and headed out the door. On the way to her car, she called Nick.

"Hello, Wanda. How you doin' tonight?" Nick asked, wondering and at the same time excited about her reason for calling so late.

"Not good, Nick. Shy is dead and Mike is being held for her murder," Wanda said and started up her Lexus.

"Did I hear you right? Shy is dead? And Black's in jail for murder?"

"That's what he told me," Wanda said as she drove.

"Did he do it?"

"I don't think so. He said that's who they say he killed, but I don't know. He hung up before I could ask him any questions. When did y'all get back?"

"We got back tonight. I just dropped him off a couple of hours ago."

"What time was that?" Wanda asked, a little put out that Nick had been back and he didn't call her.

"It was after eleven, I know, but I couldn't say for sure what time it was. Our plane landed at ten-till ten. I dropped him off at his house and I came to the club."

"What airline?"

"American."

"Okay, Nick, I'm at the precinct now, so I'll call you later," Wanda said and got out of the car. She opened the trunk and took out her briefcase.

"You want me to meet you down there?"

"For what, Nick?" Wanda asked.

Nick didn't have an answer that he felt like sharing with Wanda.

"You see if you can find out what happened."

"I guess that would be a better idea," Nick admitted.

"You think," Wanda said and hung up the phone.

Nick got up from his desk and got ready to hit the street. On the way out the door, he called Freeze. "Yo, what's up, Nick?"

"Black's in jail."

"For what?" Freeze asked and sat up in bed.

"For killin' Shy."

"Get the fuck outta here," Freeze said and then he thought for a second. "How'd you find out?"

"Wanda called me. She just got to the station."

"Where'd it happen?"

"I don't know. Black hung up on Wanda before she could ask him any questions," Nick told Freeze.

"I'll call you back."

Freeze hung up on Nick and called his contact in the department. A female voice answered the call on the second ring. "Property, Sergeant Adams," she answered.

"What's up, Sergeant Adams? You got a minute for me?" Freeze asked.

"I always got time for you, boo. What's up?"

"Something happened to Black tonight. I need to know everything."

"I'll call you back."

"Thank you, baby." Freeze hung up the phone and looked

over his shoulder at the woman laying next to him. He stood up and reached for his pants. Her name was Tanya, he met her several months ago at Impressions. She was there with her man when she happened to run into Freeze at the bar. "Make it a double this time," Freeze said to the bartender.

"You look like a man who's had enough and is heading for the door," the bartender said as he poured.

He handed Freeze the drink. "That obvious?"

Freeze drained the glass, "Hit me one more time, then I'm out."

The bartender handed Freeze the glass and he turned to leave and bumped into Tanya, spilling his drink on the floor. "I'm sorry," Freeze said quickly and looked Tanya over from head to pumps. She was beautiful.

"No, I'm sorry. I wasn't looking where I was going. And I made you spill your drink."

"It's cool. Better the floor then on that beautiful dress."

"But still, let me buy you another one."

"You don't have to do that."

"I know, but I insist. What were you drinking?"

"I'm drinkin' Rémy XO."

She looked at Freeze, and then she looked around for her man and smiled. "Rémy XO, got it."

"What's your name?"

"Tanya. Tanya Price."

"I'm Freeze," he said and held out his hand.

Her hands were soft and warm. "Oh, really."

"Yes, really," Freeze said to her and smiled.

"That's really your name; Freeze?" Tanya asked in disbelief. "Like your mama named you that?"

"No, my mama didn't name me that, but that's what everybody calls me."

"Well, I wanna know what your name is. I mean it's only

fair, I told you my name. I didn't tell you my name was Diana, princess of the Amazon, did I?"

"No. But you are a Wonder Woman."

"Very good. Most guys don't pick up on that," Tanya said and stepped next to Freeze at the bar.

Freeze turned back to the bartender, who already had another double waiting for him. "Can I get something for you?"

"Rum and coke, please," Tanya answered, still looking around. "But I told you I would get that."

"It's cool," Freeze said and looked Tanya over. She had a beautiful smile, big pretty eyes and a body that screamed for attention. "I don't pay for drinks here."

"So you work here?"

"No, I'm a friend of the family."

When Freeze handed her the drink, Tanya quickly explained that she was there with somebody and handed Freeze her business card. "Real estate agent." Freeze put the card in his pocket. "Next time I'm looking to buy some property I'll give you a call."

"I was hopin' you'd call before that," Tanya said and walked away. Freeze finally called her a month later and they got together.

Tanya sat up in the bed and watched Freeze get dressed. "I guess you're leaving?" she asked.

"Yeah, somethin's up." Freeze removed his pistol from under the pillow. "I'll call you," he said and walked out of her bedroom.

Tanya got out of bed and followed Freeze to the door. She grabbed his arms before Freeze walked out. "Will I see you tomorrow?"

"I never make plans that far ahead."

Freeze left Tanya standing in the doorway and walked down the hall. He passed up the elevator and took the steps down to the ground floor. Freeze really didn't care too much for riding in elevators because of the surprise ending. *You never know who on the other side of that door when it opens,* Freeze was famous for saying.

As he walked down the steps, his cell rang. He looked at the display before answering. "What's up, Sergeant Adams?"

"Hey, sweetie. We got him. And you were right, it's bad."

"What you got?"

"Word is they found Black at his house kneeling over a woman's body, covered in blood. And they think they got the murder weapon, they're testin' it now."

"The woman?"

"They think it's his wife, but she's been beaten pretty badly."

"Thanks, Sergeant Adams. I owe you one."

"I know. I get off at six, I'll be home by seven."

"I'll see you then," Freeze said and ended the call. He immediately called Nick back. "Meet me at Cuisine. We got work to do.

CHAPTER 5

When Wanda walked in the interrogation room, she saw Black sitting handcuffed to the table. As she sat down at the table next to him, she was shocked to see him covered in blood. "Are you all right, Mike?"

"I'm all right, Wanda," Mike said and leaned close to her. "They haven't charged me yet, but they printed me."

"That's not good," Wanda whispered, thinking that the police would probably run his prints against every unsolved drug-related homicide for the past fifteen years. Wanda sat back in her chair. "I tried to call Bobby, but he's not answering."

"Bobby took Pam and the kids on a ten-day cruise. He promised her—no business this trip. No cell phone. He said he would check in when he got to Puerto Rico."

"What happened, Mike?"

"Somebody killed her." Mike closed his eyes and Wanda reached out and held his hand.

"I'm sorry, Mike," Wanda said and squeezed his hand a little tighter. It was as if Wanda could feel his pain and her eyes got moist. "I'm so sorry, Mike," she said and wiped her eyes. "Tell me what happened?"

"I found her on the floor in the kitchen. Somebody beat her and then shot her in the back."

"What did you do?"

"I held her," Mike said and looked at Wanda. "I held her until the cops got there."

"How did the police get there? Did you call them?"

"No."

"I know this is hard, Mike, but I need you to walk me through the whole thing. Don't leave anything out."

"I know the routine, Wanda." Mike paused. "When Nick and I got back from Miami I called Cassandra—" Mike paused and took a deep breath. It was obvious to Wanda that this wasn't easy for him. She'd never seen him this way. "I called her to let her know that I was back and that I would be there in about an hour."

"Was she all right then?"

"As far as I know. I mean, if anybody was in the house with her, I couldn't tell it."

"What time did the flight arrive from Miami?"

"About ten minutes till ten."

"Do you know the flight number?"

"No."

"That's all right, I can find that out. Okay, so Nick dropped you off at the house at what time?"

"I guess it was about eleven."

"When you got in the house what happened then?"

"The TV was on but she wasn't in the living room, so I called for her, and when she didn't answer I went looking for her. I looked upstairs, checked the bedrooms. Then I called her cell phone because I thought maybe she had gone out. I heard it ringing and followed the sound to the kitchen."

"That's when you found her?"

"Yes. She was laying on the floor. It was obvious she'd been beat up pretty bad and then they shot her in the back." Mike dropped his head again, but looked up quickly. "Get me outta here, Wanda. I got things to do."

"I know, Mike. Just cooperate with them and we'll be outta here," Wanda said confidently.

CHAPTER 6

Detectives Goodson and Harris walked into the interrogation room, smiling. Wanda rose to her feet. "I'm Wanda Moore, attorney for Mr. Black."

"Ms. Moore, I'm Detective Harris and this is Detective Goodson."

"I remember you, Detective Harris," Wanda said and shook the detective's hand. Then she turned to Goodson. "I definitely remember you, Detective Goodson," she said to him without offering her hand. "It was an incident involving a Bruce Matloski if I'm not mistaken."

"That's correct," Goodson said and pulled out a chair. "That case is still open, but we're hopin' to get some fresh leads."

Hearing that made Black smile. *I definitely had my gloves on for that one.* Wanda saw the smile on Black's face and she smiled, too.

"Shall we get to the reason we're all here this time?" Harris said and placed one of the crime-scene pictures on the table in front of Black. "You wanna tell me what happened here?"

"First of all," Wanda interrupted. "Would either of you gentlemen like to tell me why my client was fingerprinted? Has he been charged with anything?"

"No, he hasn't been charged with any crime. However, Mr. Black was found by the uniformed officers at the scene of a crime, which does make him a suspect," Harris explained. "Them having him printed, that was a mistake. Overzealous rookie cop. Please accept the apologies of this department," Harris offered and Goodson rolled his eyes.

"I'll accept that for the time being," Wanda said, knowing that once he was released she would move to have those records destroyed as well as any evidence obtained as a result of that action, but now wasn't the time to bring that up.

"Who is the victim?" Goodson asked.

"She's my wife, Cassandra Black."

"We're gonna need somebody to identify the body," Goodson said and Black cringed at the thought of his beautiful wife.

"I'll take care of that once we're finished here," Wanda said.

"Can you tell us what happened here?" Harris asked, pointing at the pictures.

"I don't know what happened. I found her that way."

For the next forty-five minutes Black told his story of how, when he returned home from a business trip he found his wife beaten and shot to death. They grilled him over and over on key points of his story.

They wanted to know where he'd been and why?

What time the plane landed at JFK?

What time he talked to Shy?

How long did it take to get there?

Who dropped him off at the house?

Each time the detectives tried to ask Black anything that wasn't in any way related to Shy's murder, Wanda would touch Black's hand. "Can you explain to me what that has to do with this case?" and for the most part that would keep the detectives on task.

"Let's go through this again. You say when you got home you couldn't find her, so you searched the house," Goodson said.

"That's right."

"So you called her cell phone and followed the sound into the kitchen and that's when you found the body."

"That's right."

"You say you searched the house for her; why didn't you look in the kitchen?"

"Cassandra rarely goes in the kitchen."

Harris laughed. "Why is that?"

"She doesn't cook, so she has no reason to go in there."

"Sounds a lot like your wife, Goodson," Harris laughed, but Goodson wasn't amused.

"When was the last time you spoke to your wife, Mr. Black?" Goodson asked, more to kill the laughter in the room.

"I called her from the airport," Black answered.

"Why?"

"To tell her I was back and that I was on my way home."

"What'd you call her from a pay phone?"

"No, I told you I called her from a cell phone."

"What time was that?"

"I don't know exactly. We got off the phone about ten after ten. I called when we got in the car."

"No luggage to pick up?"

"No."

"That would make it about ten, maybe five or ten after."

"That sounds about right."

"The officers didn't find a cell phone on you at the time of your arrest."

"If you were listening the first time I said it, you would know that it wasn't my phone," Mike said, becoming increasingly annoyed with answering the same questions asked a different way.

Goodson sat back and smiled.

Harris flipped through the notes he'd been taking. "That's right, you said that the phone belonged to a Nick Simmons. And he was with you on your trip to Miami, he was the one who dropped you off, right?"

"Right."

"Did he come inside?" Harris asked.

"No."

"Why not?"

"'Cause I didn't invite him."

"This Nick Simmons, you say he's a private investigator?"

"Yes."

"We're gonna need to talk with him," Harris said.

Wanda wrote down Nick's number and handed it to Harris as Captain Keys stuck his head in the door. "I need to see you gentlemen for a minute," he told the detectives.

"Excuse us for a minute," Harris said and he and Goodson followed the captain out of the room.

Wanda turned to Black. "What do you think that's about?"

"I don't know, but let's hope they're ready to cut me loose. I gotta get out there, find who did this to her. I can't just sit here," Mike said and tugged on his handcuff.

Just then, the detectives came back in the room. Goodson sat down, but Harris stood back with his hands behind his back. "Now, you say you got off the plane and called your wife to tell her you were on your way. This time of night, not much traffic, when did you get there, quarter to eleven?"

"No, it was later than that."

"The medical examiner placed the time of death at some-time between ten-thirty and eleven." Goodson moved closer to Black. "Tell me something," he said in a more re-laxed tone. "How was your relationship with your wife?"

"Fine. I love my wife."

"No problems? You cheatin' on her, or she cheatin' on you maybe."

Wanda touched Mike on his hand. "What are you getting at, Detective?"

"The nine-one-one operator received a call at ten-forty-five from a woman who identified herself as Cassandra Black sayin' he's gonna kill me." Goodson leaned forward so his face was inches from Black's. "You wanna know who she said was gonna kill her?" Goodson paused a second. "Mike Black. She said Mike Black is gonna kill me. Let me tell you what I think happened. You called your wife, you argued. Then you rushed home, got into it again and that's when you kicked her ass and shot her in the back when she tried to run."

Before either Black or Wanda could say anything, Harris stepped forward. "Mr. Black, do you own any firearms?"

"Yes."

"What about a forty-five automatic, a Colt?"

"Yes."

"This your gun?" Harris asked, holding a plastic bag with a gun in it. "It's registered to you."

"If it's registered to me then it must be mine." Mike

looked at the gun. "I keep that gun in the house for protection." He knew what was coming next.

Goodson stood up and began to unlock the handcuffs from the table. "Stand up, asshole."

"This is the murder weapon, Black," Harris said. "You're under arrest for the murder of Cassandra Black."

CHAPTER 7

"So what are we doing here?" Nick asked as Freeze drove past the Spot.

"We're here to talk to Birdie," Freeze answered and parked his truck down the street.

"What about? You think he got something to do with this?"

"He might," Freeze said definitely and turned toward Nick. "Night before last, while you and Black were in Mexico, Birdie, Albert, and a couple of their boys came lookin' for me at Cuisine."

"He came lookin', for you?" Nick asked sarcastically. "He knows you don't do business there anymore. What'd he want?"

"It never got that far. Shy was there that night. Workin' the room, playin' hostess, you know, goin' around to every table makin' sure they havin' a good time. I guess she rolled up on Birdie's table. He must have said some out the way shit to Shy, 'cause by the time me and Mylo got there, they up in each other's face and Shy said she don't know how he get any pussy, as ugly as his ass is. He was about to back-hand her when I put my gun to his head. Birdie left, but he told Shy that she would see him again and she wouldn't like it."

"You think that he killed her over that shit?" Nick asked, obviously unconvinced.

"Let's go ask him," Freeze said and got out of the truck.

The Spot was a small club that was always crowded with ballers, male and female, along with the usual array of wannabes and hangers-on. The last time Nick was there the place was run by Rocky. He used to deal for Chilly, who controlled most of the drugs uptown until Nick killed him. Something about Nick having sex with Chilly's wife. Rocky ran the club until him and two of his associates were found dead at the red light in front of the club.

After that, Derrick "D-Train" Washington took over the Spot. Birdie took the place over when D-Train was found shot to death in his girlfriend's bed. The only suspect was his girlfriend, Melinda Brown. Her whereabouts are un-known.

Nick and Freeze made their way through the crowd at the Spot looking for Birdie or one of his crew. Just about everyone in the place knew Freeze and most acknowledged his presence as he passed. They stepped up to the bar. "Rémy XO, and Johnnie Black, both straight up," Freeze or-dered as two of Birdie's men came up behind them.

"What up, Freeze!" he yelled over the music. He was a young buck, wearing a wife beater and way too much bling.

Freeze nodded and Nick put his hand on his gun. "What's up, Lonnie? You seen Birdie in here tonight?"

"What you want with him?"

"I need to talk to him."

"What you wanna to talk Birdie about?"

"What business is that of yours?" Nick asked.

"Who the fuck are you?"

"Fuck all that," Freeze said and got in the man's face. "Is Birdie here? If he is you go tell him that I wanna talk to him."

"Fuck that! You don't come up in here tryin' to run shit. The fuck you think you are?" Lonnie yelled.

Freeze looked at Nick. "There's always some mutha-fucka tryin' to make rep."

"I believe the man asked you a question. He wants to know who the fuck you think you are," Nick laughed and Freeze punched Lonnie in the face.

Nick pulled out his guns and covered Freeze as he grabbed the back of Lonnie's head. Freeze slammed his head face-first into the bar, "You wanna know who I am?" Freeze slammed his head again. "I'm the muthafucka that asked you was Birdie here." He slammed his head again and then Freeze put a gun to his head. "Now, is he here?"

"What the fuck is goin' on here?" a man asked as he pushed his way through the crowd.

Nick pointed a gun in his face and he put up his hands. Freeze turned and looked at him. His name was Albert Web. He was the brains behind Birdie and everybody knew it. "What's up, Albert?" he asked and let Lonnie go. "I'm lookin' for Birdie."

"He's not here," Albert said and looked at Lonnie's bloody face. "All you had to do was ask."

"I did." Freeze stepped to Albert. "Since he ain't here, I'll talk to you."

"Follow me. We can talk in my office," Albert said and walked away. Freeze put away his gun and followed Albert. Nick followed behind them slowly with his guns still drawn.

Once they reached the office, Albert sat down behind the desk. Freeze and Nick stood in front of him. "What can I do for you gentlemen?"

"I wanted to talk to Birdie about the other night at Cuisine."

"Yeah, I'm glad you got there before it got ugly."

"I know when he left he said that she would see him again and she wouldn't like it. Birdie say anything else about it?"

"Nah, he just laughed it off. No big deal. Why, she tryin' to make something more of it?"

"You know where he was tonight?" Nick asked and leaned over the desk.

"I haven't seen him all night. But I can tell you right now, Birdie didn't mean anything by that. That ain't even the direction we're tryin' to move in. We don't want any problems between us, Freeze. Problems are bad for business."

"You talk to Birdie you tell him I'm waitin' to hear from him."

Once Freeze and Nick had left the office, Albert sat back in his chair and thought about what just happened. The look on their faces told him that whatever this was, it was about more than just the little beef Birdie had with Shy.

"What has that nigga done now?" He picked up the phone and tried to call Birdie, both at home and on his cell, but got no answer. Albert started to get up, but picked up the phone and dialed another number. The phone rang five times before it was finally answered. "Albert, you know what fuckin' time it is?" Mylo asked.

"Of course I do. Freeze and Nick were just here looking for Birdie. You know what they want? Is something going on that I need to know about?"

"Slow up, slow up. You say Freeze and Nick came lookin' for Birdie. They say what they wanted?"

"Are you listening to what I'm sayin'? They wanted Birdie. They didn't say what they wanted or I wouldn't be callin' you. The only thing Freeze said was about the other night at the club when Birdie and Shy got into it. What happened after we left, Mylo?"

"Nothing happened. Shy chilled out the people that was sittin' nearby with free drinks and shit. Me and Freeze left right after ya'll did."

"Did she say anything else about it?" Albert asked.

"Not to me," Mylo said. "But Shy don't talk much to me."

"I wouldn't think so, you are way below her level," Albert said and tapped his fingers on the desk. "I need to know what's going on, Mylo. If she wants to make more of this than it was I need to know."

"I'll see what's up and call you back," Mylo promised.

"I need to know it soon. I don't need anything fuckin' up our position. Do you understand what that means?"

"I ain't stupid, Albert, damn. I know what the fuck it means."

"I don't think you do, so let me break it down for you. You've been making big cash with us these last couple of months, so if we get fucked, you get fucked."

"I understand," Mylo said and hung up the phone.

Albert got up and went into the club. He made his way through the crowd to the bar looking for his men. He found them with two young ladies who were tending to the cut on Lonnie's face. "Can I see the two of you in my office," he said and walked away.

Lonnie and Smiley excused themselves from the ladies and made their way through the crowd to Albert's office.

Smiley knocked on the door. "It's open," Albert yelled from behind his desk. As soon as they closed the door, "What happened out there?" he asked.

Lonnie took the bloody bar towel away from his face. "He said he wanted to see Birdie."

"He say what he wanted with him, I mean before he busted your face?"

"No."

Albert looked at Smiley. "Where were you when they were bustin' his face?"

Smiley smiled and shrugged his shoulders.

"They didn't come over here just to bust your face," Albert said. "Something is going on. Something big. I need to know what's going on."

"What you want us to do?" Smiley asked.

"Take him and have someone look at his face." Albert looked at Lonnie and laughed. "What'd he do, pistol-whip you?"

"No," Smiley said quickly. "Freeze grabbed him by the back of his neck and slammed his face into the bar," he said, acting the scene out with his hands.

Albert shook his head in disgust. "Once you get your face looked at, you two ask around, find out what's going on and how it involves Birdie. And do it quick. I got a feeling this is gonna be bad for business."

CHAPTER 8

Detective Kirkland arrived at his desk ready to start another day, but since he came through the door he'd had a feeling that something wasn't quite right. As he made his way through the precinct, it seemed like everyone was talking about him. It was as if something was going on that everybody knew but him, and nobody was willing to tell him.

He sat down at his desk and picked up a case file. As usual, his partner, Richards, wasn't there yet. Richards was a good cop, had good instincts, but he was always late, and Kirk was getting tired of it.

Kirk looked around the room; he couldn't shake the feeling that everybody was whispering about him. He was about to get up and ask somebody when the captain came out of his office to end all the drama. He called Kirk in his usual manner. "Kirk! My office, now."

Kirk got up and made his way to the captain's office. When half of the detectives stood up, he was sure that something was wrong. "You wanted to see me, Captain?" Kirk asked as he sat down.

The captain had a big smile plastered on his face. "Late-shift officers from this precinct answered a domestic violence call. When they arrived on the scene, they found a woman badly beaten and shot in the back. Victim was dead when they got there." The captain paused. "They also found the suspect on the scene, kneeling over the body and the murder weapon with his prints all over it."

"Don't you just love it when they come to you gift-wrapped, Captain?" Kirk mused, making light of it and wondering what any of that had to do with him.

"Kirk, the suspect was Mike Black."

"You're kiddin'?"

"I'm dead serious," the captain said.

"Who the vic?"

"His wife, Cassandra Black."

"Whoa, hold up," Kirk said and held up his hand. "You're sayin' Black killed his wife?"

"That's exactly what I'm sayin', Kirk."

"What's he sayin'? Has anybody questioned him yet?" Kirk said and stood up.

"Sit down, Kirk," the captain said and Kirk slowly reclaimed his seat. "Of course he said he didn't do it. Goodson and Harris are on the case."

"Goodson and Harris? Those two assholes, you gotta be fuckin' kiddin' me," Kirk said, knowing that Goodson and Harris were famous for cutting corners and at times, just plain sloppy police work.

"They interrogated him late night."

"Last night? Why didn't you call me?"

"You know how things work around here, they were up."

"Damn it, Gus, you know how long I been waitin' to nail this guy."

"Luck of the draw, it was your night off, they caught the case. Let's not lose sight of what's really important here."

"What's that?" Kirk asked.

"What's important here is that we finally got his ass," the captain said enthusiastically.

"I guess you're right. I can barely contain myself, I'm so fuckin' happy."

"Look at the bright side, Kirk."

"There's a bright side in this for me?"

"You mean other than the fact that he's off the street."

"Yeah, Cap, other than that."

"You might be able to close some of your old cases."

"Yeah, big fuckin' deal. Damn it, Gus, you still shoulda called me," Kirk said as he got ready to leave the office, but he stopped at the door. "Can I at least talk to him? Maybe he'll talk to me."

The captain looked at his watch. "You better hurry. He's being arraigned this morning at nine."

Kirk shot his captain a dirty look as he left the office. "Thanks." It was the same dirty look he gave every cop he passed on the way out of the building.

On the way to the courthouse, Kirk was pissed. He felt that he should have been the one to bring Black in. He had dreamed about that day for years and now it would never happen. As he began to calm down a little, he thought about what the captain said about how the officers found Black. The more he thought about it, the more it didn't make sense to him. Why would Black allow himself to be caught at the scene of a murder? The Black he knew was smarter than that. He wouldn't be careless enough to leave the murder weapon with his fingerprints on it laying around for the cops to find. No, it didn't make sense at all.

What made the least sense to Kirk was the fact that the victim was his wife. *Black adored that woman. They always seemed so happy together, so in love with each other. Why would he kill her?*

When Kirk made it to the courthouse, he quickly found out what courtroom Black was being arraigned in and headed in that direction. He arrived in the courtroom and took a seat. He sat through the other cases, laughing at how stupid some of the perps had to be to commit the crimes they had been accused of. *Whatever happened to common sense?* When he saw Wanda enter the courtroom he knew they were about to bring Black in. Wanda glanced in his direction and acknowledged his presence. Kirk always had a thing for Wanda and she was looking exceptionally delicious that day.

"The docket number five-six-two-four. The state versus Mike Black. The charge is murder in the first degree."

"Is the defendant represented by counsel?" the judge asked.

"Yes, your honor. Wanda Moore for the defense."

"The charge is murder in the first degree, how do you plea?"

"The defendant pleads not guilty, your honor," Wanda said as she stood by Mike's side.

"Remand?" the judge asked.

"Your honor, the defendant is charged with the brutal beating and murder of his wife. He maintains residences in the Bahamas and Trinidad. The state considers Mr. Black a considerable flight risk. We recommend that he be held without bail," the prosecutor stated.

"Ms. Moore?" the judge asked, directing his attention to Wanda.

"Your honor, my client is innocent of the charges and

wants nothing more than to stand and face his accusers," Wanda said, knowing nothing that she said would make any difference at this point. There was very little chance that he would be released on bail.

Mike turned to Wanda and gave her a *is that the best you got* look. Wanda shrugged.

"I see." The judge paused and smiled. "I order the defendant be held without bail. Good to see you again, Ms. Moore. Next case."

Kirk stood up and left the courtroom as they led Mike away. There was no way he was leaving the courthouse without talking to Black. He talked with a deputy sheriff friend of his and made arrangements to speak with Mike before they took him away.

CHAPTER 9

Kirk sat alone in a room waiting for the deputies to bring Black in. He couldn't get past Black getting caught at the scene of a crime with the murder weapon. And not just any crime scene; his wife was beaten and shot to death. *Black was going to be the main suspect anyway, why make it easy for them by hanging around?* Kirk thought. No, this was a story he'd pay money to hear.

When the door opened, Kirk stood up. When Black saw that it was Kirk he was being brought to see he almost smiled. Kirk stood by quietly as Mike was handcuffed to the table and the deputy left the room.

"Good morning, Detective," Mike said as he rubbed his wrist with his free hand.

"Never expected to see you here."

"Neither did I."

"And if I did see you here, the only reason would be because I was the one who brought you in."

"So you came here to gloat, Detective?" Mike asked.

"No, Black," Kirk said as he sat down. "I just wanna know what happened."

"I didn't do it."

"Then tell me who did."

"I don't know. Cassandra was dead when I got there."

"I hear the case is a slam dunk."

"But it's not."

"I don't know about that, Black. Goodson tells me that you're a done deal."

"Come on, Kirk. You know as well as I do that Goodson couldn't find pussy in a ho house."

"Oh, I don't know about that, this one sounds pretty solid. I hear they found you covered in blood at the scene, murder weapon's registered to you, sounds like a slam dunk to me."

Mike leaned forward quickly. "I didn't kill her!"

"Then tell me what happened!" Kirk shouted back.

Mike sat back in his chair and took a deep breath, then proceeded to tell his story. "I had just got back from Miami."

"What were you doing there?"

"I had business there."

"Wait a minute, you want me to run out and find Wanda?" Kirk stood up. "She needs to be here."

"No!" Mike said and Kirk stopped. "Sit down, Detective, Wanda has work to do."

"Fine by me." Kirk sat down. "You said that you went to Miami." Kirk took out a pad and began to take notes. "Did you go by yourself?"

"No, Nick was with me."

"What time did you get back here?" Kirk asked.

"About ten."

"Exactly," Kirk demanded.

"Ten minutes till ten."

"Somebody pick you up or did you drive there?"

"Nick drove."

"He park at the airport?"

"He drove to the airport and parked his car in long-term parking. I don't remember the space number."

"That's okay, I can find that out easy enough. What kind of car was it?"

"Black Cadillac XLR."

"Nice. Yours?"

"Nick's."

"You remember what time you parked it?"

"Tuesday, around nine in the morning."

"So you caught a flight to Miami. Ticket in your name?"

"Can't fly without ID, Detective."

"Not that getting fake ID would be a real problem for you, but we'll skip that for now. You say you and Nick got back here at ten minutes to ten. What you do then?"

"I called Cassandra to tell her that I was back and that I was on my way. Then Nick took me home."

"You go straight there?"

"Yeah."

"Didn't stop anywhere. How was traffic?"

"We didn't stop anywhere, and traffic wasn't bad for that time of night. We got there a little after eleven."

"You sure about the time?"

"Yes."

"How can you be so sure?" Kirk asked and took notes.

"I remember when I got in the house the news was on."

"Where did you find the body?"

"In the kitchen."

"Was she dead when you found her?"

"Yes."

"What happened then?"

"The cops came."

"Where were you?"

"In the kitchen, holding her." Mike dropped his head. "I didn't kill her," he said without looking at Kirk.

Kirk looked at Mike; it was obvious to him that he was hurting over what happened. *Maybe he's telling the truth,* Kirk thought. For him the realization that Black might be innocent was a bittersweet pill for Kirk to swallow. On the one hand, here sitting before him in handcuffs, was the man that he'd been trying to lock up for years. On the other hand, Kirk was a cop; a good cop. He had sworn an oath to uphold the law and protect the rights of citizens. If Black wasn't guilty, then it was his obligation to investigate, *and if the facts say he innocent then he's innocent.* Kirk took a deep breath. "You resist when they took you in?"

"No."

"You say anything to the officers when they took you?"

"No."

"You know anyone that would want to kill her?"

"No."

"So walk me though what happened when you got to the house. Tell me every detail, don't leave anything out," Kirk told him.

"I went in the house and turned off the alarm."

"You always have the alarm on when people are in the house?"

"When she's in the house by herself; always."

"Go on."

"I called her, but she didn't answer. I went in the living room, the TV was on. I called her again, I picked up the remote and turned off the TV and went up upstairs."

"Did you notice anything out of the ordinary when you came in the house or when you checked the living room?"

"Not that I can think of."

"Okay, so you went upstairs."

"I looked in all the upstairs rooms, then I went back downstairs. I went in the living room, I sat down on the couch, and picked up the phone. I figured maybe she went out, so I dialed her cell phone. When I heard the phone ringing in the house, I followed the sound to the kitchen. I opened the kitchen door and Cassandra was lying on the floor."

"How was she laying?"

"With her arms out in front of her."

"How long were you in the house before you found the body?"

"Couldn't have been more than five minutes."

"You call the cops?" Kirk asked.

"No."

"Who called them?"

"I thought you knew all this?"

"Tell me anyway," Kirk said and smiled.

"Goodson said that Cassandra called nine-one-one and said that I was tryin' to kill her."

That raised an eyebrow on the detective. He didn't ask any more questions about it, but made a note that he needed to hear the recording of that call. "You said you found the body and then the cops came."

"Right."

"How long after you found the body was that?"

"Almost right away," Mike said and noted the puzzled look on Kirk's face. "I been thinkin' a lot about that."

"What's that?"

"How did the cops get there so fast?" Mike asked the detective.

Kirk leaned back in his chair. "Did you tell all this to Detectives Goodson and Harris?"

"Yeah."

Kirk sat back in his chair. "What he say?"

"You're under arrest."

When Kirk left the courthouse, he sat in his car and reviewed the notes he had taken. There were some things about Black's statement that he wanted to check out. Kirk knew how Goodson operated and how he felt about Black. He knew that Goodson liked to take the shortest path to close a case, which may or may not include investigation. With that thought in mind, Kirk decided that he would operate under the impression that Black was innocent of the crime that he was charged with and investigate the crime to prove his guilt or innocence.

Innocent until proven guilty. What a concept.

Kirk decided that it wouldn't be a good idea to talk with Goodson or Harris. After all, it was their case and he didn't want to appear as if he was stepping on their toes, even though that was exactly what he was doing. The thing to do now was to verify the timeline that Black laid out. His first stop would be Kennedy Airport. Then he would go to see the medical examiner and then visit the crime scene.

CHAPTER 10

It was 9:45 in the morning when Albert got to Birdie's apartment. He'd been trying to get in touch with him all morning, but since Birdie wasn't answering, Albert got in his car and drove to his apartment. On the way there, Albert called Mylo to see if he'd found out anything.

Their business relationship began one night when Mylo was drunk, broke, and complaining about it. He told Albert that he couldn't live off the scraps Freeze was throwin' him. Albert told Mylo when he was ready to man up and make some real money to come see him. Mylo was at the Spot looking for Albert the next day. Without telling Birdie, Albert gave Mylo a little package to see what he could do with it. Mylo flipped it and was back for more in days. Since then, Mylo's buys have gotten bigger and bigger. "And you're able to do this without Freeze knowing?" Albert asked Mylo after one of their exchanges.

"I'ma tell you this one more time, Albert. They ain't organized like they used to be. Black and Bobby is out, they don't even fuck with the shit no more. I couldn't tell you the last time I even saw Bobby. I'm tellin' you Freeze ain't the nigga y'all think he is," Mylo said.

As time went on, Mylo was bringing in so much money that Albert had to tell Birdie. He was pissed at first, until Albert told him how much money they were making. At this point they considered Mylo one of their best earners, but now Mylo wasn't answering Albert's calls either.

Albert rang Birdie's doorbell and waited. When nobody answered he began banging on the door. When Birdie finally opened the door he was furious. "What the fuck is wrong with you? You lost your goddamn mind, bangin' on my fuckin' door at this hour of the morning?" Birdie said and walked away from the door.

"We need to talk," Albert said as he went in the apartment.

"Yeah, well, you coulda tried callin'."

"I did. All last night and early this morning."

"What's so damn important, Alley?"

"You alone?"

"No. Asia is in the back," Birdie said and plopped down on the couch.

"Can she hear us?"

"Alley, just say what you came here to say."

Albert took a deep breath and sat down in the chair across from Birdie. "Freeze came looking for you at the Spot last night."

"Freeze? What the fuck did he want?"

"That's what I came to ask you."

"What the fuck is you tryin' to say?" asked a frustrated Birdie.

"I'm sayin' he didn't say what he wanted, only that he wanted to talk to you."

"What would Freeze want to talk to me about?"

"That's what I'm askin' you." Albert got up and went in

the kitchen to pour him a drink, leaving Birdie confused and scratching his head. Albert returned with his drink and sat down.

"Kinda early for you, ain't it?" Birdie said about Albert drinking.

"I need a drink, is that all right with you? I mean, you drink like a fuckin' fish all day."

"Calm down, Alley. All I'm sayin' is you don't usually drink this early."

"All I'm sayin' is that Freeze and some other guy came in, Freeze talked to Lonnie and ended up slamming his face into the bar."

Birdie frowned. "He fuck him up bad?"

"Busted up his face."

"Nigga thought he was cute anyway. Maybe a few scars will bring him back to earth." Birdie laughed. "What did Lonnie say to him?" he asked.

"That you weren't there."

"That's it?"

"That's all he said," Albert replied.

"Did you talk to Freeze?"

"Of course I talked to him. The only thing he said other than he was waiting to talk to you, was he asked about you and Shy the other night."

"What about it?"

"He reminded me that you said that you'd see her again and she won't like it."

"Why didn't you tell me that shit before?"

"I wanted to know if this was about something else," Albert said quietly and Birdie gave him a look.

"Something like what?"

"I don't know, could have been anything. You might have been fuckin' Freeze's woman, like Clark Kent," Albert said, making note that a man known by the name Clark Kent had been fuckin' Freeze's ex-girlfriend Paulleen.

Birdie laughed. "That new bitch he got is fine as hell, but she don't get around like Paulleen used to."

"That's because she's a different class of woman altogether. This one has class," Albert informed him.

"What's her name again?"

"Tanya Price."

"Yeah, well, as much as I'd like to fuck her ass," Birdie said. "Whatever he wants, it ain't got nothing to do with her."

"Good to know, but that doesn't change that fact that this is about you and Shy."

"What you think's up with that?"

"I don't know what's up with it, Bird, but if I had to guess . . ." Albert said and paused.

"If you had to guess what?"

"Maybe she told Black about it."

"I never thought about that," Birdie said and dropped his head.

"You did threaten his wife."

"Shit! I didn't mean that shit. I was just—"

"You was just what, Bird, tryin' to fuck up everything that we worked so hard to build here. Is that what you were tryin' to do?" Albert stood up and began pacing. "I knew as soon as you said that dumb shit that it was gonna be bad for business. You gotta stop doin' shit like that, Birdie. You ain't slingin' rocks on the corner no more. This is fuckin' business, can't you see that?"

"Shut up, Alley! Let me think."

Albert rolled his eyes, but remained quiet while Birdie thought about what they should do next. "All right, the first thing to do is to find out what the deal is with this. I

want you to send somebody to ask around, see if Black
wanna make an issue of that shit."

"I'll get on it right away," Albert said, knowing that he
had already told Lonnie and Smiley to get him that information. "I'll call Mylo and see if he knows what up."

"Then we need to make sure all our shit is runnin' correct. I'll take care of that."

Albert sat back in his chair and took a sip of his drink.
"Remember what we used to talk about?

"What's that?"

"How we wasn't gonna make the same mistakes everybody else did. You remember that?"

"Yeah, Alley, I remember."

"We said—no, swore to each other—that it wasn't about
all that gangster shit. All that shit does is cost money, and
then niggas start dyin'," Albert said.

"Too busy playin' gangster to really make that money. I
remember what I said. Meant it. This is business. But sometimes you just gotta let your balls hang, Alley. You know
what I'm sayin'?" Birdie laughed. "So I talk shit sometimes,
but I'm about business. But it ain't all about business all the
time. I think you forget that shit sometimes."

"I understand that there is a time and a place for everything. There are times when we gonna have to crush a
nigga, but this was not one of those times. We are trying to
work around Black, not take him on," Albert argued.

"You sayin' we should be scared of this nigga? 'Cause I
ain't afraid to go up against him."

"No, that is not at all what I'm sayin'. But, Bird, we talked
about this, talked about Black specifically."

"We said we wasn't gonna fuck with Black."

"You wanna end up like D-Train? And I don't believe for
a minute that Melinda's dumb ass killed him and disap-

peared. You can't tell me that Black didn't killed the both of them."

"Why would Black kill her? Melinda used to fuck Black. That bitch wasn't nothin' but a trick ho, that Black dropped for Shy."

"A fine-as-hell trick ho, that Black dropped for Shy," Albert said and raised one finger to emphasize his point.

"Yeah, but Black is about business. If it wasn't about business, why would he kill her? That shit don't make no sense. Yeah, I believe Black had Dee killed, but that bitch bounced."

"Yeah, like Adriana bounced on *The Sopranos*," Albert said and both he and Birdie laughed. "It doesn't matter, man. All I'm sayin is that we gotta be smarter than that. Chilly had it right, he made peace with Black. But then he went up against him and now he's dead."

"I heard it was 'cause dude fucked Chilly's wife."

"Whatever, Bird." Albert got up and went toward the door. "I meant what I said, you got to watch your temper. You see how it's bad for business."

"I hear ya, man, I hear ya. Ain't nobody more aware then I am about where we are and what we tryin' to build here."

"Good, then we agree that startin' an argument with Mike Black's wife was a stupid thing to do."

"All I did was tell her how fine she is."

"Maybe if you had left it at that this shit wouldn't be happenin'." Albert opened the door and left.

CHAPTER 11

When Wanda left the courthouse she drove back to her office. She had called Nick and Freeze and told them to meet her there. As Wanda drove, she thought about the fact that with the exception of representing a woman named Nina Thomas, when her case was heard before the grand jury, she hadn't tried a case in years. On top of that, Wanda had never tried a murder case before. That fact made her a little apprehensive. She picked up her phone and dialed Marcus Douglas, an old friend of hers that she went to law school with. Marcus was currently practicing in Atlanta where he had recently won a high-profile murder case, involving a man that was on trial for brutally murdering his wife and her lover with a golf club.

"Law office," a female voice answered.

"Marcus Douglas, please."

"Who should I say is calling?"

"Wanda Moore."

"Please hold."

While she was holding, Wanda thought about Mike and

how he looked. She could tell the pain that he was in. She knew in her heart that he could never have killed Shy. *He loved her so much.* Once upon a time, not so very long ago, that thought used to make her very jealous. Now, since she and Shy had an opportunity to get to know each other, Wanda realized that Shy was good for Mike. She had come to consider Shy a good friend and great shopping buddy. Wanda would miss her, too.

One of the hardest things Wanda ever had to do was going to the morgue and identifying Shy's body. She was terrified to see her face, it was so badly beaten. It was a task that she hoped she would never have to perform again.

"Wanda!" Marcus yelled as soon as he came on the line.

"Hi, Marcus," Wanda said with a smile in her voice.

"You know when Janise told me that you were on the line, I could hardly believe it. How long has it been since we talked?"

"Three years."

"Has it been that long?" Marcus asked.

"At least that long. So how have you been, Marcus? And how is Randa?"

"Now I know it's been a while since we talked, Wanda. Randa and I are not together anymore."

"What?" Wanda said in shock, knowing how close Marcus and Randa were.

"Our divorce has been final for a few months now," Marcus told her.

"Well, you sound pretty happy about it."

"To be honest, Wanda, I have mixed feelings about it, but overall, yeah, I'm pretty happy about it."

"Then I'm happy for you. So I guess you've gone back to your playboy ways?"

"See, Wanda, there's where you'd be wrong. I've been dating one woman for a few months now and it seems like it's getting pretty serious. And I guess that's what's responsible for me sounding so happy."

"I'm glad to hear it, I hope it works out for you this time," Wanda said. "How's the practice doing?"

"The practice is doing great, Wanda. I don't know if you know this or not, but I recently won a high-profile media trial. Ever since then business is booming."

"I heard all about the case, Marcus. Congratulations. In fact, that's what I wanted to talk to you about."

"So I guess this isn't a social call?"

"Of course it is, Marcus. Any time two old friends can get together and catch up, it's a social call."

"Okay, counselor, we'll consider this a business-related social call, how about that."

"Did that sound too PC?" Wanda said.

"Very, but tell me what I can do for you."

"You are still licensed to practice in New York, aren't you?" Wanda asked.

"Yes." Marcus hesitated. "Why do you ask?"

Wanda cleared her throat before she began. "Marcus, a very old and dear friend of mine has been charged with murdering his wife. To be honest with you, Marcus, I've never defended anyone on a murder charge before and—"

"And you want to know if I'd defend him."

"Yes," Wanda said softly.

"I'm honored. You usually don't ask anybody to do anything for you, especially if you can do it yourself."

"I know, but this is very important to me, Marcus," Wanda explained to him.

"Well, Wanda, like I said I'm flattered, but aren't there plenty of good defense attorneys in New York?"

"Yes there are and I know most of them personally, but I didn't call any of them, Marcus, I called you. Like I said, this is very personal to me. Mike Black is family to me," Wanda said, choking back tears. "I need you, Marcus."

Marcus took a second or two before answering. "No murder cases, huh?"

"Not one; closest I got to a murder case was ruled self-defense by the grand jury."

"You still . . ." Marcus paused, thinking about a delicate way to ask his question. "You still working for the same people?"

"Yes, Marcus."

"And you've never had a murder case, huh? I would have thought that murder cases, I don't know—I just had this picture of you, you know."

"Marcus, most of my practice is entertainment law. I do very little criminal law at this point."

"I just thought that you were defending gangsters, but I stand corrected," Marcus said, feeling just a little uncomfortable. "What's our client's name?"

"Mike Black."

"The guy you used to always talk about. Isn't he like—the boss?"

"Yes, Marcus." Wanda almost smiled.

"So how strong is their case?"

"He was just arraigned this morning. We haven't gotten to the discovery phase yet. At this point, all I can tell you is that the murder weapon is registered to him, and naturally his prints are all over it," Wanda said as she pulled up in front of her office.

"I know it shouldn't matter to a good defense attorney, but did he do it?"

"He couldn't have."

"Okay, Wanda, I'll take the case. But you'll have to do a lot of the preliminary work, and I'll come to New York for a day or two to work with you on preparing for the trial."

"Thank you, Marcus. I owe you one," Wanda said and sat down at her desk.

"No, Wanda, this makes us even. Remember, you're the one who got me through constitutional law."

"You mean I let you copy all my papers, 'cause you were too busy with what's-her-name to be bothered with something as trivial as that."

"I'll have you know that I rewrote them before I turned them in," Marcus laughed.

"Anyway, thanks. We'll talk soon, Marcus," Wanda said and hung up the phone.

It wasn't too long after Wanda got off the phone with Marcus that Nick and Freeze walked through the door. Wanda told them what happened with Black, both the night before with the police and that morning in court.

"What did Black say happened?" Freeze asked.

"He said when he got home he found her dead in the kitchen." Wanda sat back in her chair. "I had to identify her body," she said and made a face that showed her repulsion. "Whoever killed her, beat her in her face. I've never seen rage like that." Wanda noticed the way Nick and Freeze were looking at each other. "What?"

"I think Birdie might be involved in this," Freeze said.

"What makes you say that?"

"The other night Birdie and Shy got into it at Cuisine," Freeze told her.

"What happened?"

"I don't know what started it, but I heard her say something like she don't know how he gets woman, since he's such an ugly muthafucka."

Wanda wanted to laugh, but she held it in. "That sounds like Shy."

"Anyway, Birdie was about to backhand her, but he changed his mind when I put my gun to his head. When Birdie left, he told Shy that she would see him again and she wouldn't like it."

"And you think that he killed her for that?" Wanda asked skeptically. "'Cause it doesn't sound like all that to me."

"She dissed him in front of his crew," Freeze explained to Wanda. "He was with Albert, a couple of females and two of his boyz. They was all fallin' out laughing."

Wanda put her elbows on her desk and massaged her temples. "You look tired," Nick said to her.

"I didn't get much sleep last night. I was at the precinct late last night and in court early this morning."

"You up for this?" Nick asked.

"No," Wanda said to two shocked faces. "That's why I hired an experienced trial lawyer."

"Who?" Freeze demanded to know.

"His name is Marcus Douglas. We went to law school together," Wanda said and glanced at Nick to gauge his reaction.

"He any good?" Nick inquired to Wanda's disappointment.

"I think so."

"Can we trust him?" Freeze asked. "I mean, we gonna be lettin' an outsider into our world."

"I wouldn't have hired him if I didn't think I could trust him. I'm going to do most if not all of the pretrial work; I'll prep him, but he'll actually try the case."

"But you'll be there with Black, right?" Freeze asked.

"I'll be sitting right next to him. It's called second chair," Wanda said.

"So, were you guys pretty close in law school?" Nick

asked with just enough attitude to make Freeze look at him like he was crazy.

Wanda, on the other hand, smiled at his delayed reaction to her announcement that she'd be working closely with a potential old boyfriend. "Yeah, we spent a lot of time together," Wanda said. "Studying," she added.

Freeze's cell phone rang and he answered it. "What's up?"

"Hey, Freeze. This is Tamia."

"What's the word, Sergeant Adams? I know you got something for me."

"Yeah, baby, I got a whole lot for you, but we'll talk about that later. I got something that I need to tell you about, but not over the phone. You still coming by here?"

"I'll be there in about an hour," Freeze told her.

"I'll have it wet for you," Sergeant Adams said and ended the call.

When Freeze hung up the phone, he turned to Nick and Wanda. "That was my contact at the precinct. She says she got something for me."

"So what are we going to do about Birdie?" Wanda asked.

"Me and Nick went looking for him last night. He definitely knows that we looking for him by now." Freeze got up. "Nick, I'll get with you after I take care of this. See if we can't find this nigga."

"Call me," Nick said without taking his eyes off Wanda.

"Whatever." Freeze left Wanda's office.

Nick stood up. "I'm gonna get outta here, too. Get something to eat."

"I haven't eaten yet. Mind if I join you?" Wanda asked.

"Sure."

*   *   *

At Wanda's suggestion, they went to lunch at Chez Napoléon, a French bistro located in the theater district on Fiftieth Street between Eighth and Ninth avenues. As Wanda looked over her menu, Nick merely glanced at his menu. He was looking at Wanda until she looked up. "What?" she asked.

"What're you gonna have?" Nick asked.

Wanda looked at the menu again. "I was thinking about the coquille St. Jacques."

"I didn't see that." *Probably 'cause I was looking at you,* Nick thought. "What's that?" he asked, this time actually looking at the menu.

"It's sea scallops in a cream sauce and melted cheese. What about you, what are you gonna have?"

"I was thinking about the escargots de Bourgogne."

Wanda looked at her menu. "Snails? Yuck. You actually eat those things?"

"Sure, they're good. You should try them sometime. Take a break from calamari once in a while."

"I'm not having calamari today," Wanda said quickly.

"That's only because it's not on the menu." Nick smiled at Wanda and she stared into his eyes. Finally, Nick looked at his menu. "Snails are good, but I gotta be in the mood to eat them."

"Chicken. You don't eat those disgusting things," Wanda said playfully.

"Whatever. I'm gonna have the baked clams Josephine. And I'll have the Napoléon complex martini."

Wanda flipped to the martini menu. "Napoléon mandarin, vodka, orange wedge. That sounds good. I'll have one, too."

Once their meals arrived, Nick and Wanda ate and sipped their martinis in relative silence. The thing that was uppermost on her mind was Black, naturally. As for Nick, he, too, was thinking about Black and what he could do to get him out of jail. *C-4 and a helicopter should do it,* Nick thought. But his mind and his eyes were on Wanda.

"So you and this lawyer, what's his name?"

"Marcus," Wanda said while she ate. "Marcus Douglas."

"You and this Marcus guy, what's up with that?" Nick asked.

"What about him?"

"You two do anything else other than study together?"

Wanda looked up at Nick. "If you're asking if anything is going on between us, the answer is no. Marcus is one of the best trial lawyers in the country. I think hiring him was the best move. I've never tried a murder case before and this is too important to mess up." Wanda gently placed her fork on her plate. "Why do you ask?" she smiled and asked playfully.

"I just wanted to know what type of guy he is. Freeze is right, we'll be letting an outsider into our world."

"That's all? I mean, is there anything else?"

"Should there be more?"

Wanda laughed a little. It wasn't like Nick was about to stand up, beat his chest and say that she belonged to him and he didn't want Marcus anywhere near her, but she would take what she got. "Like I said, Nick, I wouldn't have hired Marcus if I didn't know I could trust him. I'll keep him away from anything he doesn't need to be involved in, so don't worry, I got this," Wanda said, but Nick wasn't listening. He was looking at her face, watching her lips move, but he couldn't hear her.

If he wanted to be honest with himself, he would have to admit that he was in love with her, in love with everything about her. The sound of her voice, the way she wore her hair, the clothes she wore, and her smile. She didn't smile often, but when she did it lit up the room, at least in his eyes. *And that body, my god! But we're friends,* Nick thought. One day he would find the courage to tell her how he felt. In the meantime, he would keep his feelings to himself and simply enjoy being with her.

CHAPTER 12

After leaving JFK Airport, where he verified the first part of Black's story, Kirk drove back to the Bronx. His next stop was the medical examiner.

"Fact," he said into his recorder as he drove. "Mike Black left the city on Tuesday morning as a ticketed passenger to Miami, returning on American Airlines at ten-fifty. Black Cadillac registered to Nick Simmons, exited long-term parking at ten minutes after ten. There were no major reported delays on the Van Wyck, give them a few ticks to get out of the airport, so that would put them back uptown, like he said, around eleven."

The next thing Kirk would need to know was the time of death. He stopped at a store near the precinct and got a couple of cups of coffee. Kirk was going to see Dr. David Frazier, the ME assigned to the case. "Afternoon, Dave," Kirk said as he came through the door.

"How's it going with you, Kirk?" Dr. Frazier said to him, barely looking up from the cadaver that he was working on.

"I brought you some fresh coffee."

Frazier looked up from his work. "You know, I was just thinking about brewing a fresh pot, but I know I'm only gonna drink a cup, maybe two at most," Frazier said and peeled off his gloves. "And if that's the case, why bother making a fresh pot; you know what I'm sayin'."

"Why don't you just make enough for one or two cups?"

"I never can get it right, either it's too weak or too strong. There hasn't been a decent pot of coffee made in here since Sondra quit."

"They tell me that some women, not all, but some women take the whole sexual harassment thing very seriously, Dave."

Frazier took a sip of his coffee. "I don't know what to tell you, Kirk. One minute I'm watching her bending over a body, you know, with that big juicy, soul-sister ass, next thing you know, I got a handful of it."

"Looks like the cut under your eye healed nicely," Kirk said and smiled.

"That's what I get for playin' grab-ass with a woman with a scalpel in her hand."

Both Frazier and Kirk laughed.

"What you got there, Dave?" Kirk asked.

"Nothing exotic, Kirk, just a simple hepatic failure. Cryptogenic cirrhosis."

"What does that mean, Dave?"

"Cryptogenic cirrhosis means that a cause of death was not actually found on examination. However, the cirrhosis, which is essentially replacement of normal liver tissue with nodules of tissue separated by bands of fibrous tissue—destroys the normal function of the liver, and this in turn leads to hypoalbuminaemia due to poor protein synthesis by the liver. Acute hepatic failure often develops on top of the cirrhosis, and it is this that actually killed the patient; the liver just stopped working," Frazier said.

"That is way more information than I really need, Dave, but thanks."

"You did ask," Frazier said and took a sip of his coffee. "So, what can I do for you?"

"Cassandra Black."

Frazier looked curiously at Kirk. "Oh yeah, but that's Goodson and Harris's case. What are you doin' here?" Frazier said slowly as he shuffled through the paper on his desk until he found the one he wanted.

"Consider me an interested party."

"Well, at least somebody's interested."

"What do you mean, Dave?"

"I mean I haven't heard from Goodson or Harris since they had me rush them the results of the ballistics on the weapon they recovered at the scene."

"And?"

"No doubt about it, that was the murder weapon, but I told Goodson that I hadn't autopsied the body yet, so I'd definitely have some more information when I got finished."

"They never checked back with you?"

"I left messages for both of them, but so far, no call."

Kirk laughed a little. "Well, tell me what you found, Dave, and I'll pass the info along."

"Bullshit, Kirk. This is Mike Black's wife, right?"

"Right."

"Everybody knows you've had a hard-on for this guy for years."

"What you got, Dave?"

Kirk followed the ME until they got to the unit that contained Shy's body. Dr. Frazier opened the unit, pulled back the cover and Kirk looked at her face.

"Damn!" Kirk said and shook his head. "You couldn't

tell it now, but that was one of the prettiest women I ever saw."

"Yeah, well, you're right, I can't tell it now," Frazier said in as deadpan a manner as he could. "Anyway, Kirk, cause of death . . ." Frazier paused for a quick review of his notes. "Victim was shot four times in the back. One bullet entered just below her left shoulder blade. It went through the superior vena cava. The second entered another a little below the other, that one went through her heart. And the other two entered through her back, one passed through without hitting any vital organs and the other pierced her right lung. If I had to make a guess about the order, judging by the angle of trajectory, the first was the kill shot, to the heart. The other rounds entered on an angle at varying degrees, which indicates that she was going down when the perp shot her. I'd say death occurred sometime between ten-thirty and eleven-thirty."

"If he got home around eleven, then he'd still have time to do it," Kirk thought out loud.

"Don't think so."

"What makes you say that, Dave?"

"Three things, four really. First off," Frazier said and pulled the cover back a little further. "I would've thought with a beating like that there would be some defensive wounds and there would definitely be some skin under her nails, but there aren't any. That's when I noticed those cuts and bruises around her wrists."

"What would cause that?" Kirk asked the ME.

"My guess—handcuffs."

"Hmm."

"That got the old juices flowing and I began to look a little further. I took a closer look at her face. Have you noticed that for the most part the wounds are limited to the left side of her face?"

"Killer was right-handed."

"Yes, nothing extraordinary there, however, if you look closely at the right side of her face you'll notice that there are small cuts on the corner of her mouth that are consistent with her being gagged."

"What's the fourth?" Kirk asked and continued to make notes of everything the ME said.

"I didn't find any evidence of drugs in her system, but I found traces of N-two-O in her system."

"English translation, please?"

"Nitrous oxide."

"Again, in English, please. What the fuck is that?"

"An colorless gas with pleasant, sweetish odor and taste, which when inhaled produces insensitivity to pain." Frazier paused and looked at Kirk. "Laughing gas."

"You're shittin' me?"

"If you asked me, and I notice that you haven't . . ." Frazier smiled. "The killer took his time with this one. The killer cuffed her, gave her the N-two-O, gagged her and then he beat her. Then he shot her."

Kirk left the ME's office with more questions than he had when he went in. The most pressing question was, why the laughing gas? If the killer wanted to beat her and beat her as badly as she was beaten, then why did he give her something that would decrease her sensitivity to pain?

Kirk got out his cell and called Lieutenant Reyes, the head of the crime-scene investigation team, to see if he could get some answers. "Reyes," the lieutenant answered.

"This is Kirk."

"What's goin' on, Kirk?"

"You worked the Mike Black crime scene, right?"

"I shoulda known that's what you wanted. Yeah, I worked it, why?"

"I just left the ME and I got some questions I need to ask you about the crime scene."

"Ain't that Goodson and Harris's case?"

"Yeah, it's their case," Kirk spit out.

"I'm kinda busy right now. Why don't we get together tomorrow? You can buy me breakfast."

"What time?"

"Seven. Meet me at the precinct."

"Be on time, Reyes," Kirk warned. "Or you're buying."

CHAPTER 13

Freeze parked his truck in front of Sergeant Adams's apartment building He was anxious to hear what she had for him, and more importantly, whatever it was that it would be something that could help Black. "It better not be just about her wantin' some dick."

He was about to go inside when his cell phone rang. "What up?"

"What's up, Freeze? This is Mylo."

"Yo, what's up?"

"Where you at?"

"About to take care of some business."

"I was just callin' to let you know that some of Birdie's people been rollin' around the way askin' a lot of questions."

"I'm lookin' for Birdie. You seen him?"

"Nah, I ain't seen him. What's up?"

"You ain't heard?"

"Heard what?"

"Somebody killed Shy last night," Freeze said coldly.

"You think Birdie had something to do with it?"

"Maybe."

"It's about what happened the other night at the club, ain't it?"

"I don't know, Mylo, that's why I wanna talk to him."

Mylo thought for a second about how he could work both sides of this to his advantage. *I get these niggas killin' each other and I'll be ready to pick up the pieces when they fall.* "You need me to do anything?"

"Yeah, get on the streets, Mylo. I know your ass is still layin' up in the bed," Freeze kidded him. "But get your ass up and find where Birdie's hidin'."

"I'm on it," Mylo said.

"I'm out."

Freeze got out of his truck and went inside. He took the stairs up to her floor and walked to her door. Before he had a chance to knock on the door, it opened. Tamia Adams opened the door to let Freeze in, wearing a see-through blue gown.

"Now that's what I call service."

"I saw you pull up from the window," Tamia said and broke into a model's turn. "You like?"

"You know you sure got the right initials, 'cause you damn sure got a whole lotta tits, Tamia, and a hell-of-a ass, Adams, for a muthafucka," Freeze said while getting his eyes full.

"I'll take that as a yes."

"Take that as a hell-fuckin'-yeah. Sometimes I wonder why you became a cop."

"Easy money, baby, easy money. When I first got on the street, me and my partner agreed that we would always be the last unit to respond. Those days, I never even had to take out my gun." Tamia touched and then jiggled her breasts. "Having these got me off the streets and it's been easy money since then."

"I'm sure that ass did some talkin', too," Freeze commented.

"Well," Tamia said and reached for his hand. "Then you need to come get some of this 'cause it comes with a whole lotta drippin' wet pussy. And your pussy is creamin' for you, just the way you like it," Tamia said seductively and attempted to lead Freeze to her bedroom.

Freeze removed her hand from his. "First things first, Sergeant Adams. What you got for me, and it better be something good."

"Trust me, baby, it is." Tamia walked over to the couch and sat down. "Can you at least sit down?"

Freeze took a deep breath and joined Tamia on the couch. She immediately moved closer to him and began to rub his leg.

"Okay, Sergeant Adams, I'm sittin' down now. What you got for me?"

"Tell me something, Freeze, if I were to say that I didn't have anything for you, would you get up and walk this dick outta here?" Tamia asked as her hand ran up and down the length of his growing hard-on.

"Yeah, I would. And I would think seriously about kickin' your ass for wastin' my time. But I know you got somethin' for me 'cause I know you wouldn't waste my fuckin' time like that, Sergeant Adams."

"Why do you always call me Sergeant Adams? You never call me Tamia."

"Would you tell me what the fuck you gotta tell me? I need to be out findin' who killed Shy. So if you ain't got somethin' for me then I'm out."

"Yeah, I know, after you kick my ass. You know that's assaulting a police officer. I could lock you up for that."

"Tamia!" Freeze said much louder than he needed to.

"Okay, okay. Last night after I talked to you, Goodson and Harris checked Black's gun into evidence."

"So. What does that mean to me? And how does that help Black?"

"What it means to you and how it helps Black is evidence disappears from there every day."

Freeze leaned back on the couch and looked at Tamia. "I want you to get that gun and bring it to me."

"That's exactly what I had in mind, Freeze," Tamia said and stood up. "You know what else I got on my mind?"

"What else you got in mind, Sergeant Adams?" Freeze said looking up at Tamia as she slowly slid her gown off her shoulders. The dainty material fell to the floor and she · stepped away from it.

"You know I could show you better than I could tell you," Tamia said and dropped to her knees. She unbuckled his belt, unzipped his pants, and pulled out his long, rock-hard dick. Tamia admired it before lowering her head to it.

She gazed up at him as she allowed her tongue to slither across the head. The look on Freeze's face never softened. So Tamia took the entire head into her mouth; she closed her eyes as if she were savoring her favorite flavor. "Emmm," she moaned.

Freeze relaxed a bit, and eased back into the sofa.

She used her free hand to rub his balls.

"Yeah, that's it," he mumbled.

Tamia slurped and sucked, first wetting his head more and more. She opened her eyes and looked at Freeze. When she thought he was ready, she deep-throated him and squeezed her jaws, tightening her grip around him. Freeze grabbed a fistful of her hair and began to guide her head closer and closer into his lap. "Yeah, do that shit."

Tamia sucked harder. She could feel his hips moving in sync with her own motions. The more she sucked, the tighter her grip became on his balls, and she stroked them, squeezed, and sucked even harder.

She could feel Freeze flinching beneath her touch and loved the power she felt. She wanted to keep him in that position for as long as possible, but she felt the floodgates release between her own thighs. By now, Freeze had reached for her nipple and squeezed it ever so tightly between his fingers.

"Damn, girl," he said.

Tamia moved faster, her head bobbing quickly up and down; she would swallow, then slurp, swallow, then slurp. A few minutes of that motion and she held him whole in her mouth. Again, she added pressure and pulled back when she felt him convulse.

Freeze's breathing was off the chart. He was all hot and bothered, just the way Tamia wanted him. Before he could move another inch, she dug behind a cushion and pulled out a black-and-gold wrapper.

Freeze looked up at her from his spot on the couch. His breathing had returned to normal. Tamia snatched the opened wrapper and used one hand to slip the condom on his throbbing erection.

Before Freeze could make another move, she straddled him. She didn't do it slow or easy; she slid right onto his dick and began to ride him unmercifully.

"Oh, shit, your dick is so hard," Tamia cried. "I like it hard," she cooed.

"Take it then, fuck this dick," Freeze encouraged.

"Emm-hmm." She rode with her back stiff.

Sounds of flesh meeting flesh filled the room. Tamia

locked her arms around Freeze's neck and used her hips to move up and down on his massive rod. He guided her by the hips, and kept up with her vigor.

"Get it girl, get this dick," he challenged.

That seemed to help Tamia pick up the momentum. "I'm trying," Tamia said, still pumpin' that ass.

"You like that?" Freeze asked.

"Oh, yeah, this is what I needed," Tamia cried.

Suddenly Freeze grabbed both of her breasts, squeezed them together, and brought her hard nipples into his mouth. He sucked and lathered them. Then abruptly Freeze stopped, held her shoulders tightly, and thrust his hip into her midsection. Tamia's eyes widened, with her mouth agape, she squeezed her walls tighter. However, Freeze shoved her up and off his still throbbing dick.

"Ww-hat are you doing? You was hittin' my spot, why'd you stop?" she questioned. Her face was drained of its color.

Freeze manhandled her body as he guided her, facedown over the arm of the couch. Before she could protest any longer, he slammed himself into her from behind. She released a gut-wrenching scream and dug her fingernails into the sofa.

"Oh yes, Freeze, right there, right there baby," she cried.

Freeze hammered away.

"Oh Freeze," she moaned.

"Yeah, you like this dick, don't you?"

"Yes Freeze, yessss, yes!"

Just as he was about to explode, he pulled himself out, ripped the condom off, and entered her again.

"Yes, Freeze, oh yes!"

He grabbed her hips and pulled her into him as he pounded her pussy.

"Yes, Freeze, cum in me, baby, fill me up!"

"Damn, this pussy is good"

"Come on, Freeze, I feel it, come on, baby!"

In a desperate frenzy, Freeze grabbed her titties, squeezed them together and pulled out just in time to spray her back with his juices.

"Damn, Freeze," she said.

Once Tamia got through screaming his name, Freeze went into the bathroom and took a shower. When he came out of the bathroom, Tamia was laying across her bed. "Come here, Freeze," she said and motioned him to come to her. Freeze sat down on the bed beside her. "I'll get the gun for you, baby, but there are two things I want."

"I'm listening."

"I want ten thousand dollars and—"

"And what?"

"I want you to spend an entire night with me."

Freeze stood up and walked toward the bedroom door.

All night? You owe me, Black. He stopped in the doorway and turned to face her. "Deal," Freeze said and left.

CHAPTER 14

After finally getting the information they had been look-ing for, Lonnie and Smiley got back in their car. The two of them had been in the street all night and most of the day talking to people, trying to find out why Freeze was looking for Birdie. Lonnie called Birdie to let him know that they had the information, but Lonnie knew this wasn't the type of thing that needed to be said over the phone. "That bad, huh?"

"Yeah, it's that bad."

"I'm at the crib. Get here as soon as you can."

Now that they knew what it was all about, Lonnie drove as fast as traffic would allow him to get to Birdie's apart-ment. "I don't know what you rushin' for," Smiley said.

"Right. He ain't gonna wanna hear this shit anyway," Lonnie said and slowed down.

"You think Birdie killed her?" Smiley asked.

"I don't think so, but you never know. If Albert thought it was good for business, you damn right they'd do it," Lonnie said. "I just don't see how killin' Black's wife would be good for business. Unless you gonna kill Black, too."

"And Freeze, and Bobby," Smiley threw in.

"That's what I'm sayin', it just don't make sense."

"That's your problem," Smiley said, doing his best imitation of Albert. "Your problem is you don't understand business. It is conducted well beyond your level."

"I understand that muthafuckas been gettin' their asses killed over fuckin' with that nigga for years. Birdie and Albert wanna be the next ones to try, that's fine, let them. But you and me need to be smarter than that. 'Cause it ain't gonna be too much longer before them niggas is dead and then it will be our time to step up."

After he got off the phone with Lonnie, Birdie called Albert and told him to get over there as soon as he could. When Albert got there, he fixed himself and Birdie a drink. Birdie rolled a blunt and the two sat quietly, smoking and drinking until Lonnie finally knocked on the door.

"What took you so long?" Albert said as he swung open the door.

"Traffic," Lonnie said as he and Smiley walked into the living room.

Once they were all seated, Birdie stood up. "Well? What you gotta tell me that you couldn't say over the phone?"

"The way I got it is that you and Black's wife got into it at his spot the other night," Lonnie said.

Albert immediately bounced up off the couch. "I told you that was what it was about. You disrespected his wife. I knew it was gonna be bad for business. Sometimes I wonder if you understand what that means," Albert said to Birdie, but it was more grandstanding for Lonnie and Smiley's benefit.

Lonnie smiled at Albert, but knowing what he knew, he

wasn't impressed. He turned to Birdie. "It's a lot worse than that, Birdman."

"What you mean?"

"I mean it's about more than you just dissin' his wife."

"Well, what the fuck is it about then?" Albert asked.

"Shut up, Alley, let the man say what he gotta say," Birdie demanded.

"Somebody killed her."

"What?" Albert asked.

"Killed who?" Birdie demanded to know.

"Black's wife. Somebody killed Black's wife."

"What that got to do with me?" Birdie needed to know.

"'Cause y'all had that beef, they think you killed her," Lonnie said looking back and forth between Albert and Birdie.

Albert and Birdie looked at each other. "They think I killed Shy? Why would I kill her?" Birdie asked, still not seeing the obvious.

"I told you, they think it's 'cause y'all had that beef," Lonnie repeated. "But that's not the worst of it."

"Please tell me what could be worse than Black thinkin' I killed his wife?"

"Black's in jail for the murder."

"Oh shit," Albert said and sat down. He took a big swallow of his drink and looked at Birdie. He could tell by the look on his face that he didn't know anything about this. Besides, he thought, *Birdie couldn't be that stupid.* "This just keeps gettin' better."

"Shut up, Alley, I need to think about what we gonna do," Birdie said and walked to the window. He stood there in a daze, looking at nothing in particular. The idea that Freeze thought he killed Shy was so foreign to him that he couldn't wrap his mind around it.

"Don't you think it's obvious what you gotta do?" Smiley asked Birdie. "You need to make sure they know that you didn't have nothin' to do with it."

"No shit. Of course, I need to talk to them. That ain't the problem."

"What's the problem?"

"You got any ideas on how I'm supposed to convince them that I didn't do it?"

"Huh?" Smiley said.

"Yeah, that's what I thought. How'd it happen?"

"You broke in their house, beat her up real bad and then you shot her in the back," Lonnie told Birdie.

"Damn," Birdie said and dropped his head. "They think I did the shit myself. Freeze should know that ain't how I do shit. If I was gonna do some shit like that I'd have you two do it," Birdie said while pointing at Smiley and Lonnie.

"You think that makes us feel better or worse?" Smiley asked. He understood that if it came to it that it wouldn't be just Birdie. Freeze would come after him and Lonnie.

Birdie turned around and reclaimed his seat. He looked over at Albert who had remained uncharacteristically quiet during the discussion of what needed to be done. Albert simply sat listening and sipped his drink. "You ain't got nothin' to say about this, Alley?"

"You told me to shut up. I thought you didn't wanna hear what I had to say," Albert said.

"Well now I wanna hear it," Birdie said. "What you think?"

"I think you're absolutely right. Freeze should know that you definitely wouldn't do it yourself. But the only problem with that is Freeze won't take the time to think about it, he'll just come after you, just like he did. It's a good thing you weren't there that night. They probably woulda shot you on sight. But I think there may be a way that we can use this to our advantage."

"I'm listening."

"The word on the street is that you killed Shy over that nonsense the other night, right?"

"Yeah."

"I say we let the word get around."

"Why, Alley?" Birdie frowned.

"People think that you took it to Black only makes our position stronger. People thinkin' you're strong makes it easier for us to expand into new market."

"You know something, Alley, you're right. Havin' mutha-fuckas thinkin' I went up against Black might even make me a legend, and that would be good for business, but there's only one problem with that plan."

"What's that?" Albert asked.

"We'll all be dead."

Lonnie and Smiley laughed.

"This shit ain't fuckin' funny, nigga!" Birdie shouted.

"Not necessarily. Like you said, Bird, them knowing this ain't your style is gonna work for us. I say we lay low for a couple of days, let the word get around. Then you reach out to them."

"Nah, that shit won't work. You said it yourself, Freeze ain't gonna think about that shit. He gonna come after me blastin'. That's all the nigga know how to do." Birdie looked at Lonnie and Smiley. "I could use a nigga like that on my team."

"It will work!" Albert shouted and got everyone's attention. Albert took a quick breath. "And I'll tell you why. We let the word get around that you did it and at the same time we reach out to Bobby Ray."

"Bobby ain't been around much lately," Lonnie added.

"Something about his wife going crazy," Smiley added.

"I know that, but with Black in jail, Bobby Ray has gotta step into the void. He has to. Him and Wanda already know havin' Freeze in charge is bad for business. They know Freeze is muscle, a soldier, not a general. That's why they been making us deal with Shy instead of Freeze. We reach out to Bobby; we assure him that we had nothin' to with it. That you were just talkin' shit, that you got nothin' but respect for Mike Black and you wouldn't be that stupid. I'll remind them that war would be bad business. This will work, Birdie, trust me."

Birdie sat back in his chair and thought about Albert's plan. If it worked out the way Albert said it would, it would definitely improve his status. However, it could also very easily backfire and get him killed. After considering his options, Birdie decided it was worth the risk, and besides, he really didn't have much of a choice. They already thought he murdered Shy; laying low for a couple of days was definitely a logical move. But it also would be logical to bring in a few new faces for protection. "Let's make it happen," Birdie said confidently. "Alley, I need you to make a call to Cleveland. Tell them I need a couple of good men."

"I got it," Albert said as his cell rang.

"Lonnie, I want you and Smiley to put the word out that I wanna talk to Bobby. If anyone asks y'all about me havin' somethin' to do with it, you just say, yeah, I heard that, too. Understand?"

Lonnie glanced over at Smiley. "I understand," they both said, almost in unison.

Albert hung up his phone. "It's confirmed."

"That your boy?" Birdie asked.

Albert nodded his head.

"All right," Birdie said as he walked Lonnie and Smiley to the door. "Go on and get outta here. I need to talk some things over with Albert."

*   *   *

Once Lonnie and Smiley were out of the building and in their car, Lonnie said, "That has got to be the dumbest plan I ever heard. This is just what I'm talkin' about, we gotta be smarter than that. All that shit is gonna do is get them killed," he added.

"Just tell them 'yeah, I heard that, too,'" Smiley mocked Birdie. "I'll tell them, yeah, I heard that, too, but I didn't have shit to do with it."

"They want us on the street talkin' this dumb shit up while they hidin', that's bullshit! We the ones that need to be layin' low."

"I think we need to put the word out that we didn't have shit to do with it, then we lay low," Smiley recommended. "And when Birdie and Albert are dead, we'll make peace with Bobby Ray."

CHAPTER 15

Mike Black

I stood with my eyes closed and my back turned when the cell door closed behind me. There was a certain finality to that sound; it was almost like part of my life had just closed behind me. I knew when I opened my eyes I would see my future.

I opened my eyes and looked around the cell.

This was my future, these walls, and this time.

There was a small Puerto Rican man on the bottom bunk, which meant the top one was mine. I walked further into the cell toward the bunk and put my new belongings down.

"My name is Pablo," the small Hispanic man said.

"Mike Black," I said.

Pablo was saying something to me, but I wasn't listening to anything he was sayin'. The only thing on my mind was Cassandra, my beautiful Cassandra.

I climbed up on the bed, stretched out and closed my

eyes. I didn't wanna think about her, I wanted to block it all out. Make like this nightmare wasn't really happening.

That she wasn't dead.

But I couldn't.

Every time I opened my eyes or felt the pain in my back from this hard-ass bed, it would reinforce that fact that Cassandra is really dead and I'm in jail for killin' her.

The harder I tried not to think about Cassandra, the more I thought about her. With my eyes closed, I saw her laying there. I saw the blood; saw her face, beaten, bruised, and bloody.

How would I go on without her?

And what about Michelle?

I really didn't wanna think about my baby being forced to grow up without her mother. The way things were lookin' she may be growin' up without a father either. I had to face the fact that even though I didn't kill her, that I may be spending the rest of my life locked down.

Caged like a fuckin' animal.

I wondered if I'd ever see Michelle again. The idea of it sent chills through me. I remembered the first time I held my beautiful baby girl in my arms the day she was born. She started screaming bloody murder. She cried, until the doctor handed her to me. She stopped crying and stared into my eyes. At that moment I was hooked. It was like Michelle held up her pinky and I wrapped myself around it.

Michelle looked so much like Cassandra. I couldn't wait to get home every day so I could hold her, make funny faces at her, feel her squeeze my finger and just marvel at this new life I held in my hands. Cassandra would tell me to put her down 'cause I was gonna spoil her, but I didn't care. For maybe the first time in my life I was happy— happy to be home with my girls.

All that is over now.

Who would do that to her and why?

I tried to think of who my enemies were. Most, if not all of my enemies were dead.

Diego?

Maybe he set this in motion before I killed him?

Maybe his father, Gomez?

He had to know by then that Diego was dead and figured I had something to do with it. But no, I doubt even Gomez, with all his connections, could have put something together this quick. This took planning, that much I was sure of. Besides, Gomez practically disavowed any knowledge of Diego's existence. But my killing his son would be enough to change his mind.

It couldn't have happened any other way. I talked to Cassandra less than an hour before I came home and found her. She didn't give me any indication that anything was wrong.

I remembered dropping to my knees when I saw her. Her body was still warm. That means that whoever killed her, had to know where I was and how long it would take me to get there.

There's one thing that bothers me the most. Goodson said Cassandra called the police and told the 911 operator that I was tryin' to kill her. The police got there right after I did. I'm not sure how fast police response times are *around the way*, but I know that it can't be all that great. At least ten—more like fifteen minutes. The call had to have been made just before I came in the house. The only question now was why. Why kill Cassandra and not me?

I knew the answer to that.

The only reason to kill her and not me is to hurt me.

Maybe I was next.

The killer had to be somebody that would want to hurt me, exact some measure of payback for what they suffered.

I always knew that Cassandra was going to be my weakness, that's why I wanted her out of the city.

I was the reason she was dead.

Like I killed her myself.

That thought made me feel worse. How could I have been so stupid, blind to the fact that this was bound to happen? I was too fuckin' arrogant thinkin' that I was so fuckin' powerful that I couldn't be touched.

I thought I heard a noise, but I was so out of it I didn't give it much thought. I tried to think of every one that I killed or was in any way responsible for being killed.

The list was long.

Then I felt a sharp pain from a blow to my head and was dragged out of my bunk. I hit the floor hard. I looked up and could see three men comin' at me. I looked over at my cellmate, Pablo; he had retreated into the corner of his bunk and covered himself with a blanket.

The three men started kickin' me and hittin' me over and over with something hard. It felt like a cop's nightstick. I covered my head to keep from gettin' kicked or hit in the face with that club. Finally, I was able to grab the foot of one of my attackers and threw him to the floor. His head hit the floor hard and that appeared to knock him unconscious. The other two backed off, but only for a second. It was just enough time for me to get to my feet.

I looked at the two men standin' in front of me. I was already mad as hell and hurt over Cassandra's death and I wanted to—needed to take that out on somebody.

To make them feel my pain.

To make them understand without question, "You muthafuckas picked the wrong nigga to fuck with tonight!"

In the small, dark cell, I couldn't really see their faces; all I could tell about them was that they were white and bald. The first man came at me with the nightstick. He swung, but I ducked out of the way. There wasn't much room in the cell to maneuver, and that would be my only advantage.

When he swung at me, again, I grabbed the club with my left hand and his face with my right. With all the power I had, I slammed the back of his head into the wall. The other man jumped on my back and wrapped his arm around my neck. His grip tightened around my neck and he tried to pull me off his buddy, but in that small cell he backed into the bunk. I kept slammin' his head against the wall, over and over again until he loosened his grip on the club. Now I was able to wrestle it away from him. I hit him twice in the head with the club and he quickly went down. Then I swung the club wildly over my head and hit the guy with his arm wrapped around my throat. He let me go and backed away.

The first man that came at me started moving, tryin' to pull himself together. I threw the club at him like a spear and hit him in the head. He went out again.

Now it was just one left.

"Come on!" I screamed at him.

He rushed at me and I hit him as hard as I could in the face. He stumbled backwards and I kept hittin' him with both hands until he went down. I stood over him and returned the favor. "Who sent you?" I yelled and kicked him in the face. "Who killed my wife?" I kicked him in the gut this time. I kept kickin' that muthafucka until he stopped moving. I stood there breathing hard and lookin' down at my attackers. Damn, I was out of shape. It had been a long time since I had to fight three muthafuckas. Shit, it's been a long time since I had to fight anybody. Too much time livin' the good life. Too much time gettin' lazy and complacent, but if I ever got outta here, that would have to stop. When I get free, everybody's gonna know that Mike Black is back!

I glanced over at Pablo. Once the commotion stopped, he

peeked out from behind his blanket. Once he saw what had happened, Pablo jumped off his bunk and ran toward the bars. "Help! Help! Somebody help, come quick!"

I laughed a little, but I understood; this was my fight and he wanted no parts of it. Smart man.

Three guards came runnin' up the cell. "Oh my god," one said as he looked to the floor at the bodies at my feet. I raised my hands. They quickly had the cell door opened and without askin' what happened, they dragged me out of the cell, cuffed me and took me away.

"How did they get in my cell?" I asked quietly as they took me away, but I got no answer.

CHAPTER 16

As hard as she tried, Wanda couldn't get to sleep. There were a million things rolling around in her mind. She couldn't wrap her mind around the fact that Shy was dead and that Mike was in jail for her murder.

That doesn't even sound right.

She knew she had done the right thing by calling Marcus Douglas to defend him, but she still felt bad about it. "I should be the one defending him," she said out loud as she fluffed her pillow and tried again to find a comfortable spot. Wanda knew that this was too important and that she didn't have the trial experience that she would need to defend him herself. It would kill her if there was a chance to get Mike acquitted of the charges and she blew it because she made a mistake.

Frustrated with her inability to go to sleep, Wanda got out of bed. She put on her robe and went to the bar in her living room. Not that she was much of a drinker, but when she did, she usually drank apple martinis. "Not tonight." Tonight she was sure that she needed something stronger.

Wanda picked up a bottle of Tanqueray gin and poured herself a drink. It burned a little going down, but she drained the glass and poured another. Wanda sat down in her favorite chair and sipped her drink.

She, like everybody else, wondered who killed Shy. Wanda didn't think Shy had any enemies, and definitely none that would go to this length to kill her. It wasn't that she knew everything there was to know about Shy, but Wanda had assumed—with Shy being out of the game for so long—that problems like this died then.

Wanda felt that it was her responsibility to call Shy's family and tell them what happened. Her mother took the news very hard, crying hysterically before handing the phone to her son Harold. He told Wanda that he would be in New York the next morning to claim the body and take her back to Baltimore to begin to make arrangements for her funeral. "And since it's Mike who's accused of her murder; when I get there you and I can have a conversation about what is going to happen to Michelle," Harold said. It was a conversation that Wanda wasn't looking forward to having.

Earlier in the day, Wanda had called Pam's sister, Monica's house to check on Michelle. In light of what was going on, Monica had agreed to keep Michelle until it was decided what to do with her. Monica said she was just fine, totally oblivious to what had happened to her mother and father. *Maybe I should try to adopt her,* Wanda thought as she sipped straight gin. *But that would make me Mike Black's baby's mama.* Wanda laughed and took a big swallow.

Once Wanda had finished her second drink, she got up and went back to the bedroom. She lay across her bed confident that after two shots of straight gin she would have no trouble at all falling asleep. But that wasn't the case. Wanda continued to toss and turn, unable to find a comfortable spot so she could relax and go to sleep.

Wanda sprang to her feet and began to get dressed. She slipped on some jeans and a T-shirt. Wanda poured herself a shot and drank it before grabbing her purse and her keys. She headed for the door thinking that maybe if she went for a ride that it would help her to clear her head. *And maybe, just maybe I could get some sleep.*

After driving around for more than an hour, Wanda parked her car in her space at Impressions. When she got out of the car, Wanda was surprised to see Nick's car parked in front of the club, but it was a pleasant surprise. She was sure that he would be out in the streets with Freeze trying to find Birdie.

Almost without thinking, Wanda made her way around the club as she always did when she came in the club. Stopping at each bar and talking to the bartenders and waitresses, checking to see what kind of night they were having. While she made her rounds, Wanda looked for Nick. She was hoping to find him somewhere in the club, which would have saved her a trip to his office.

I don't want him to think that I came here looking for him, she thought, and that was the truth, she didn't come there looking for him, but she was excited that he was there.

They had been spending a lot of time together and she really enjoyed being with him. She and Nick got along so well together and she'd always thought that he was sexy. If she really wanted to be honest with herself, she'd have to admit that she wanted him, and that was the problem. First of all, she didn't know how he felt about her, other than being friends. The last thing Wanda wanted to have happen was for her to break down and tell Nick how she felt and for him not to be feelin' her. Second, they were friends, very old and dear friends. *What if we got together and it didn't work out between us*? Wanda would lose a good friend and good friends, real friends, are truly hard to come by.

Once Wanda made it up the stairs to the office, she put her hand on the doorknob and was about to open it when it occurred to her that Nick might not be alone in there.

What if he's got some waitress bent over the desk? she thought as she turned the knob and walked in. Nick was seated behind his desk going over that evening's paperwork. He looked up when he heard the door open. "Wanda!" he said.

Nick was surprised and very glad to see her, especially since he had been thinking about her since they had lunch earlier that day.

"Hey, Nick," Wanda said softly, but the enthusiasm in Nick's greeting made her smile inside. She took a seat in front of the desk.

"What brings you out this evening?" Nick asked as he filed the paperwork he'd been reviewing.

"I couldn't sleep, too damn much on my mind," Wanda replied.

"I can only imagine. Can I make you an apple martini?"

"I already tried drinking myself to sleep. Tanqueray gin, straight of course."

"Of course."

"It didn't help, I'm still wide awake. But go ahead and fix me one anyway."

Nick got up and walked over to the bar. "You think that Tanqueray mixes well with apple martinis?"

"I don't know. Make it Tanqueray, then."

"How about on the rocks this time?" Nick asked.

Wanda didn't look or act like she was drunk, but he knew all too well how Tanqueray had a nasty habit of sneaking up on you. While Nick fixed Wanda's drink and a Johnnie Black for himself, he looked at Wanda. He'd seen her dressed in her big fuzzy robe, in a sexy evening dress and more business suits and dresses than he could remember, but this look, dressed in a tight T-shirt and tight jeans, Wanda looked delicious to him.

You should just tell her how you feel.

"So what are you doing here, Nick?" Wanda said to snap Nick out of his trance. "I thought you'd be out ridin' with Freeze."

"He said he had to go handle some business. I asked if he wanted me to ride with him, but he said he had to ride solo on this one, Tonto," Nick said and Wanda giggled. He handed Wanda her drink. "After I dropped him off I came by here to see how things were goin'."

"Everyone says it's been a good night."

"Crowds been steady and they're spendin' money. Got a couple of wannabe ballers in the VIP ordering Dom like it's water."

Wanda raised her glass. "Here's to them," she said and took a sip. "So, did you find Birdie?"

"Nope, haven't found him or Albert. Freeze heard that a couple of his boyz been rollin' around puttin' the word out that they don't know where Birdie is, but they had nothin' to do with it. They're probably the ones that did it," Nick said and paused. "We can't find them, either."

"Not having a good night, huh?"

"I've had better."

"It's so frustrating not being able to do anything for Mike. I mean, we're not even sure that Birdie had anything to do with it. Have you heard anything else?"

"Nobody knows anything, if they do they're not talkin' about it. Right now Birdie is all we got. You talk to the police?"

"I talked to Goodson," Wanda said and took another sip.

"What's he got?"

"What he's got is Mike. The murder weapon with his

fingerprints on it and him found at the scene. Case closed, so let's all go out and eat doughnuts!" Wanda laughed and so did Nick.

She finished her drink and stood up. "I'm gonna get outta here, Nick. Go home, try and get some sleep."

"You gonna be all right to drive?" Nick asked and drained his drink. He stood up and followed Wanda to the door. "Do you want me to drive you home?"

Wanda stopped and turned to face Nick. "No," she said and paused. "But you could be a gentleman and walk me to my car. Make sure I get there safely."

As Nick and Wanda made their way through the club the lights dimmed and the DJ played the LeVert classic, *Baby I'm Ready*. "That used to be my song!" Wanda screamed as soon as she heard it. "I used to love this song back in the day."

"Would you like to dance?" Nick said and extended his hand like a gentleman.

Wanda looked at Nick. "I'd love to." And took his hand.

As the music played and Gerald LeVert crooned, Wanda fell into Nick's arms. "Do you remember the last time we danced together?" Wanda asked.

Nick smiled an uncomfortable smile. "I don't remember ever dancing with you. Something that feels this good, I'm sure I'd remember."

"Do you remember Darrell Cook?" Wanda asked, choosing not to say anything about the flirtatious comment Nick just made. *So, I feel good to you?* Wanda thought and held Nick tighter. *Well, you feel pretty good yourself.*

"Yeah, I remember him," Nick said. "Tall fat guy, used to break into white folks' houses. He used to always say he'd never rob no black people 'cause they ain't got shit worth stealin'."

"Yeah, well, robbing white folk got him fifteen years on a

burglary case," Wanda mused. "Do you remember the night we were at this party in Section Five and I got into an argument with him?"

"No," Nick laughed as he held onto Wanda like his life depended on it. "That's probably because I was drunk."

"Probably—we were all pretty drunk that night." Wanda paused. "You don't remember me and Darrell gettin' into an argument? We were all up in each other's faces, we were cussin' each other out, when all of a sudden you grabbed me by the arm and dragged me away from there. You said, *'Would you like to dance?'* I don't remember what the song was, I was so mad."

"But you calmed down pretty quick," Nick said, suddenly remembering it all now. What he remembered was that Black, who was always aware of everything going on around him, saw Wanda arguing with big Darrell and told Nick to go dance with her before it got out of hand. But that didn't stop Nick from taking credit for it. "You looked like you needed to be dancing instead of arguing."

Wanda buried her head deeper into Nick's chest. "Maybe this is what I needed to do tonight. Just go somewhere and dance."

"It's still early."

"No, I got a lot of work to do in the morning," Wanda said sadly. She looked up at Nick. "Do you dance, Nick?"

"I'm dancing now."

"That's not what I mean. I just don't remember you being much of a dancer. I remember you spending a lot of time drunk with your back on the wall," Wanda laughed. "Or in some woman's ear."

"That was a long time ago, Wanda. I'm not the same guy I used to be."

"I know that." Wanda paused and then she laughed. "You spend too much time with me to be out chasing women."

"What does that tell you?"

"I don't know," Wanda said as the song ended. She slid her hand into his as they left the dance floor. "You tell me, Nick, what does that say about you?"

"It means that I like spending my time with you," Nick said as they passed by one of the bars. "Do you wanna get a drink before you go?" he asked.

"No, thank you. I might have one before I get in bed."

"Need some company for that drink—before you get in bed?"

Wanda stopped and looked at Nick. She tipped her head to one side and thought, *why not*. "I just might," she said and started to leave the club. "Follow me home, Nick. Make sure I get there safely."

CHAPTER 17

"So you're a LeVert fan?" Nick asked.

"I say we take that conversation inside." Wanda blushed. She unlocked the door, invited him in and turned on the lights. She walked over to the CD player and with one touch of a button, soft music filled the air as Gerald LeVert's deep baritone bounced off the walls. Nick swept Wanda in his arms. "Now, where were we?" They began swaying to the music again. "*Oh Girl, oh Girl—Baby, it's time for me to give you all the love you need. Baby, I know that you deserve the best—*" Nick sang.

"It seems I'm not the only LeVert fan in the room?"

Nick stopped singing.

Wanda pulled back. "Why'd you stop? You were sounding good." Before she could say another word, Nick's lips locked with hers. She tried to keep up with his tongue's vigor, but the strength was too overwhelming. Wanda could feel herself getting caught up in a powerful tidal wave of pleasure. Soon, she began tugging at his shirt as if it was a barrier to her satisfaction. Once she managed to get it off, she covered his chest with kisses. "I have wanted to do this for so long," Wanda said almost in a whisper and bit softly, and tugged harder at his nipples. Nick held her head as she slowly kissed her way down to his waist.

Abruptly, he stopped her, gently holding her head between his hands. Their eyes met. "I have dreamt of this since the day I met you," Nick confessed.

Wanda kissed his belly button, but kept her eyes locked on his. She could feel the heat rising from deep within. Her nipples had hardened the moment he took her into his embrace for the dance. She felt the moisture that had gathered between her thighs. Nick helped Wanda undress him. He stood before her in nothing but his briefs and Wanda stepped back. When she began to undress, Nick watched closely, but he stopped her. "No, not yet. I told you I've dreamt of this for so long. Let me do this my way."

Wanda forced her lips to his, kissed and sucked his tongue, until he couldn't keep up. Nick pulled Wanda to his chest and kissed her. He reached under her T-shirt and ran his hands over her lace cups. He wanted to tear the damn thing off her, but that might ruin the moment. *Maybe it wouldn't.*

Slowly he pulled it over her head and immediately began kissing her neck, across the exposed area of her chest and down to her navel. Nick unbuckled her belt and unfastened her jeans. He stared into her eyes while he pulled down her zipper. Nick smiled at Wanda and kissed his way down. Once he reached the lace on her thong, Nick dropped to his knees and as slowly as he could, pulled down Wanda's jeans, all the while sliding his tongue along her skin.

Nick stood up and guided her to the sofa and stepped out of his briefs. Her eyes looked down at what he had to offer and a smile curled across her face. Wanda took his length in her hands and stroked it. "Ssssss, it's everything I thought it'd be," she moaned.

Make sure you fuck me like you mean it, he thought as they sank into the sofa and began kissing. While Nick enjoyed the taste of Wanda's tongue, he reached behind her and unhooked her bra, and then eased it off her shoulders. He had always wondered, fantasized about her breasts. They always looked so perfect in all of the clothes she wore. He took her nipple into his mouth. Wanda grabbed the back of Nick's head with one hand and her breast with the other. He slid his hand in between her legs Wanda moaned softly and her head drifted back. While Nick continued to feed, he wasted no time in removing her thong.

Wanda eased Nick's back against the couch and stood up. Nick looked up at Wanda as she moved, his dick throbbed in anticipation of what he was about to receive. His mouth opened like he wanted to say something, but he simply couldn't find the words. Wanda straddled him, grabbed her hips and slowly slid down on him with such ease that Nick could tell just how much she'd been anticipating this. She moved up and down with precision. Their bodies rocked in sync, Wanda rode his dick like she was in a competition and things were getting rough.

"I love this ass," he whispered, but Wanda couldn't hear him. She bounced up and down, while he sucked and squeezed her nipples.

"Oh god, Nick, that drives me insane!" she cried. He thrusted his hips, matching her rhythm stroke for stroke.

Suddenly, Nick grabbed her and rose from the sofa. "I forgot; which way is the bedroom?" he asked.

"You're gonna drop me!" Wanda laughed.

Nick looked at Wanda like she was crazy. "Please." There was no way he was going to drop her. "Which way?"

"Straight ahead to the right," she said.

"Oh yeah." While he remained inside her, Nick carried her into the bedroom and placed her onto the bed as gently as he could in that position. When he did, he stepped back to look at her. "Damn, I can't believe this," he mumbled.

Wanda laid on her back and spread her legs wide. "Come on, don't keep me waiting," she cooed.

With an invitation like that, Nick laid down on the bed next to Wanda. She began kissing him passionately and stroking his erection; his hands were all over her body. Nick closed his eyes as the sensation of hands gave way to the sensation of her lips, soft and wet, against his chest and then to his throbbing dick.

Nick rolled Wanda on her back and kissed her navel, and kept kissing her until he was between her thighs. Nick inhaled her scent. Soon his lips and tongue were engaged with her lips and clit. Slowly tonguing her lips and sucking lightly on her clit. "That's it, baby. Take your time, Nick," Wanda said and closed her eyes.

Wanda's excitement grew as Nick used the flat of his tongue and then the tip of it to make her feel different sensations. He listened to her moan, to the sound of her breathing and increased his pace. He opened his eyes and looked at the expression on her face.

Wanda was in ecstasy.

Nick felt her thighs quiver on his arms and then the sound of her toes curling up against the sheets. Suddenly her eyes sprang open. "You're gonna make me cum!" When she released, Wanda held his head in place and called his name. "Oh, Nick!"

Wanda was so wet that Nick guided his entire length in her with no problem. She wrapped her legs around him, once again holding him in place as he eased in and out of her.

"Right there, Nick!"

When he felt her body tremble beneath him, Nick stroked her harder to make sure she'd come back for more. "Cum for me, Wanda. I wanna feel your pussy tighten around my dick."

Wanda's eyes narrowed and she grinded her hips into him and gave him exactly what he asked for. The sensation pushed Nick to his limit. Wanda saw it in his eyes and rocked her body harder.

She had him, and she knew it.

CHAPTER 18

Kirk sat on the hood of his car outside the precinct, waiting for Lieutenant Reyes to arrive. Very early that morning Kirk spent some time with the 911 operators, listening to the recording of Shy's 911 call. It left the detective with more questions than it provided him with answers.

Nine-one-one operator. What is the emergency?
My name is Cassandra Black—he's trying to kill me.
Can you give me your location?
He's trying to kill me—Mike Black is trying to kill me.
Ma'am, can you give me your location?
Please come. He's trying to kill me.
Have you been injured? Do you need an ambulance?
Please come. He's trying to kill me.
Is the suspect present?
He's coming for me.

And then the phone went dead.
Kirk asked that the recording be played again. After lis-

tening to it for a second time, Kirk thanked the operator for his time and left the office. Once he was in the hallway, Kirk said, "Something ain't right."

The first thing that raised Kirk's eyebrow was how calm Shy sounded for somebody who had just taken a beating. When Kirk got in his car, he took out his recorder. "The caller's voice was very calm and even-toned. The caller wasn't crying or hysterical, she didn't sound nervous or the slightest bit stressed. In fact, it sounded more like the caller pronounced every word very clearly to be sure that she was understood. The call came in at ten-fifty-five. The ME puts the time of death sometime between ten-thirty and eleven-thirty. So that fits. Something else, the caller never really answered any of the operator's questions.

"When the operator asked where she was, *Ma'am, can you give me your location?* She said, *Please come. He's trying to kill me.* When the operator asked, *Have you been injured? Do you need an ambulance?* Instead of saying yes, or he beat me up or whatever, please send an ambulance, she says, *Please come—Mike Black is trying to kill me.*" Kirk turned the recorder off. "It just doesn't make any sense."

When Lieutenant Reyes got there he parked his car across the street and walked over. "*Mi amigo,* Kirk," Reyes said and shook hands with Kirk. "How are you, my friend? And more importantly, where are we having breakfast?"

"I got a box of doughnuts and a couple of cups of coffee in the car," Kirk replied and pointed to his car. "You're a little late so the coffee is probably cold."

"That is not the answer I was looking for."

"I'm only kiddin'," Kirk laughed and started to get in the car. "We can eat anywhere you want. I just wanna ask a couple of questions. And I wanna roll by the crime scene, if you have time."

Reyes laughed a little and got in the car. Once he had his seat belt fastened, he asked, "What did the ME say that got you up early in the morning?"

"Well, let me ask you something first."

"Go ahead."

"Tell me how you think it went down?"

"He beat her, she tried to run or at least turned her back, and then he shot her. Pretty cut-and-dry. We bagged it and tagged it and moved on to the next call."

"You think she fought back? Tried to defend herself"

Reyes paused and thought for a second about the body he saw. "Ass-kickin' like that, definitely."

"You check under her fingernails?"

"Now that we're talkin' about it, I do remember being surprised that they looked clean."

"ME thought that, too. That's when he noticed small cuts on her wrists. He also found small cuts on the corner of her mouth."

"I know he told you what he thinks caused them, so spit it out, Kirk," Reyes demanded.

"He thinks she was handcuffed and gagged."

"Wow, that changes things a bit. What else did he say?"

"He found trace of N-two-O in her system."

"N-two-O?" Reyes said in surprise. "What would nitrous oxide be doing in her system?"

"Good question."

"There's no way to know which came first, the N-two-O or the beating, but there's no reason for him to give her nitrous oxide and then beat her like that."

"Unless," Kirk said, prompting Reyes to reason his way through the problem.

Reyes thought about how badly Shy was beat. "So she could take more of a beating. The fucker took his time and beat her slow." Reyes took a deep breath and ran his fingers through his hair. "Forget breakfast, Kirk. I need to have another look at the crime scene."

Kirk smiled. "I was hoping you'd say that," he said and put the key in the ignition. "We could grab something on the way."

"Cool. But I'll drive. I got a feeling I'm gonna need my stuff."

After a quick stop for breakfast bagels and coffee, Detective Kirkland and Lieutenant Reyes headed for Black's house. They rode in silence for most of the trip, as each seemed intent on finishing their bagel before the other. Kirk finished first, a combination of Reyes having to drive and him being very hungry.

"So what's your deal here, Kirk?" Reyes asked.

"What do you mean?"

"This is not your case. So are you investigating Harris and Goodson's case to make sure they get the guy? I know how they do things. Or do you just wanna have some part in bringing him down?"

"Fair question. And the answer is neither."

"So what's up?"

"When the captain first told me about it I couldn't believe it. Mike Black fucked around and got caught. I'll admit it, I was a little pissed off that after all the times that I knew he did it and couldn't prove it, he finally got sloppy and got caught. Then the captain tells me that one, he killed his wife." Kirk counted on his fingers. "Two, he killed her in his house, and three, they caught him on the scene with the murder weapon, just waiting for the police to come. It just didn't add up."

Once they were inside the house Kirk and Reyes went straight to the kitchen. Kirk looked around the room. "Now the way it supposed to have gone was it all happened in this room. That he beat her and then shot her." Kirk looked around the room again. "Where's the phone?" he asked, noticing the phone jack on the wall but no phone.

"Evidence. We found it on the floor over there by the sink, along with some kitchen utensils and shit that was probably on the counter."

"Okay, so she calls nine-one-one, he caught her, ripped the phone of the wall. That stuff gets knocked on the floor somehow, then he beats her and shoots her. The call came in at ten-fifty-five and the report says the first officer was on the scene at twelve minutes after eleven. That gives him seventeen minutes to handcuff, gag her, and give her nitrous oxide. Doesn't give him much time."

"Maybe he beat her first, then she called, he caught her and shot her."

"Okay, let's say he did. Where are the cuffs?"

"Huh?" Reyes stopped what he was doing and looked at Kirk.

"And whatever he gagged her with, and whatever he gave her the nitrous oxide with; I didn't see any of it in your report."

"We didn't find any of those things," Reyes said nervously.

"So he disposed of all that stuff, but not the murder weapon, then he waited for the cops to get there. Didn't happen that way."

"I know where you're going with this, Kirk. We did everything by the book. We didn't know anything about no handcuffs or N-two-O. We found signs of a struggle, a body, and a murder weapon."

"Take it easy, Reyes. I'm not here to run heat on you. We're just two cops following up on some new leads we got from the ME, that's all. All I'm sayin' is the shit didn't happen that way. Let's get to work and figure out how it did happen. Now what did he handcuff her to?"

"One of those chairs would be my guess," Reyes said and began walking toward them, while Kirk looked around the rest of the room. Reyes checked the chairs and the rest of the area carefully, and couldn't find any marks on the chairs or anything else that indicated that Shy was handcuffed and beaten there. "Nothing."

"Anybody check the rest of the house?" Kirk asked.

"We didn't."

"What about Goodson and Harris; they clear the rest of the house?"

"I really don't know."

"Well, let's have a look around," Kirk said, shaking his head as he left the room. Once the two men got to the foyer, Reyes looked puzzled as Kirk reached for the doorknob.

"I thought you wanted to look around the house?" Reyes asked.

"I wanna have a look around outside the house, too."

Kirk and Reyes walked around the house, looking carefully for anything out of the ordinary. They made it around to the kitchen door and checked it over before moving on. When they got to the basement door the result of their search was different. "Take a look at this," Kirk said, kneeling in front of the door. Kirk stood up and moved out of the way so Reyes could get a look. He reached in his bag and looked at the doorknob through a magnifying glass. "What do you think?" Kirk asked.

"This lock's been forced. The marks are small, almost unnoticeable. At night, with just a flashlight, I might of missed this," Reyes admitted.

"Black told me that the alarm was on when he got home and it was always on when she was in the house by herself."

"If the alarm was on, forcing that door would definitely set it off. Unless somebody disabled it. But he says the alarm was on, so that would also mean they would have had to disable the alarm, forced the lock, and reset the alarm."

"Then how do you explain those marks?" Kirk asked.

Reyes thought for a second before answering. "Maybe Black was setting it up to look like somebody had broke in."

"So what you're saying is that after he killed his wife, he came out here and jimmied the lock to make it look like a break-in. And while he was doing that he got rid of the handcuffs, and the rest of that stuff." Kirk paused for a second. "He wouldn't have a lot of time, so he couldn't have gotten far, it's all gotta be around here somewhere. But why not stash the gun?"

"Maybe he stashed that stuff and went back for the gun."

"Or the gun and the body?" Kirk added.

"And he just ran out of time."

"He said he got a ride here. Maybe Simmons waited for outside for him. He could have taken the stuff out to the car and been going back for her and the gun. Or if Simmons was gone, he could have put it in his own car." Kirk looked around. "Did you check the garage?"

"No," Reyes said flatly.

Kirk turned to walk toward the garage. "Let's have a look inside."

Once they were back in the house, Kirk went into the living room. "Black said when he talked to her that she was in here watching TV." The living room was a good-size room, nicely decorated with two chairs on opposite sides of a picture window that faced the street, and an entertainment center with every device imaginable, with a big-screen television that covered one of the walls. A couch lined the other wall and a highback chair sat facing the television. Next to the chair was a table and a lamp on it. "If it's anything like at my house, that's her spot on the couch and this is his chair. The only thing missing," Kirk said and looked around the room and then pointed, "is the footstool. And what is it doing in over there? It's not really close enough to that chair for somebody to be using it with that chair."

"Somebody sitting on the stool talking to somebody sitting in the chair, maybe."

"Maybe."

"Hello, what do we have here?" Reyes said, staring at the lamp shade. He turned on the lamp to get a better look.

"What you got?" Kirk asked.

"Blood. A couple of small spots." Reyes stepped aside to let Kirk have a look. While Kirk examined the blood on the lamp shade, Reyes looked at the chair. "I got more on this chair. Definitely blood splatter," he said and went in his bag to get his collection tools to get a sample of the blood for testing.

Kirk stood in front of the chair. "Okay, this is where the beating took place. That's why the stool is over there. I think she was cuffed to this chair and the killer stood right where I'm standing and hit her." Kirk made mock swings with both hands, then pointing to what was now an obvious pattern.

Reyes pulled out his cell phone. "I need to get my team down here."

"I think that's a good idea."

When Reyes's team got to the scene, they wasted no time covering the house. This time it wasn't just a bag it and tag it exercise. If they had done everything by the book the last time, this time was much more thorough. By the time his team arrived, Reyes had set up barriers around the property. He assigned a man to control the entry or exit of all people entering and leaving the established boundaries. Now Reyes was very concerned about maintaining the integrity of the scene. He quickly assigned two officers to examine the basement door, the basement itself and the surrounding area.

Before the team left the crime scene, they had accumulated more evidence. Although they didn't find the handcuffs, or the gag, or whatever instrument was used to administer the nitrous oxide, a partial footprint was discovered in the area of the basement door. A cast was made of the partial footprint. However, there was no way of determining when the footprint was left or when the lock was forced. What they discovered inside provided more information on how the crime was actually committed. Now they were certain that the beating took place in the living room. In addition to the blood on the chair and lamp, they found several small drops of blood leading into the kitchen. "What's surprising is that the trail stopped at the kitchen floor."

"I think the killer had to have cleaned the blood from the kitchen floor so the trail wouldn't be followed back to the living room," Reyes speculated and Kirk agreed.

Detectives Goodson and Harris heard about what was going on at the crime scene and came over. "What the fuck is going on here?" Goodson demanded to know. He didn't appreciate Kirk checking behind him.

"We're investigating a crime, Detective," Kirk said and stepped closer to Goodson.

Reyes quickly got in between the two detectives and explained what they had found, but Kirk never mentioned the issues he had with the timeline. Knowing how the crime was committed didn't prove that Black didn't kill her. "None of this changes anything. As far as I'm concerned, we got the right man!" Goodson said and stormed off.

CHAPTER 19

Freeze hung up the phone with Mylo and got back in his truck. He had been in the street since early that morning trying to find Birdie or any information about Shy's murder. Tanya had been calling him at various times throughout the morning, but he didn't answer. When he finally did answer, he was surprised that Tanya wasn't trippin'. "I only wanted to know if you were all right. I was worried," Tanya said.

"Yeah, I'm a'ight. Just got some shit I need to handle."

"When can I see you again?"

"I don't want you anywhere around me until this is over."

"But you can't tell me when that will be?"

"No."

"Can't you at least tell me what's going on?"

"Look, Tanya, the less you know about what I do the better. You're not part of this world and that's how you gonna stay," Freeze told her.

"I love you," Tanya said and hung up the phone.

Freeze closed his phone and cracked a smile. Tanya was so different than Paulleen. If it had been Paulleen calling, she'd be losin' her mind because he was never around. *I guess that's why the bitch was out fuckin' everybody.*

Just like Tanya had been calling Freeze all day, he'd been trying to call Nick, but he wasn't answering either his home phone or his cell phone. He had driven by Nick's house, but Freeze didn't see Nick's car, so he drove on the first time. The second time he drove by Nick's apartment, even though he didn't see Nick's car, he stopped and went inside.

Since Freeze had a key, he let himself in. He searched the apartment and didn't find anything out of place from the last time he had been there. He sat down on the couch and wondered where Nick would be. It wasn't like Nick not to take his calls no matter what he was doing. But to not hear from him at all, especially at a time like this, with Black in jail and Shy dead, really worried him. He had called Wanda at her office, but her secretary told Freeze that Wanda called and said she wouldn't be in for the day. Freeze called her at home, but got no answer. He tried her cell, but the result was the same, voice mail. *Where the fuck is everybody?*

Freeze began to think about the possibility that something may have happened to them. *Why else wouldn't I be able to get in touch with either one of them?*

The idea that Birdie had killed Shy, and may have killed Nick and Wanda made Freeze furious. He sprang to his feet and left the apartment, slamming the door behind him. Freeze walked a very determined walk to his truck and got in. He banged both fists against the steering wheel. Although he hadn't told Nick or Wanda, Freeze felt responsible for this entire situation. Not only for what happened between Shy and Birdie at Cuisine, but he was supposed to come by the house that night and see Shy. She called Freeze and told him that Black was on his way home and that he wanted Freeze to wait for him. He resented Shy and the way she ordered him around, so that night he said, *fuck it! If Black wanna see me when he gets there, he knows how to call.* He was probably the last person Shy talked to. If he would have just went over there when she called him, none of this would be happening.

Freeze started up the car and sped away. He was responsible for Shy being dead and Black being in jail. The thought kept rolling around in his mind as he drove. It didn't matter how long it took or what he had to do, Freeze vowed to make this right. He would find Birdie and everyone involved and kill them.

Freeze tried to call Nick again, but still didn't get an answer. It wasn't long before he found himself driving down Black's street. There were police vehicles parked in front of the house and the area around the house was taped off. Freeze drove slowly as he passed the house. He picked up his phone and called Sergeant Adams. "Property, Sergeant Adams," she answered.

"What's up, Sergeant Adams?"

"How you doin', baby?"

"Not good. There are a lot of police at Black's house."

"Now? What would they be doin' there now?"

"That's what you need to find out. Call me back," Freeze said quickly and hung up the phone.

Freeze drove up on the avenue and passed a liquor store. Figuring that he could use a drink, Freeze parked his car and went inside. He brought a half-pint of Rémy Martin VSOP, and left the store. Freeze cracked the bottle as soon as he got out of the store. When he started walking back to his car, Freeze saw two faces he knew drive by in a white Rodeo. He recognized them from the other night at the

Spot. "That's the muthafucka got his face slammed in the bar."

Freeze knew that Birdie was too much of a bitch to do the shit himself, *wouldn't wanna get his hands dirty.* No, Birdie was the type of nigga that would send somebody. *He would send them.*

Freeze drained the bottle and threw it in a nearby trash can. He walked quickly toward the Rodeo, which was now stopped at a red light. Freeze removed his gun from his waist just as he got to the passenger window. He raised his weapon and fired into the car. When Freeze lowered his weapon, the clip was empty and Lonnie and Smiley were dead. Freeze put his gun back in his waist. As the car rolled into the intersection, Freeze walked back to his car, got in and drove away.

CHAPTER 20

Mike Black

Now what was that all about?
I sat on the floor in the corner of my cell, thinking. I didn't come out of the fight too bad. A few bumps and bruises on my arms and ribs from being kicked. And my neck is still sore from getting choked, other than that I'm all right. One of the men who came after me got a fractured skull, the other two were just knocked out. So far, nobody's said anything to me about the fight, or about charging me with assault.

A couple of suits came in and looked in on me while I was in the infirmary. They were more interested in what I was saying. One of them asked the guard that brought me in if I had said anything. "The only thing he said, sir, was he wanted to know how'd they get in there. Other than that I haven't heard a peep out of him," the guard answered. Then he came and told me that I was being taken to administrative segregation for my own protection and left.

I haven't slept much, couldn't sleep, too much on my mind to sleep. Those were Aryans. I haven't done any business with any Aryans, ever. So why would they come after me?

My head felt like it's gonna bust open.

What the fuck is going on?

If I wasn't sure of it before, I'm convinced now that this was a setup. Killing Cassandra was just the first part of it. That's why the cops were there so fast. Killing her was set up so I'd be caught at the scene. Arrested and in that cell. That's where they wanted me. I was supposed to die in that cell. That was their plan for me.

But who?

Why not just kill me, why kill her just to get me arrested and killed in here. I'm sure that all that will turn out to be very useful for Wanda when we go to trial, but I still had to live that long. One thing that I was sure of was that if somebody wanted you dead in here you're gonna die. Nowhere to run, don't know who your enemies are, who sold you out for a pack of cigarettes. Was it safe to eat the food? Or would I hang myself in my cell? Or maybe I'll sharpen that plastic fork and stab myself in the juggler vein. I know that there had to be at least one guard involved, maybe more. No way I was safer in segregation.

Somebody went to a lot of trouble to set this up. Somebody with resources. Power and money.

Who did I piss off with power and money?

Gomez would fit into the category, but I still don't think he could pull something together that fast. Besides, he wouldn't send Aryans to kill me, there's plenty of homeboys in here that Gomez could reach out to.

I laid down on the bed, and thought about Cassandra. I wondered, but knew I couldn't think of a time when I ever felt this much pain. She was everything to me. I loved her so much. I changed my life for her. I never thought about a future that didn't include her. Now she was gone.

That took everything from me.

And maybe that was the point. I took something from somebody and this is their revenge. They wanted me to feel this pain before I died in that cell. And maybe I should have let them. Let them stab me in the heart, 'cause I have nothing left.

I rolled over, thinking that changing positions would somehow change the things I was thinking about. But it didn't work, Cassandra was still on my mind. I thought about the dream I had on the way back from Miami. Interesting that I would dream about the day I met Regina on the day Cassandra died.

I should have died that night. Them muthafuckas had me, no gun, hands up, waiting to die. I didn't see him coming up behind them, I just heard the shots.

Bobby stepped out of the shadows. "I can't let you out of my sight for a minute, can I?" Bobby asked. "Can't even take a piss in peace. I'm standin' there with my dick in my hand and I heard gunshots."

"How did you find me?"

"Followed the gunshot and banged up cars until I found yours. Knew you couldn't of gone too far on foot, so I drove around until I saw this asshole goin' down the alley with his gun out. The rest was pretty easy," Bobby said as we got in his car.

"Thanks, Bob."

"Yeah, I know, I saved your life, again. But I'll tell you what, next time I go to the bathroom you're comin' with me. You wanna act like a little kid then I'ma treat you like one."

"Yeah, whatever."

After that we went by André's. He got a kick outta my *I*

almost got killed tonight story, then he put us back to work. André sent us out to Long Island to collect fifty grand for a guy name Gordon Hicks. Gordon wasn't involved in the game, he was in construction. He was the little brother of some guy André used to run with. Gordon was subcontracting the electrical work on some big job. He needed the money to make payroll and other expenses until he got his draw down from the general contractor. When the banks wouldn't loan him the money against the contract, he came to André, who gladly give him the money in exchange for the fifty he loaned him plus part of his company.

"After the night you had you can use an easy run," André laughed. "He's havin' a party tonight, celebrate finally gettin' that money. You and Bobby go on out there, drink up his liquor, fuck some of his women and bring me my money. You shouldn't have any problems, he called and said come get it. But if he don't have it all, make sure you give him to a new understanding."

So me and Bobby drove out there, and Gordon had the money waitin'. Bobby wanted to head back to the city right away, but I saw a few women that I was interested in so I wasn't ready to go. "Why don't you take the money and go?"

"You sure?"

"Yeah, shit, yeah, I'll be all right. I need to fuck new pussy tonight, and I saw a big amazon bitch that I wanna see naked. And what's up with you? I saw a couple that are your type. Skinny as a rail, flat as a board, with a juicy ass."

"Yeah, that's me. But I got somebody to do tonight," Bobby said. "So I'll go take André this money, and you get their numbers for me."

After Bobby left, I wandered around and mingled with Gordon's guests. He hadn't actually invited me to stay, but he didn't seem to mind. The whole time I got my eye on the amazon, patiently waiting for my opening, and when she stepped away from her group to get another drink, I went after her like a predator goes after his prey.

Her name was Cézanne; she was a registered nurse and worked in an emergency room. She was there with a friend of hers who knew Gordon's secretary. Cézanne was at least five-eleven, with long powerful legs and big thighs. Cézanne had big, delicious looking titties and fat, juicy nipples that were fighting to get out. All tucked neatly into a tight black minidress, and you know how I love a woman wearing black.

Sometime I feel like they're wearin' it just for me.

We were having an interesting discussion about treating gunshot wounds. I was especially interested since I almost got shot that night. While she was talkin' I noticed that somebody was watching me. There were two women standing off in a corner and neither of them were taking their eyes off me. They were both fine as hell, although I thought one of them was more Bobby's type than mine. She was rail-thin and had the kind of ass he likes, but she had nice-sized titties. They were both definitely fuckable. I tipped my head in their direction and they both smiled and waved.

I kept on listenin' to Cézanne talk about her life in the ER when I noticed that one of the women that was watching me had moved. I looked around the room and saw she had gone to the bar and gotten a drink and now she was coming my way.

She walked up and said, "Excuse me," like Cézanne was in her way. Cézanne stepped aside and she passed between us. Then she looked around like she was looking for somebody. Of course, Cézanne was oblivious to all this and was still talkin' away. Next thing you know the three of us are talkin', only now she's telling us about her job as a receptionist at a doctor's office. Finally, it got around to me and what I do. "I'm a collector."

"You mean like you call people on the phone and try to get them to pay their bills?" she asked.

"No," I laughed. "Not quite."

"So what do you collect? Stamps, coins, something like that?" Cézanne asked.

"No, people owe the people I work for money and I collect it for them."

"You mean like a gangster?" Cézanne asked.

"You could say that."

"Do you, like, kill people?" she asked.

"If I did, and I told you . . ."

"I know, you would have to kill her," Cézanne said. I swear it looked like her nipples swelled when she said that. Now the conversation was all about me, until Cézanne excused herself to the ladies' room.

"I thought she would never leave," I heard her mumble as Cézanne walked away, but looking back at me the whole time.

"What did you say?" I asked even though I knew.

"I said my name is Regina."

"I'm Mike Black."

That was how it started for me and Regina. At the time, I had never met anybody like her. Regina had style and she was interesting to talk to. Regina was the most articulate woman I had ever been with, and that includes Cassandra. Regina said she spoke that way because her grandmother always insisted in her speaking perfect English no manner how the other kids were talkin'. All I can say was that Regina was a lady, a lady in every sense of the word.

Regina introduced me to a whole new world. It was her that introduced me to fine dining, and goin' to plays, and art museums, and recitals. And we used to dance, every night, out on the dance floor having the best time. When she left me, the way she left me, I swore I would never dance again.

I loved Regina.

But I cheated on her relentlessly.

At the time I met Regina, I was fuckin' Vanessa, Victoria, and Lisa and a couple of others that I can remember their faces, but not their names.

My angel Vanessa, she had the prettiest ass I'd ever seen. I was with Bobby when I met her. "If you told her to haul ass, she'd have to make two trips," Bobby said at the first sight of Vanessa's ass. You might expect, with an ass like that, that she'd like doin' it doggy style, which she did but it wasn't her favorite. Her thing was having me squeeze her head with my thighs while she was blowin' me.

No lie.

Now, Victoria, that woman had so much raw sexuality. She would take a deep breath and my dick would get hard. I remember one time I took her to Atlanta to see her father at the VA hospital. We wheeled him outside and had a picnic. Actually we had a picnic and he smiled at her and seemed to have fun watching us have fun. On the way out, Victoria said she wanted to take one more walk around the beautiful green grounds before we went back to the concrete jungle we called New York City. So we're walkin' along and Victoria started walkin' off the path. I followed her into the woods and behind some bushes. I was about to ask what we were doin' there, but before I could get my question out, Victoria started takin' off her clothes and throwin' them on the ground. "Hurry up, take your clothes off," Victoria ordered.

And who am I to argue with a half-naked woman.

Once our clothes were off and on the ground, Victoria laid down and I laid down on top off her. While we were fuckin' we could hear people walkin', kids playing, and one guy who was tryin' to get his girl to do what we were doing. After that, New York City became our bedroom. We would fuck anywhere.

And Lisa, good pussy, but damn that bitch could lie her ass off. You never knew if what she sayin' was true or just more of her usual bullshit. Lisa didn't weight much so she used to love it when I'd pick her up and fuck her against the wall.

Now during the years that Regina and I were together, I fucked Tish. She was friends with both Vanessa and Victoria. Vanessa and Victoria knew each other through Tish, but they weren't friends. One night me and Tish was hangin' out and she said, "I know you fuckin' both of them. I just wanna know if there's any of that dick left."

Then there were Alisha, Gwen, Arlene; they were all waitresses at my club, the Late Night. Alisha was a small-time hustler on the run from some Miami boyz that threatened to cut her throat the next time they saw her. Her skin was jet-black and beautiful. Alisha had a nice ass too, but she was flat-chested.

I'm a tittie man from way back.

But the nipples on the girl must have been at least a half-inch long. When I was inside her, and her legs were on my shoulders, squeezing her nipples used to drive her insane.

Gwen was one of the few married women I've ever dealt with. I always thought it was bad business. Anyway, Gwen was a fine little Puerto Rican, maybe five-feet-one, at best. She would come by the office on the nights that she worked while she was on break. She'd have a drink, smoke a cigarette, powder her nose and talk shit with me. But before she went back to work, she'd kick off her heels, come out of those tight-ass waitress pants and we'd fuck on the desk.

And Arlene liked doin' it on the pool table, so she'd always try and find an excuse to hang around after the club closed.

Then there was Yolanda. Bobby used to call her *hair* because she had a high top fade, at a time when more people had gone past that. We fell out when she tried to play the pregnancy game with me. There was Marva, I really liked her, but she liked to fuck all the time and couldn't wait around for me to have time for her, so she moved on.

Damn. Angela. Damn, I wanted to fuck her ass, wanted to fuck her so bad that I hit the pipe with her just to get a shot of that ass. After I fucked her, I came to my senses and realized that that was the shit the muthafuckas is losin' their minds and their lives over, and in some cases, it was my job to take their life, so I knew that wasn't something that I wanted to get involved in.

And then there was my baby Brenda. She was much older than me and she told me once that if she ever got pregnant that I would never know about it, which was fine with me after I played that game with Yolanda. Things were goin' along fine until she stopped calling me, then she moved. A few months later, I hear from a friend of hers that she was pregnant. So I tracked her down and asked her if it was my baby. I was even thinking about doin' the right thing 'cause, like I said, Brenda was my baby. But Brenda said that it wasn't mine, that she had been seein' some nigga and it was his baby, but I didn't believe her. I never saw her again after that, I called her for a while, but she changed the number and eventually moved away. It's been years, but I still wonder if that really was my baby. And oh yeah, I fucked Cézanne, too. That night at the party she told me that she worked at Long Island Jewish Hospital. I found out what shift she worked and sat in the emergency room and waited for her.

I didn't feel good about the way I was doin' Regina, but I didn't feel bad about it either. It was just the way it was, I loved Regina and that was just sex. One had absolutely nothin' to do with the other. That was the way it was until I found out that she had been cheatin' on me, and it had been goin' on in one form or another with the same muthafucka for years.

Even though I was doin' the same thing, it still ripped my heart out. I felt like she wasn't mine anymore. Like the three of us had been sharing a bed. Until now, losing Cassandra, I had never known pain like that. I had never known what the pain I had knowingly put Regina through felt like. The roles had flipped and it was me and I hated the feeling. We were able to work things our and get through it, but things were never the same.

Regina was the type of person that was always worried about what people were sayin' about her. I would tell her, let 'hem talk. You ain't gonna stop 'hem no matter what you do. Even though Regina would smile in his face, she used to hate Bobby and tried to convince me that I should, too. Until Pam told her that she was marryin' him, after that Bobby was the greatest. He was willing to stand up and committed to his woman. When using Bobby to pressure me into marrying her didn't work, Regina started givin' me ultimatums. It finally ended at Bobby and Pam's wedding, when she told me that she hated me, and I never saw her again. I wished things had ended differently for us, I wish things had been different, I wish I was different.

But, there are a lot of things I've done that I regret.

Everything was different with Cassandra; she wouldn't have it any other way. I changed my life to be with her. I gave up everything I was before to be with her. There were no other women; I didn't want anybody else but Cassandra. I didn't need any other woman, because Cassandra gladly gave me everything I wanted and so much more. She was the total package, everything I thought a woman should be. Cassandra was everything to me, and I built my world around her. I loved her more than I loved life. Now she's dead, gone, and I don't know how to, or if I even want to, go on without her.

CHAPTER 21

Wanda woke up at 7:30 that morning when the alarm went off. She didn't want to get up, but she had work to do. Wanda sat up in her bed and looked over at Nick; he was still sound asleep. He deserved to sleep.

Wanda laughed a little and got out of bed. On her way to the bathroom she thought, *My god, Wanda, what have you done?* Wanda stopped and looked at Nick as he rolled over in bed. *Got satisfied! Finally!*

When Wanda got in the bathroom she looked at her reflection in the mirror. She had just had sex, great sex; okay, it was fantastic. But it was with somebody who, until last night, she called a friend. Although Wanda had thought about being with Nick many times, she never really thought that it would happen. She never thought that Nick was interested in her that way. They were friends, and Wanda simply accepted that no manner how she felt about him, that he wasn't interested. If he was interested he had plenty of time to mention it. "We're together all the time. He should have said something." Wanda turned on the shower and thought it funny that all it took was him saying, *Need some company for that drink—before you get in bed?* for her to drive home like a maniac and throw herself at Nick.

Now that the water was just the right temperature, Wanda stepped in and let the water beat down on her body. It was as if she could still feel Nick's hand all over her. It had been a while since anybody had made her feel the way she was feeling then. Wanda had dated a few guys throughout the years, nothing steady and definitely nothing that lasted long. As the relationship developed, Wanda would always find something that irritated the hell out of her or she would finally invite them over to play, only to find that they were lacking in certain important areas. There were doctors and other lawyers, agents, managers, the odd client or two. At one point, a young thug pushed up on her with a strong game, but his bark was so much worse than his bite.

Don't you hate it when that happens?

Shortly after they made love, both Nick and Wanda passed out, and she was glad for that. If they had stayed awake they would've had to have the *what do we do now?* conversation. But it was still a valid question. What would happen to their friendship? They could both agree that it was something that just happened because they were both under stress. *You know, because of Mike,* Wanda reasoned. They would agree that it would never happen again, and they would never mention it to anybody. *Especially Mike.*

But that wasn't what she really wanted.

Once she dried herself off, Wanda wrapped the towel around her and went to the closet to pick out something to wear. Before she and Nick could decide what they were going to do, first Wanda needed to be sure of what she wanted. It was obvious that she liked him, *liked him a lot*, but what did she want? Wanda wasn't sure. Fact is, she had known Nick for years. She knew how he was. Nick had sat on her couch and told her that he had sex with two women.

"One of them was to get information," Nick told her when she asked him about it. "And the other one threw herself at me. What was I supposed to do?"

"You were supposed to say no, thank you and got the fuck outta there. And maybe you shoulda worked a little harder and found another way to get the information other than stickin' your dick in her!" was what Wanda wanted to scream at Nick. Instead she rolled her eyes and said, "Whatever, Nick."

She selected a Kay Unger printed silk dress and got ready to leave for the office. After one last look in the mirror, Nick had made a shocking mess of her hair, but she was able to do something with it. On her way out the room, Wanda bent over and kissed Nick on the cheek and said, "Keep it hard for me. I'll be back for more later."

Wanda stepped outside; it wasn't even 9:00 yet, and it was already hot. She got in her car, turned on the air and began her trip downtown. As she drove, Wanda thought more about want she wanted for her and Nick. The one thing she was sure of was that she wanted to have sex with him again. But she really wanted more than that. Since they already spent so much time together, it would be easy to add a sexual element to their relationship. *A relationship. There, I said it. That's what I want, a relationship. One that will last.*

It wasn't too long before Wanda found herself on the Major Deagan, going absolutely nowhere. The traffic did give her more time to think. Although she did want a relationship, Wanda was by no means convinced that Nick was the right person to get involved with. *I think it's a little late for that now.*

Sure he spent a lot his free time with her, he did run Impressions. There were many nights when she watched women wearing next to nothing throw themselves at Nick. Now Wanda considered herself an intelligent woman, so there was no way she believed that Nick was passing up all that free pussy.

After thirty minutes of moving about a quarter of a mile, Wanda had had enough. She picked up her cell phone and called her secretary. "Cancel all my appointments and hold all my calls. I'm working from home today." Wanda forced herself into the slow lane, got off at the next exit, and went home.

When she got back to her house, Nick was still sleeping. Wanda slowly took off her clothes, watching Nick as he slept. After she returned her dress to the closet, Wanda slipped in bed next to Nick. He rolled to her right away. "Good morning." He looked at the clock and noticed that it was after 10:00 in the morning. "Don't you have to go to work?" Nick said and put his arms around Wanda.

Wanda laughed a little. "I tried that already. I've been up, took a shower, got dressed, left the house, got stuck in traffic, turned around, and here I am."

Nick smiled. "So you're not goin' to work?"

"Nope."

"Good," Nick said and rolled on top of Wanda.

For the rest of the day they alternated between making love and sleeping. Now it was after 4:00 and the two looked exhausted after their last session. "What are we doing?" Wanda asked and rolled away from Nick. Before he could answer her question with something clever like, *fuckin'*, Wanda said, "I mean, you should be out looking for Shy's killer and I should have gone to work and tried to find a way to get Mike out of there. Instead look at us."

"If you're tryin' to make me feel guilty about this it's not gonna work. There is no place I'd rather be."

"Neither do I, Nick. This has been so good, but what if something happened? I'm surprised your phone hasn't been ringing off the hook. I know Freeze has got to be looking for you."

"I turned it off last night when I got here. What about you? I noticed that your phone hasn't rang either. Anytime you worked from home and I've been here, your phone rings constantly."

"I told my secretary to hold all my calls," Wanda said and laughed.

"See there."

"I guess I'm no better than you."

Nick rolled out of bed and got his phone, but Wanda stopped him before he turned it on. "Before you do that, there's something I want to talk to you about."

Nick quickly got back under the covers. "What do you wanna talk about, Wanda?"

"Us, Nick," Wanda said, just a bit aggravated with Nick for not knowing the obvious. "What are we doing here?"

"Didn't you ask me that before?"

"I'm serious, Nick." Wanda frowned.

"Yes," Nick laughed a little. "I see that."

"I really need to know what's going to happen with us next."

"What do you mean, Wanda?"

"I mean you and I have been in this bed making love all day."

"I thought you said you left for a couple of hours?"

"Nick."

"I'm sorry, Wanda, I know what you're talkin' about. I know we made love all night."

"And all day today," Wanda quickly added.

"And it was great, Wanda." Nick paused. "I really feel

you." Wanda smiled and took Nick's hand in hers. "If it's all right with you, I'd love to do it again."

Wanda moved closer. "I do, too. It was—it was fantastic, that's what it was. But we're friends, Nick. I don't want this to ruin our friendship."

Nick shook his head. "I can't speak for you, Wanda, but makin' love to you won't change the way I look at you, or the way I feel about you." As far as he was concerned, he would never do anything to change that. Nick wanted to tell her that he knew things wouldn't because there was so much more that he was feeling. He had waited so long to be with her and now that they were finally together, she was acting like she was ready to call it a one-night stand that they would never mention again or to anybody.

"I understand that, Nick. I cherish our friendship and would hate for this to ruin it, that's all I'm saying," Wanda said and rolled over. "It was probably just because we're both just stressed about what's happening with Mike."

Nick got out of bed and walked over to the window. Wanda rolled over and watched him walk. He stood there, peeking out the window for a while, trying to decide what to say. Should he tell her now? Should he tell her now that he was in love with her, and run the risk of Wanda saying that she was, you know, flattered, but she wasn't interested in it being more than what it was, sex. They were friends, and that was the way she wanted to keep it.

Well, at least she wants to fuck some more, maybe in time, Nick thought and then knowing that wasn't what he wanted, Nick said *fuck it!* "It might have been like that for you, Wanda, it wasn't like that for me."

"What are you talking about?"

"I mean I'm in love with you, Wanda." Nick turned to Wanda and said, "Don't you know that, Wanda? I love you.

That's why I spend all my time with you, Wanda, 'cause I love you, and I have been so hooked on everything about you for a long time." Nick exhaled. "There, I said it."

"You act like it was a problem." Wanda smiled, and then she started to laugh a little. She knew that laughing in front of a man after he confesses his love for you was a bad idea so she held it back.

Truth be told, Wanda couldn't believe her ears. Even though she was feeling Nick, more so now since he made her scream like an animal, and that could even be stretched to include her feeling the same way, but it still caught her off guard.

"You don't know how long I've wanted to tell you that," Nick said and slowly walked back to the bed.

"What stopped you?"

"I didn't want you to get that look on your face and tell me that you were flattered, but you wanted to stay friends."

"Come back to bed, Nick," Wanda said and patted a spot on the bed. Nick walked around to his side of the bed and got under the covers. Wanda moved next to him and he put his arm around her. "You don't have to worry, even though I am flattered, I'm not going to say that. Not when I been feelin' you, Nick. All this time that I've been spending with you, I thought that's all you were interested in. I think I started feelin' you that night I got you out of jail."

"I started diggin' you that night, too," Nick lied and kissed Wanda on the cheek. "How come you never said anything?"

"I didn't wanna make a fool of myself. Let's just say I didn't wanna hear about how flattered you were."

They both laughed. Nick reached out for Wanda's face. He kissed her softly and then with real passion. Wanda ran her hand across Nick's chest. "So, now that we found love, what are we gonna do with it?"

"Oh, now you wanna know?" Wanda asked.

"Yeah," Nick laughed, "Now I wanna know."

Wanda moved closer. "Take it one day at a time."

CHAPTER 22

Now that Nick and Wanda had confessed their love for one another, Wanda recommended that they get back to the real world. Nick reluctantly turned on his phone and checked his messages, while Wanda called her secretary. "You were right, Freeze been callin'," Nick said.

"He called me, too," Wanda told him as she continued getting her messages from her secretary. Once she had gotten them all, Wanda hung up the phone and checked her home messages. "Damn!" Wanda said and deleted the message. She slammed the phone down and turned to Nick. "Bobby called."

"What did he say?"

"Where is everybody? He's in St. Maarten and that they're all having a great time. It's really doing a lot for Pam. He's at sea tomorrow and he'll call from the next island." Wanda sighed

"You think he'll call Freeze?" Nick asked.

"No. He said Pam was lookin' at him crazy because he was on the phone. Mike said he promised her no phone."

"Maybe you shouldn't tell Bobby."

Now it was Wanda lookin' crazy at Nick. "Why not?"

"You just said it's doin' a lot for Pam. Them and the kids are havin' fun together."

"And."

"What's Bobby gonna do when you tell him that Shy is dead and Black's in jail accused of the murder?" Nick got out of bed. "He's gonna make everybody pack their shit and drag them all back here to do what? He's right where he needs to be. Takin' care of his wife."

"You're right, that won't do Pam any good. I don't know, I'll ask Mike. I was supposed to go see him this afternoon. He probably thinks I forgot all about him."

"If you're still tryin' to make me feel guilty about how we spent the day . . ." Nick laid down next to Wanda. "Okay, it just worked, now I feel guilty. But I still don't regret it." He kissed her.

"I don't either," Wanda said and kissed him again. "Oh, I almost forgot, Kirk called me, too."

"Kirk has your home number?"

"He called the office," Wanda said and then she thought, *oh, no he's not jealous.* Wanda smiled a satisfied smile.

"What does Kirk want? He's not on the case, is he?"

"No, he's not, at least to my knowledge, but he called and said he wants to talk to you, and he doesn't have your number."

"Me? What does Kirk want with me?"

"He said it's about Mike."

Wanda copied down Kirk's number and handed it to Nick.

"Well, if it's about Black it must be important," Nick said and dialed the phone.

Kirk answered on the second ring. "Kirk."

"What's up, Kirk? This is Nick Simmons. I heard you wanted to talk to me."

"Yeah, Simmons, I want to talk to you about Black and the murder of his wife."

"You on the case, Kirk?"

"I stuck my hand in."

"What do you wanna talk about?"

"Black said that you dropped him off the night of the murder. I just have a few questions. When can we get together?" Kirk asked.

"I could meet you in about an hour," Nick answered.

"Make it two, I'm right in the middle of something."

"Two hours it is."

"I'll meet you in front of Black's house in two hours," Kirk said and hung up.

"What does he want?" Wanda asked.

"He wants to meet in two hours to talk about Black."

"Two hours, huh?" Wanda said very sexily.

"That's what he said," Nick said and started to grab his pants.

"Then you've got time."

Nick turned around and saw that Wanda had pulled back the covers and spread her legs. "You're right. I do have time."

"I'm always right."

Two hours later, Nick pulled up in front of Black's house. Kirk was already there waiting for him. He walked up to Nick's car and got in. "Hope you don't mind if we talk in here? It's hot as hell out there."

"You want me to turn up the air?"

"Shit—it feels good in here." Kirk admired the interior. "What model is this?" Kirk asked.

"XLR."

"Nice," Kirk said, nodding his head. "What's a heap like this cost, about eighty thousand?"

"Eighty-two."

"What's it like to drive something like this?"

"You wanna drive, Kirk?"

"Nah, I'm not that kind of hater. But anyway, I wanted to ask you a few questions about Black."

"What do you want to know?"

Kirk took out his notes. "Black said that you and him just got back from a trip, where'd you go?"

"Miami. But you already know that." Nick smiled and reclined his seat. He made himself comfortable while Kirk asked questions that he already had verified as fact. But being the thorough cop, he asked Nick, what business did they have in Miami? What time did they get back here? Did you park at the airport? How long did Black talk to Shy? Did you stop anywhere? How was traffic? What time did you get there? Then he asked, "What was the tone of the conversation?"

"What do you mean?"

"I mean did he sound upset, or anxious, did his mood change after he talked to her?"

"No, he was glad to be home. He was cool while he talked to her. They talked about the baby."

"Wait a minute. What baby?"

"What kind of detective are you? They have a five-month-old baby girl, her name is Michelle."

"Damn, I didn't know that. Where's the kid now?"

"She's with Bobby's wife's sister."

"Where is Bobby? I haven't seen him around lately."

"His wife got sick and he's been takin' care of her." Nick told the detective. Kirk didn't need to know that Pam had an emotional breakdown after she killed two people. "They're on a cruise right now."

"What happened when you got to his house?"

"He got out and went inside. I guess that's when he found her body."

"You talk to him after that?"

"No. I haven't talked to him since he got out of the car."

"What'd you do when you left there?"

"I went to the club."

"You go straight there?"

"Didn't stop anywhere."

"Anybody able to verify you were there?"

"Just the whole staff, there might have been a few that didn't see me."

"You didn't hang around the house, make sure everything was okay?"

"No Kirk, I didn't hang around, I went straight to the club," Nick said, thinking that Kirk was trying to drag him into this. "What are you gettin' at, Kirk? You think I had somethin' to do with killin' Shy?"

"No, I'm just asking questions. Why, did you have something to do with it?"

"No."

"I didn't think so," Kirk said and started to get out of the car, satisfied that if his story checked out, that it couldn't have been Nick that removed the evidence from the crime scene. "Thanks for talking to me."

"Kirk," Nick said quickly and Kirk turned and faced him. "Black didn't kill her. He couldn't. He loved her."

"I believe you," Kirk said and paused. "To be honest, I don't think he killed her."

"Then why is he in jail?"

"Wasn't my case."

"Then what are we doin' here?"

"I already told you, I stuck my hand in and pulled out a few—let's call them inconsistencies—that interested me."

"So if it's not your case, what are you doin'? Tryin' to make sure that Black gets life?"

"Why does everybody keep asking me that? Look, when I heard the story, it didn't quite wash for me. So I got involved."

"What do you mean, didn't quite wash?"

"I know you'll never admit to this, but Black's killed a lot of people and I've never been able to make a case against him. You wanna know why?"

"Tell me why, Kirk."

"Because he's a smart killer as killers go. No prints, no shells, no witnesses, nobody talking. That's the kind of killer Mike Black was in his day. Not the type that the cops catch at the scene, covered in blood with the murder weapon laying around."

"Yeah, he would have at least got rid of the evidence," Nick said, and then he thought about it. "That why you asked me if I hung around, to get rid of the evidence."

"Not if your alibi checks out. What about you, you heard anything I need to know?'

"No." Nick thought about telling Kirk about Birdie. "Like you said, nobody's talkin'."

"You got any idea who would wanna kill her?" Kirk asked.

"No idea. But somebody killed her and it wasn't Black."

"I'll let you what I think, I think that whoever killed her set it up to look like Black did it. They set it up to look like Black came home, lost it, and just got caught. The timing it took to pull this off took some planning. If I'm right it was planned down to the point that even with the inconsistencies I found that without another viable suspect, Black is gonna get life for murdering his wife."

CHAPTER 23

As soon as Kirk got out of the car Nick called Freeze. "What's up, man? Where the fuck you been?"

"I had to take care of something," Nick told Freeze, thinking about what he had taken such good care of.

"Whatever it was, it must have been real fuckin' important."

"Believe me, it was real fuckin' important."

"Whatever, Nick. All I'm sayin' is that with all the shit that's goin' on I need to hear from you."

"Yes, Daddy."

"Fuck you, Nick. Where you at now?"

"In front of Black's house."

"What the fuck you doin' there?"

"Talkin' to Kirk."

"What he want?"

"He wanted to know if after Black went inside, did I wait and take evidence away from there."

"What? That don't make no fuckin' sense. What evidence Kirk talkin' 'bout? They got the gun."

"Doesn't make sense to me either."

"Fuck Kirk, let him do what he gotta do, I got some shit I need to tell you about."

"What shit?" Nick asked.

"Meet me at Cuisine in about an hour."

Nick drove off and looked at the dashboard clock and thought about going back to Wanda's house and bending her over some piece of furniture, but he called her instead. "Hello, Wanda."

"Hi, Nick."

Nick could tell by the sound of her voice that something was wrong. "What is it?"

"Three men attacked Mike in his cell last night."

"Is he all right?"

"He is, but they aren't. One of them is hurt pretty badly. Mike's in administrative segregation for his protection."

"It happened last night and you're just hearin' about it now?"

"They left a message with my secretary. Even if she tried to call me, my ringer was off and my cell was on silent."

"Oh."

"How'd it go with Kirk?"

"He doesn't think Black did it."

"Then why is he still in jail?"

"That's exactly what I asked him." Nick smiled.

"See how close our minds are?" Wanda mused. "What did he say?"

"He said whoever killed Shy, set up to make it look like Black killed her. He said he found some, what he calls inconsistencies, but he said unless we find who killed her, Black is goin' down for this."

"Well, whatever inconsistencies Kirk found will come out in the discovery phase, so that will help us. What else did Kirk say?"

"Kirk said the setup took planning and timing to pull it off, and that means somebody with resources and a reason to want to kill her and make it look like Black did it."

"Has anybody considered that maybe this has nothing at all to do with Mike?" Wanda asked. "Shy used to do business and I'm sure she made enemies."

"You're right, but all I'm sayin' is Kirk said it took planning, right?"

"Right."

"Kirk gave me the impression that however it went down it took a lot of planning. The thing with Birdie and Shy happened the night before the murder. That's not enough time to set anything up, and to me that lets out Birdie. So we need to stop fuckin' around with that nigga and find out who really killed Shy."

At that moment, Birdie and Albert were relaxing in Atlantic City, on the boardwalk at the Trump Taj Mahal casino resort, in one of their rajah suites. They caught Smokey Robinson in the Xanadu lounge and hung out in the Casbah nightclub. Birdie hit the crap tables, while Albert played poker. Their plan was to stay a few days there, have some fun, then go back to New York. They would say that Birdie was in Atlantic City on the night of the murder. When Albert found out what it was all about, he went down there to tell Birdie, and since Birdie didn't know anything about it, they didn't see any reason to rush back.

When Albert got the call that Freeze had killed Lonnie and Smiley, he was in the Jacuzzi with a blond hooker that latched on to him while he was playing poker the night before. She was working the casino that night and saw Albert raking in big pots, so she angled her way to a spot right behind him. She had been there a while before Albert turned around and noticed her. The woman was absolutely stunning, in that red Badgley Mischka satin cocktail dress. Albert picked up a hundred-dollar chip and put it in her cleavage. "Don't go anywhere. I won't be long." Thirty minutes later, they were at the bar, sharing drinks and making arrangements. Thirty minutes after that they were in his suite.

Now that he had the news, Albert hung up his cell and thought for a minute. He looked over at his blond companion and said, "This is working out better than I expected." Albert excused himself and got out of the Jacuzzi. Once he'd dried himself, Albert put on the hotel robe and went into the living room. Birdie was laid back on the couch; he, too, had picked up a working girl. She was a tall black woman with very pretty lips and an ass you could sit drinks on. When Albert came in the room, her ass was the first thing he saw. Ass up, face buried deep in Birdie's lap.

"Bird, we need to talk."

Birdie gave Albert a wide-eyed look. "Now," he said, about to cum.

"Hurry up, this is fuckin' important."

"So is this," Birdie said to Albert and looked down. "Gohead, baby."

Albert turned away and tried not to look at the woman's ass, but the temptation was too great. He looked just in time to see Birdie make a cum face.

Albert laughed and went back in the bathroom to laugh some more. "What's so funny?" his blond companion asked.

"Nothing, sweetie. You just had to be there."

Albert waited enough time for Birdie to regain some sense of composure, before going to talk to him. By the time Albert came in the room, the woman was sitting on the couch next to Birdie, who had pulled his pants up, but she was still naked. "Honey, could you, like, wait in the Jacuzzi for me?"

The woman looked at Birdie, he motioned for her to go.

"But isn't somebody already in the Jacuzzi?" she asked as she walked by Albert.

"Yeah. I'll be in a little while to watch," Albert said, staring at her ass until she got to the door and turned around.

"Okay, but that's gonna cost extra," she said and closed the door behind her.

"Damn, she got a big, pretty ass," Albert remarked.

"Know what I'm sayin'?" Birdie agreed. "Wait till she sucks your dick."

Albert sat down in the chair across from Birdie, but he couldn't resist laughing a little when he thought about that cum face. "What's so funny?" Birdie asked.

"Nothing, Bird. You just had to be there."

"All right, what's so important?"

"Freeze killed Lonnie and Smiley," Albert said flatly.

"What?"

"You heard what I said. Freeze killed Lonnie and Smiley," Albert repeated.

Birdie bounced up from the couch. "When this happen?"

"This afternoon."

"You know how it happened?" Birdie snatched the bottle of Henny off the table.

"Pour me one, too," Albert said and continued. "Lonnie was stopped at a red light, Freeze walked up to the window, popped them both, and walked away like it wasn't shit."

"Where'd it happen?"

"On the avenue, a couple of blocks from Black's house."

"What the fuck were they doin' there?"

"I don't know."

"Damn. Just walked up and shot 'hem in the daytime, and just walked away. You can say what you want about Freeze, but that muthafucka got heart."

"What you gonna do, start his fan club?" Albert asked, but Birdie ignored him.

"Here, take your damn drink," Birdie handed Albert his drink and sat down. "This is fucked up."

"What is?" Albert asked. "I mean, other than Smiley and Lonnie being dead, what is so fucked up about this?"

"Sometimes, Alley, you so smart you stupid as hell. That's what's fucked up about it. They're dead! I knew I shouldn'ta listened to your ass. We shoulda went right to Freeze, stood up and said nah, we didn't do no foul shit like that. You want us to go ride on the niggas that did it? He woulda respected that."

"And he still will when you say it. I mean, don't you see how this is working out exactly like we planned it."

"You planned on Smiley and Lonnie being dead?"

"I said we all need to lay low. Not go ridin' around the dead zone. What the fuck were they doin' there?" Albert said and stood up. He looked around the room and announced, "This is layin' low. In AC, gettin' our dicks sucked."

"A'ight, they fucked up. They got caught slippin', but I still gotta do somethin' about it."

"I agree, we need to stick to the plan."

"The plan? Why you can't see this."

"See what?"

"That it was a stupid plan. Muthafuckas is dead behind your plan."

"It's an acceptable loss!" Albert yelled. "Those aren't your homies! They're soldiers! Soldiers, Bird, and you are the general and like it or not this is a war now."

"That's why I gotta bust back. If I don't do nothin' muthafuckas will try to roll over me."

"But if you escalate this, it will be bad for business."

"Then business will have to suffer."

"Okay, but think about this for a minute. We go back tomorrow, we put the word out that we wanna meet with Freeze or Bobby. You still make that same speach about ridin' the niggas who did it. But you tell them that you're willing to consider Smiley and Lonnie a misunderstanding, because it's bad for business. They'll respect that."

Birdie thought about what Albert said. "No, Alley, this time we gonna do things my way. We bust back. End of story."

"Who you gonna kill then?" Albert asked and turned away.

"Freeze."

Albert turned back quickly. "Now that's another matter entirely."

"What you talkin' about?"

"Think about it, you kill Freeze and that takes this to a whole other level. If Freeze is dead, Shy is dead, and with Black in jail, Bobby will come talk to us."

CHAPTER 24

Mike Black

I understand why some muthafuckas lose it in here. Time ain't no easy thing to do. Especially in here, nothin' to do but think. Think about shit you don't wanna think about.

I can see Cassandra's face, beaten.

I wondered if I'd ever get that picture out of my mind and be able to remember her like she was, beautiful, and mine. No one ever had a hold on me the way she did. I would have given her anything she wanted, done anything for her.

I wondered what was goin' on in the world. Maybe Wanda will visit today. I definitely could use it. I needed to know what was goin' on. Information makes the world turn and I'd made my livin' on it. Knowing what to do and when, was the key to it all. It's served me well, until now.

You know what's funny about this, of all the shit I've done, all the people I've killed, I'm in jail for a murder I didn't do, couldn't do. What goes around, comes around, right?

Over the years I've done a lot of shit, some of it—okay, a lot of it—I'm not proud of. I've heard a lot of people say that they've never killed anybody that didn't deserve it or never killed anybody that wasn't in the game. "They don't count," I've heard. "When you livin' that life, that's the risk that comes with it."

There are two people that I've always regretted killin'. One was stupid, I was drunk. But the other, he didn't have to die. Like I said, the first one, I was drunk, that's my only explanation. I was hangin' out with Angelo Collette.

So we're out in Long Island when Angelo saw this guy. "Hey, Mikey."

"What?"

"You see that guy over there?" Angelo slurred.

"Which one?"

Angelo pointed. "The white guy."

I looked at Angelo's finger and followed it. "They're all white guys, Angee."

"The one wearin' sunglasses at night."

"Oh."

"That fucka owes me money," Angelo said.

"So what you wanna do? You gonna kiss him or we gonna get your money?"

"What are you, Mikey? A fuckin' fruit or somethin'? Hell no, I ain't gonna kiss him. But the chick with him, now her I'd like to fuck."

I looked closer. "Damn, Angee, that's a fuckin' man!"

"It is?"

"What are you, Angee? A fuckin' fruit," I laughed.

"No, I'm fuckin' drunk!"

"Shit, so am I. But I ain't talkin' about fuckin' no man.

What are you? A fuckin' fruit!" I laughed so hard my head started hurtin'.

"Come on, Mikey," Angelo said and stumbled in that direction. "Hey, hey. Hey you, fuckface. You with the glasses," Angelo said as we staggered up.

"What's up, Angelo?"

"Fuck that, fuckface. Where's my fuckin' money?" Angelo demanded to know. He grabbed the guy by the collar and led him around behind the club. "Now, fuckface. Where's my fuckin' money?"

"I don't have it on me. I'll bring it to you tomorrow, I swear to God, Angelo."

Angelo turned to me and when he turned back it was with one to the gut. "Hey, fuckface. I'm fuckin' talkin' to you, fuckface. Where's my fuckin' money, and you better not tell us no shit about you ain't got it."

"Really, Angelo, I'm gonna give you your money. I just ain't got it on me."

"You hear this shit? You hear this shit, huh, Mikey? This piece a shit don't have my money."

"Yeah, I hear him."

"This fuckin' fuckface piece a shit don't have my money. Shoot this prick, Mikey."

I took out my gun and shot him.

"What the fuck!" Angelo screamed. "Are you out your fuckin' mind, Mikey?"

"What? You said shoot him, so I fuckin' shot him," I slurred and put my gun away.

"I was fuckin' kiddin'. I was just tryin' to scare the bastard," Angelo said as he paced back and forth over the body. "Fuck it, let's get outta here."

Back then, I was young, dumb, drunk, and armed. A deadly combination.

* * *

Then there was one other guy. He didn't deserve to die either, but I killed him. I was goin' to collect from a guy named Herman Epps. He was a nice guy, I mean it. Herman Epps was really a nice guy. But one thing about Herman, he was all about business. He was a consistent buyer, never late with the paper. He wasn't gettin' rich with it, but he was doin' well. Herman's downfall, like most men, was women. He loved them and he loved to love them. I'd see Herman hangin' out at all the hot clubs. Always with a different woman, but then he met Anastasia. After that Herman was never the same. After that his game got sloppy, but Herman could never see what kind of poison Anastasia really was.

Anastasia was an attractive woman, but she wasn't a star or anything close to it for that matter. But to hear Herman tell it, Anastasia had a gift. He told me once, even though I didn't really wanna hear it, that he didn't know what cummin' was until he met her. Long story short, he was pussy-whipped. Herman said the only thing wrong with her was that Anastasia was insanely jealous. If a woman ever got near Herman, she'd make a fool of herself and Herman, too. After a while, Herman laid back, cut loose all of his women and married Anastasia.

So like I said, Herman had gotten a little slow with the money, but he always came through. At the end, Herman was tryin' to step it up, making bigger and bigger buys. Until this one time, he had re-upped on the product, even though he owed fifty grand. It was Herman, always straight with the paper. So when he assured André that he would have his money in a few days, nobody thought twice.

But all of a sudden, Herman goes missin', nobody and I mean *nobody*, had seen or heard from him in weeks. I had gone by his apartment, Herman wasn't there. Wasn't in any of his usual spots, he was ghost. One night about two in the morning, I was in the area hangin' out with Cézanne and I see a light on in his apartment. I told her that I would be right back, put my gloves on and went inside. When I got to the door, I heard music playin' softly. I knocked on the door, Herman didn't answer. "Herman! It's Black! Open the door, I just wanna talk." Still no answer. "Come on, Herman, I know you're in there. I can hear the music." He still didn't answer, so I used this size fourteen key I got.

When I kicked in the door and went inside, the place was a mess, and it smelled bad. It was hard to breath, it was so funky in there. My first thought was, *I would think Anastasia would at least keep the place clean, but maybe cleanin' ain't her thing. Herman said she could fuck, not clean.* I went into the living room and found Herman sittin' in a chair, listening to Teddy Pendergrass, staring at the snow on the TV screen, but he had a nine-millimeter in his lap. At first, he didn't seem to realize that I was there. "Herman! Herman!" I yelled and got a step closer. "Herman!"

Slowly he turned toward me. "Black," Herman said softly. "How'd you get in here?"

"I kicked in the door."

"Oh." I looked at Herman, he was dressed in black, but it was wrinkled, like he'd slept in those clothes for a while. He needed a shave and his hair was matted to his head. And I found out what I smelled was Herman. I had never seen him look so bad.

"What the fuck is wrong with you, man?" I asked Herman.

"I know you come here for money, Black, but I ain't got it," Herman said slowly.

"What is wrong with you?" I asked again.

"I ain't got it, Black. I wish to god I had it, I wish—" Herman said and started cryin'. I'm not talkin' about a tear or two, he was cryin'. "I wish Anastasia was here."

I hate to see a woman cry, I admit it, it's one of my weaknesses. But a man cryin' is the worst. "Dude, dude, what you talkin' about? Where's Anastasia?" I asked as Herman continued to cry.

"She took everything from me, and left me here with nothing, Black. And I loved her, Black, and I trusted her. I fuckin' trusted her!" Herman yelled and swung the gun around.

"Who, Anastasia? She left you? Damn, Herman, I'm sorry."

Here I come to collect money or administer pain and I'm feelin' sorry for the guy. "It's gonna be all right, man. Just watch how you swing that gun."

"She left me, Black. Ran off with some nigga she used to get high with," Herman cried. "I thought she loved me. I gave her everything."

"Sometimes that's a mistake. Some women take you for weak when you give them too much," I reasoned. "But chill out, it'll get better. There's plenty of other fine-ass women out there," I said thinkin' about the one I left in the car.

"You don't understand!" Herman swung the gun again. "I don't want anybody! I love her!" Again with the tears.

"Look, man. I'm sorry Anastasia left you. I didn't think she was like that, but I guess you never know." I thought about Regina. At the time, I wouldn't have thought she was capable of cheatin' on me, but you know how that turned out. "You gotta get your shit together. Clean yourself up, clean this place up," I said and pointed around the room with my gun. "Get your package back and find you some new pussy. I guarantee it will make you feel better. I ain't gonna fuck you up, 'cause you shootin' bad like this and shit. Just tell me when you think you'll have some money and I'm out."

"But you don't understand. Anastasia's gone, Black. She took everything."

"Hold up. You tellin' me that Anastasia bounced with the money?"

"And the product. She took the money and the product. That's what I been tryin' to tell you. Anastasia took the money and the product and ran off with that nigga." Herman began to cry again.

Damn.

Ain't that a bitch?

Or should I say, ain't she a bitch.

"How could she do me like that, Black? I ain't no bad guy. I treated her good. Didn't kick her ass, even though she needed it sometimes. Never called her out her name."

"She took the money, Herman? The fuckin' money!" I yelled.

"All you care about is the money, but I lost everything. I don't have anything any more."

"Yeah, Herman, that's all I care about," I lied. I really did feel for him.

"There's nothin' left for me now. Anastasia was all I had. I just wanna die, Black. I wanna kill myself, but I just don't have nerve. I been sittin' in this chair for I don't know how long, with this gun, but I just can't do it."

"Fuck that, Herman, don't kill yourself, she ain't worth it."

What was I sayin'? I was supposed to be killin' him about this money.

"Kill me, Black."

"What?"

"Kill me, Black. I just don't wanna live without her. She took everything from me. She took away my future. Please, Black, just put your gun to my head and pull the trigger."

"No!"

"You can use my gun, Black, just kill me please," Herman said and tried to hand me his gun.

"No! Nigga, is you crazy? I may kill you about not havin' this money, but I ain't gonna kill you 'cause that bitch left you. What I need to do is find her ass."

"No, Black, please, don't hurt her. Please, I'm beggin' you, Black, don't kill her, kill me. I'm the one that don't deserve to live."

"Look Herman, I'm gonna get outta here, man. You're depressing the fuck outta me. I'll be back to check on you, see if you know where she is. I'm not gonna hurt her, Herman, I promise. Just don't do nothin' stupid, a'ight?"

Just as I turned to leave I heard Herman call me. When I turned around, he was pointing his gun at me.

"I can't let you hurt her, Black! This stops here!"

I shot him.

Two shots in the head.

"Damn, Herman!"

I looked at Herman's dead body slumped over in that chair.

I picked up my shells, got outta there and went back to Cézanne. "Took you long enough." Cézanne pouted and folded her arms.

We drove away in silence, or at least I drove in silence. Cézanne on the other hand, was goin' on and on about how rude it was for me to leave her in the car and take so long. That went on until I screamed, "Enough!"

After that, I made it a personal mission to find Anastasia. It took me five months to find her. Her and her new man relocated to Dallas and got into the game. With a quality product that they didn't pay for, they were able to be very competitive on price. Anastasia and her new man were livin' the life.

The life she sucked out of Herman.

One night me and Freeze paid them a visit. It was hot as hell down there. We didn't kill them, I just wanted the money. Freeze tied up Anastasia and held a gun to her head. "Now, if you don't give me my hundred grand, he's gonna kill her. But we're gonna fuck her first 'cause I hear she got good pussy." We stayed down there for two days; eating their food and suckin' up their air, but we didn't fuck Anastasia. It took him that long to get up the money.

I've always regretted killin' Herman. No matter what he said or how he felt, he didn't deserve to die. Thinking back, I really don't think Herman was gonna shoot me. *It stops here.* He wanted me to kill him. I wonder if it was because I was goin' after Anastasia, and he thought I would hurt her or because he just wanted to die. Either way, I didn't have to kill him. And whatever this is about, they didn't have to kill my baby.

CHAPTER 25

Despite the fact that Black was in jail and Shy was dead, business still had to be done, and that included Cuisine. Freeze entered the club through the back door and went through the kitchen to the office. He unlocked the door and went in. This was the first time Freeze had been in there since it became Shy's office. In spite of the fact that Freeze had the office swept for bugs once a week, Shy would never talk in the office. After their experience with DEA and the surveillance, she felt it was safer if they'd always meet outside. They would meet in plenty of delis, diners, and pizza shops, because Shy loved to eat, but couldn't cook.

Freeze always thought it was funny how Black would sit quietly and eat, while Shy told him exactly what Black told her to say. *Black's puppet*, was what Freeze used to jokingly call her. He told Nick once that Black was the world's greatest ventriloquist, because Black's mouth never moved, but you knew it was him talking.

There was a knock at the door. "Come on," Freeze said.

Lexi, the club's manager, came into the office. "How you doin', Freeze?" she said and sat down in front of the desk.

"How is it you always know when I'm in here?"

"You really wanna know?" Lexi asked.

"Yeah, I really wanna know."

"My nipples get hard whenever you're in here," Lexi said, smiling shyly.

Freeze gave her a look. "You serious?"

"No," she giggled. "I just do, that's all."

"Somebody's coming to see me tonight. I told her to ask for you. Her name is Aynna Thomas. Now listen, when she gets here, tell her to meet you at the back door. Then you bring her here to me."

"Not a problem," Lexi said. "Any news about Black?"

"No. I haven't heard from Wanda all day."

"You think he did it?" Lexi asked reluctantly. When Shy came and took over the club, first person she came to was Lexi. While she was working for Freeze her title was hostess, but Lexi ran things.

When word started to get around that Shy was taking over the club, Lexi really didn't know Shy. Of course she'd met her when Shy first became involved with Black. But shortly after that Black took Shy away to the Bahamas, and to Lexi, Shy became nothing more than at-work gossip about the adventure that she and Black had. Now here she was, her new boss. The idea that Shy was in charge and would more than likely bring in somebody to run the club or worse, she would try to run it herself, wasn't something that she was looking forward to. Lexi liked working for Freeze, he let her run the club for him and do pretty much whatever she wanted.

That first day, Shy sat where Freeze was seated and explained to Lexi that, "I know you've been running this place," Shy told her at their first meeting. "And everybody says you're doing a good job."

"Thank you," Lexi said graciously.

"I know you're probably thinking that I'm gonna come in here and change a whole lotta stuff, but I only want to make one change and it involves you. So I wanted to sit down with you first."

"I understand. What type of change do you have in mind?" Lexi asked, thinking *no, this bitch don't think I'm gonna train somebody to take my spot. That bitch is crazy. I'll quit first.*

"I worked with Michael, running the Paradise before we moved back up here. My first thought was to manage the club myself."

Lexi thought, *I knew it.*

"I would have to rely on you for, well, for everything, 'cause I wouldn't know anything," Shy laughed out loud. Lexi laughed, too, but hers was a guarded laugh. "I mean, I would have to ask you where do we keep the silverware, I wouldn't know prices, menus, and then there's the staff. And I don't even wanna think about the vendors." Shy rolled her eyes and shook her head. "So, the only change I'm gonna make is a new manager, Lexi, and I'd like you to consider taking the position, with an increase in pay of course."

So it was set, Shy wandered around the club and played hostess, making sure the guests were having a good time, while Lexi ran the club. Over time, Lexi had come to not only like, but respect Shy. She couldn't stand Shy at first, but as you got to know Shy, you start to like her. That was just the way she was, and now she was gone.

*   *   *

Freeze looked at Lexi. To him it didn't matter if Black was guilty or not, Freeze would still be fiercely loyal to him. But the question still stood and deserved an answer. Did he think Black killed Shy? "No. No, Lexi, I don't think Black killed her. I don't think a nigga could kill something he loves the way Black loved that woman," Freeze said and Lexi stood up.

"I'm gonna get back on the floor. I'll bring that woman back here as soon as she gets here."

"A'ight."

Lexi started to walk out, but she stopped. "You gonna be here until we close?"

"Doubt it."

"Okay," Lexi said quietly with her head hanging low.

About an hour later, there was a knock at the door. "Come on!" Freeze yelled. When the door cracked open, Lexi stuck her head in. "I have Aynna Thomas to see you."

"Bring her in."

Lexi opened the door and into the office came Sergeant Tamia Adams, walking nervously past Lexi wearing an auburn wig and dark sunglasses. Freeze laughed a little when he saw her. Feeling like her plans for an evening with Freeze were dead, Lexi excused herself politely and left the office.

"Sit down, Sergeant Adams. Welcome to Cuisine."

"Thank you," Tamia said, choosing to sit down on the couch instead of one of the chairs in front of the desk. "You just don't know how long I've wanted to come here."

"What stopped you?"

"I'm a cop, and this is the so-called legitimate front of an illegal gambling, loan-sharking, and prostitution operation."

"I guess you're right. So what brings you here today? And by the way, the wig is a nice touch. I think I like your hair that color."

"Do you?"

"Yeah."

"Then I'm dyeing it tomorrow," Tamia said definitely. Even though she was a cop, Tamia was madly in love with Freeze and would do anything to make him happy.

Freeze laughed. He knew how Tamia felt about him, but discouraged it. All he really saw in Tamia was inside information on what the cops were doing. That was how it began between them. Tamia was his very well-paid confidential informant. That arrangement was mutually beneficial to the two of them, and lasted in that manner until one night Freeze got a call from Tamia saying that she had some important information for him. Freeze was in the area, but he was drunk. He never liked taking care of business when he was drinking, obviously because it impairs your judgment. That night was no exception. It was late when he got to Tamia's apartment, and she was dressed in a big T-shirt and flop-flops. Nothing else. Well, the next thing you know, Tamia was bending over her dining room table, and Freeze was standing behind her, wearin' that ass out.

It's not that Freeze minded fucking Tamia; she was an attractive woman, in fact, he enjoyed it. He just didn't like the mix of *business and pussy*. Freeze would want information, and Tamia would wanna fuck. She'd called him that evening and said that she needed to see him, rather than her usual, I got something for you. "What are you doing way over there?" Tamia said. "Why don't you come sit over here next to me?"

Freeze glanced at his watch. He still had time before Nick got there. Freeze came from behind the desk and walked toward the door and locked it. When he turned around,

Freeze saw Tamia doing a silent clap. Freeze shook his head and sat down next to her. "What's up, Sergeant Adams? Tell me what brings a cop to the den of thieves?"

"I got something for you."

"Let's see it."

Tamia reached in her purse and showed Freeze an evidence bag that contained Black's gun. "You got what I want?"

Freeze stood up and went to the wall safe. Once it was opened he gladly counted out ten thousand dollars. When he returned to the couch, Freeze handed Tamia the money and she gave him the gun. It would be very difficult to convict Black of murder without the murder weapon.

Tamia put the money in her purse, while he walked toward the desk with the gun. "So about what time can I expect you?"

"Not tonight, I got something to do."

"See, I knew you was gonna say that shit!"

Freeze came at Tamia quickly. "What did I tell you? I said we had a deal, right?"

"Whatever," Tamia said quietly, but his aggression always made her wet.

"I give you my word. You did your part and I'll do mine. Just not tonight, Tamia! I got something to do later."

"Okay. What about now?" Tamia stood up, and stepped out of her panties. She turned around and bent over. "How about a down payment."

Freeze laughed, however, he did comply with her request.

After about fifteen minutes, there was a knock at the door. "Freeze! You in there?" Nick yelled as he rattled the doorknob.

"Yeah!" Freeze yelled. "Wait for me outside, I'll be out when I'm done!"

Nick walked away shaking his head and waited outside. After Freeze finished off Tamia, they left the club through the front door. Freeze introduced Tamia to Nick as Aynna Thomas, even though Nick knew who she was. Freeze had told Nick about his police informant and that was the name she chose as cover. After Freeze walked Tamia to her car, he came back to Nick. "Where fuck you been all day, nigga?"

"I told you, I had something real important to do."

"Damn, Nick, don't you think whatever that shit was it coulda waited. We need to find the muthafuckas that killed Shy and you out fuckin' around."

"I need to talk to you about that," Nick said, but Freeze continued his rant.

"Both you and fuckin' Wanda pick today of all days to decide y'all gonna just disappear." Freeze stopped and looked at Nick. He knew Wanda had cleared her schedule for the day. Then it came together. *Nick and Wanda both disappeared.* "Were you with Wanda all day?"

Reluctantly Nick said, "Yes." He did give some thought to the fact the maybe Wanda didn't want everybody to know. But Nick was proud as hell and wanted everybody to know.

"Y'all niggas fuckin'. Black in jail and y'all niggas fuckin'! If it was any other time I'd be happy for you, but this ain't the time for it," Freeze said very seriously. "Let's ride, we got business."

As soon as they turned to walk away, Freeze saw a car coming at them fast. Once he saw two guns come out of the passenger-side windows, Freeze yelled to Nick, "Get down!"

Nick and Freeze dropped to the ground, as bullets rained over their heads. Once the shooting stopped, they got to their feet and fired back, but the car was too far away to even give chase.

CHAPTER 26

"What the fuck was that all about?"

"Something happened today," Freeze said as he reloaded and put away his gun.

"What happened?" Nick demanded to know, as Lexi and two of the club security guards came running out of the club.

"Freeze!" Lexi yelled. "Are you all right?" She ran up and hugged him.

"Yeah," Freeze said, still looking around in case there was a second wave. "I'm fine. We're both fine."

"Is everybody all right inside?" Nick asked, looking at the bullet-riddled front of Cuisine.

"As far as I know everybody's fine," Lexi said as guests began to trickle out of the club. Lexi immediately turned her attention to her guests, and their attention away from Nick and Freeze.

"We gotta get outta here, Nick," Freeze said and started toward his truck.

Once they were in the truck and away from the club, Nick turned to Freeze. "What happened today?"

"I shot two of Birdie's boyz."

"What? Why?"

"There's somethin' I gotta tell you."

"Just tell me why!" Nick shouted.

"That's what I'm tryin' to do!" Freeze shouted back.

"All right, all right, let's both calm down," Nick said as Freeze drove. "Just tell me what you gotta tell me."

"It's my fault she's dead."

"Who, Shy?" Nick looked curiously at Freeze. "What the fuck are you talkin' about?"

"Shy called me that night, and asked me to come over there, but I never went."

"Why not?" Nick thought for a second. Than he looked at his friend. "You didn't go 'cause you don't like the way she talks to you?"

Freeze looked over at Nick, but didn't answer.

"Before me and Black went to Mexico I talked to Shy about that," Nick said.

"What you do that for?"

"Because I'm you're friend," Nick answered. "I told her how you felt about it. She had no idea. She called you over there to apologize to you."

Freeze didn't say a word.

"So tell me what that got to do with you killing two of Birdie's men?"

"I fuckin' lost it! I was mad and I fuckin' lost it!"

"Just tell me what happened," Nick said.

Freeze explained to Nick how he saw Lonnie and Smiley parked at a red light and he shot them. Nick shook his head in disbelief and looked out the window.

"What?" Freeze asked.

"I don't think Birdie had anything to do with Shy's murder," Nick said calmly.

"What you talkin' about?" Freeze asked.

"I talked to Kirk, he said whoever did it, it took a lot of planning. That shit with Shy happened the day before. Ain't no way Birdie could act that fast. I don't think he had anything to do with it, he couldn't have," Nick said as Freeze pulled up in front of Wanda's house. He wasn't looking forward to having this discussion with Wanda, but Freeze knew it had to be done. "Let's get this over with," Freeze mumbled as Nick rang the bell.

"You know what she's gonna do," Nick said.

Wanda looked through the peek hole and smiled when she saw Nick standing there. Thinking that he had come back to ravage her again, Wanda swung the door open. When she saw Freeze standing next to Nick, Wanda's entire facial expression changed. She looked at Nick and noticed the frustration across his face. "What's wrong?" Wanda asked.

"Freeze got something to tell you," Nick said as he walked past Wanda and headed straight for the bar to pour himself a drink.

"Make mine a double," Freeze said.

"Okay, what happened?" Wanda asked as she took a seat in her favorite chair.

"I shot two of Birdie's boyz today," Freeze answered and followed Nick to the bar.

Wanda dropped her head into her hands. When she finally looked up she mumbled, "This just keeps getting better and better. Nick, could you make me an apple martini, please?" Wanda turned her attention back to Freeze. "So tell me, why you shoot 'em?"

Nick handed Freeze his drink and he drained it before he

started talking. "Shy and Birdie got into it at Cuisine's while Nick and Black were in Mexico."

Wanda rolled her eyes, and then she sighed. "When you first told me about this, it didn't sound all that serious, when did things change? Did you talk to Birdie?"

"No!" Freeze snapped.

"Well, what changed things?" Wanda asked.

Freeze didn't respond.

"I'm going to assume since you can't tell me what changed, that nothing changed. You just saw these two people and shot them. What were you thinking?"

"I had to do something," Freeze said softly.

"Birdie didn't have anything do with it. You know he couldn't have. He ain't that smart, and he definitely ain't that gangsta, so again, I ask, what made you believe that he killed Shy?"

By this time, Nick had finished the drinks. He walked over to Wanda and placed her martini in front of her. They exchanged knowing glances, but Wanda was still mad. "Were you with him when he did this?" she asked even though she knew exactly where he was and what he was doing all day.

Nick took a swallow of his drink. "I ain't had shit to do with this one."

"It happened this afternoon." Freeze smiled at Wanda. "I don't know where Nick was all day." Even though he knew.

"Did you ever stop to think that maybe you should check with someone other than yourself before you do something like this? What the fuck were you thinking?" Wanda yelled.

"I had to do something!" Freeze yelled back.

"Great," Wanda said. "This is just fucking great! You know they're gonna have to do something about it, you know they're gonna come after us. Mike's been in jail two days and you're trying to take us to war!"

"Tell her the rest of it," Nick said.

"What? There's more?" Wanda asked and rolled her eyes.

"Why don't you fuckin' tell her," Freeze snapped at Nick.

"They just tried to hit us outside Cuisine," Nick said.

Wanda gulped down her drink. Without being told, Nick immediately got up and started fixing her another one. Wanda got up from her chair and went over to the window. "Do you know three men tried to kill Mike last night?" she asked calmly as she continued to stare out at the streetlights.

Freeze jumped up and said, "What!"

"Yeah, while you were out playing gangsta, Mike's in there fighting for his life," Wanda said as she turned to face them.

"Who did it?" Freeze asked with his fists in balls.

"I don't know, he's in administrative segregation, I'm gonna try and see if I can visit him tomorrow," Wanda said.

"That still leaves Birdie," Nick said.

"What are you talking about?" Wanda asked.

"What are you, fuckin' kiddin' me?" Freeze yelled. "They just tried to fuckin' kill us!"

"But Birdie didn't have anything to do with it," Wanda said.

"But they still tried to kill us," Nick said calmly.

"It doesn't matter whether Birdie killed Shy or not. The fact is, them muthafuckas just tried to kill us!" Freeze shouted.

"How do you know it was even Birdie?" Wanda challenged.

"Who else could it be?" Nick asked.

"I don't know, maybe we should find out before we start shooting at people again," Wanda said. She sighed in frustration and shrugged at her own commonsense suggestion. Wanda walked back to the couch and sat down next to Freeze.

Wanda looked at Nick. "I think we all need to calm down. This is not a war we need to be fighting right now. We need to focus on clearing Mike."

"You ain't got to worry about that. I got that shit covered," Freeze said.

Wanda's eyebrows shot up. "I hope you don't mean like you handled the thing with Birdie's men, 'cause if that's the case, I don't even wanna hear about it," Wanda said.

"Tell me," Nick said. "How you got this shit covered?"

"I got the murder weapon," Freeze said.

"What?" Nick said.

"How'd you get it?" Wanda asked immediately.

"Don't matter how I got it, fact is I got it, and Black ain't gettin' convicted of shit without the murder weapon."

"It does make his chances a whole lot better," Wanda said. "That and whatever inconsistencies Kirk found may just be enough to save him."

"But that still leaves Birdie," Nick said in a voice that didn't hide his anger.

"As far as I'm concerned Birdie is a nonissue," Wanda said without looking in Nick's direction. "Like I said, we need to concentrate all of our efforts on getting Mike out of jail. That's the only thing that's important."

"I think you're wrong, Wanda," Nick said, demanding her attention.

Wanda turned slowly toward Nick. "It's bad enough that Mike's in jail, now we gotta fight a war."

CHAPTER 27

Kenneth DeFrancisco had just rolled over on his side when the guard passed and made the announcement. "You have an attorney visit," he said.

DeFrancisco moved his head slightly; thinking that the guard must be talking to the inmate in the other cell next to his. He yawned and resumed his position trying to reclaim comfort. He closed his eyes again and started thinking about the ridiculous scheme he had heard the night before after lockdown.

"Yo, DeFrancisco!" the guard yelled this time. "I said you got an attorney visit. He's waiting for you in the meeting room."

DeFrancisco lifted his head ever so slightly. He felt the frown lines creep into his forehead and he struggled to understand what he was hearing. Ain't no way in hell he'd have an attorney visit. DeFrancisco had fired that worthless son of a bitch the moment he was sentenced to fifteen years for his role in a drug-trafficking scheme that, had it been successful, would've had Mike Black in his shoes at that very moment. He had considered hiring a new one, but things had happened so quickly he didn't even get a chance to get the ball rolling with his appeal. Twelve months into his fifteen-year sentence, of straight time, since it was a federal charge, the best his years of service as a DEA agent had afforded him, was confinement in the Federal Prison Camp in Atlanta. And for DeFrancisco, who was in segregation for the duration of his stay, this was two steps above hell.

He spent twenty-three hours alone in his small cell. There were no letters, no visitors and certainly no contact with the outside world. So to hear that he had an attorney visit, well, that was just a little bit more than a surprise to him. He swung his legs around and planted his feet firmly onto the cold cement floor. He yawned and stretched. "What's this shit about?" he muttered.

He really hadn't felt like being bothered lately. In the last few months he thought about how quickly his life had spun out of control. His conviction and sentence was enough to force even the strongest man to give up, but he would've never guessed his life would turn out this way. He still to this day blamed that useless son of a bitch, Mike Black, for all of his troubles.

Two days after he was taken into custody, the government, his former employer, confiscated everything they had previously frozen. All of his assets were gone. His sprawling home, the condo on the coast, his prized cars, motorcycles, even the cash he had neatly stashed in offshore accounts. Everything was gone.

As he made his way to the front of his cell, he thought back to the last time he spoke to his wife Jane. "They're putting me out!" she had cried.

"Wait, what are you talking about?" DeFrancisco had

asked. He squeezed the phone until his knuckles turned white. "Who's putting you out?" He tried to understand.

"The agents, they're from the IRS, they're going through all our stuff, everything. They say we haven't paid taxes on millions of dollars. Can they do this?" she screamed into the phone. Before he could think of an answer, he heard her wail again. "Where am I supposed to go? What about the kids? You need to fix this! You need to fix this, now!"

"Okay, wait, hold up, lemme see who I can call." DeFrancisco had no clue who he could call. He had fired the lawyer the minute the verdict came in. He didn't stop to think about what would happen to his family. He wanted to try to calm Jane as best he could. If only he had a few days, he could think of something, maybe one of his buddies could go over and help until he could figure things out.

"Where are you now?" he asked frantically.

"I've locked myself in the bedroom. The kids are still in school," she answered.

Of course the kids are still in school, he thought. He had paid up their tuition at the boarding school his wife insisted they send them to. That's when he knew for sure Jane was unstable. She rarely discussed the kids; he often had to remind her that she was a mother.

"What's everyone gonna say about all of this?" she asked.

"What?"

"I can't live like this," she said.

DeFrancisco heard the banging on the bedroom door.

"Who's that?"

"Who the fuck do you think it is? The house is crawling with agents, confiscating everything they can get their hands on and you're wondering who that is? Hold on a minute, Kenny. I know how to fix this," she snapped.

Suddenly DeFrancisco heard a noise he didn't recognize. There was more banging on the bedroom door. Then a shot rang out. That's all it was, a single shot. Seconds later, there was a crashing noise. He'd learn later that the crashing noise was the agents kicking in the bedroom door. They found Jane's body lying across their California king-sized bed. That last conversation with his wife woke him up every night and reminded him of just how helpless and alone he really was, and how much he hated Mike Black.

As he walked down the corridor that led to the private attorney-meeting rooms, he knew he was a broken man. But he still had a quest for revenge. His desire was even stronger now that he had twenty-three hours a day to think of the many ways he'd exact his revenge against the man he held responsible for the misery now called his life.

DeFrancisco was not prepared for the visitor who was waiting for him in the room. A smile curled at the corners of his lips.

"Holland Johnson," the man said and stood up as soon as DeFrancisco entered the room. Holland Johnson was actually DEA agent Pete Vinnelli. He and DeFrancisco had worked together for years. In reality, they were partners with Diego Estabon trafficking drugs, and if DeFrancisco had been willing to roll over on Vinnelli, he'd be sharing the cell with him. After DeFrancisco's wife committed suicide it was Vinnelli who took care of her final affairs and made sure that the children were taken care of.

Vinnelli was dressed in black jeans and a black T-shirt underneath a leather vest. He had a long ponytail with a full beard and three earrings dangling from his right ear. His head was covered with a Harley-Davidson skullcap. "Hey buddy," they quickly embraced. "How you holding up in here?" Vinnelli asked. He patted DeFrancisco on the back and both men took a seat.

In the many cases that DeFrancisco and Vinnelli had worked together, there were times that they didn't know if they'd live to see another day. When DeFrancisco was arrested, Vinnelli was out of the country, but he knew his partner would somehow catch up with him again, and maybe then he would find peace of mind. After DeFrancisco's conviction, he and Vinnelli did get a chance to talk. Their conversation was brief, coded, and to the point, but Vinnelli knew exactly what had to be done. Now, Vinnelli's visit confirmed a few things for DeFrancisco. "I know you said you didn't want anybody visitin' you, but there are some things I need to go over with you," Vinnelli said.

"That's okay, Holland. It's good to see you."

"Sorry to hear about Jane."

"Thank you for taking care of things for me."

"Not a problem, buddy. But I think her death was not in vain," Vinnelli said. He used his index finger to scratch his beard.

"Thanks, I'm really glad to hear that." DeFrancisco's eyebrows inched upward. "You just don't know how happy hearing that makes me, Holland."

Vinnelli nodded and winked. "Let's just say even a suicide, well, um, you know what I'm tryin' to say, right?"

"I do," DeFrancisco said.

"I'm sure right now our friend is feeling a lot like you do."

The happy look on DeFrancisco's face very quickly turned to a frown. "It was my understanding that now wasn't going to be a possibility. What happened to change that?"

"I thought I had the right bait on the hook, but—" Vinnelli said but DeFrancisco cut him off.

"But what, Pe—" DeFrancisco said angrily. He was about to call him Pete, but he caught himself and tried to calm down.

"The big one proved to be too strong for the line."

DeFrancisco put his elbows on the table and buried his head in his hands. "Was any of the line broken?"

"One break, the rest of the line is still intact, but in time I'm sure that the entire line will have to be retired."

This was not what DeFrancisco needed or wanted to hear, but in his position, what could he do about it? He longed for the days when he was free and could get things done. Vinnelli never was good at this type of stuff, DeFrancisco thought. If he had been on the street this would have been handled with clockwork accuracy, and the op would have been completed.

DeFrancisco looked at Vinnelli for a long time. "Tell me something, Holland, have you taken steps to correct the matter? Maybe this time you could use a much better quality line, perhaps?"

"Not to worry." Vinnelli glanced at his watch. "I'll be going fishing tomorrow and I'll be using a top-rated line."

"Well, let's hope you catch something. Next time you visit I hope you got a better fish story than that one. Come on, Holland, you are a much better fisherman than that."

"I got the small fish," Vinnelli said, pleading his case.

"And that's important."

"Right, you know how these things go. Cut me some slack, will ya."

DeFrancisco leaned back in his chair and smiled, but he was still pissed off. "I'm just bustin' your balls, Holland. I know you'll do your best to catch the big fish next time."

"I will, I promise you that. I owe you that much. And I wanted to assure you that things will get better. I just need you to hang in there," Vinnelli said sincerely. "We're all still pulling for you, man."

DeFrancisco nodded. "So how long do we have?"

"I think about two hours," Vinnelli said. He leaned in closer to DeFrancisco. "You need anything in here? I mean, can I get something for you?"

"This place is wild." DeFrancisco sat upright. "I can get anything I want in here, including a woman. That is, if you can call them crackhead nigger bitches *women*. You wouldn't believe the type of shit that goes on around here." DeFrancisco shook his head. "I'll give you an example of how out of control things are here. There's this guy here, they call him the chicken man. I don't know how he does it, he says he's got a guard in his pocket, I don't fuckin' know. So I'm sure you saw the projects that are adjacent to this place, right?"

"Yeah, that tripped me out, it's fucking right next door, literally," Vinnelli said, amazed.

"Yeah, that's Thomasville Heights. Well, the chicken man, he says he got him a soul sister in the projects that cooks for him. So twice a day after count, he slips off and when he comes back, this nigga's got a bag of homemade fried chicken. All individually wrapped in foil. Sells them for five dollars apiece and makes a killing!" DeFrancisco ended with a laugh.

"You're shittin' me, right?"

"I swear to fuckin' god! That's the type of shit that goes on around here. It's wild."

Vinnelli started cracking up.

"Did you ever get any of those new M and M's?" DeFrancisco asked, referring to their other partner, New York State Senator Martin Marshall. He provided political cover for their trafficking operation. When things went south for

DeFrancisco, and Marshall faced the very real threat of De-
Francisco rolling over on him, he found cover in the form of
the New York City Department of Investigations. Under
the grant of immunity, which he hoped to extend in case he
had to testify against DeFrancisco, Marshall cooperated in a
case against a city councilman who was accused of extor-
tion. Marshall gave an affidavit stating that the councilman
demanded 1.5 million dollars' worth of property and fifty
thousand dollars cash from a real estate developer who
wanted the councilman's vote in favor of a development
slated for Brooklyn. Marshall didn't have to worry, though,
Kenneth DeFrancisco was no snitch. After surviving that
near-miss, Marshall became a crusader against corruption.

"No, haven't been able to find any. Every time I go to get
some they're gone."

"Stay on that. M and M's could be a big help," DeFrancisco said, thinking that after a while Marshall could pull
some strings and maybe get him to one of those country
club prisons.

For the remainder of the visit, they shared small talk, rem-
inisced about the past, and Vinnelli vowed to visit again.

"So how are things looking," DeFrancisco asked as he
walked to the door at the end of their session.

"It's all good. It's all good, matter of fact." Vinnelli stood.
"I should be back in a few weeks, with better news. In the
meantime I've got a friend in here who's gonna take care of
you."

"I'm straight. This visit alone was enough to make things
better. I look forward to our next meeting."

DeFrancisco knocked on the door. "Guard," he yelled.

CHAPTER 28

Detective Kirkland slammed his car door shut and went into the precinct like a man on a mission. "How's it goin', Ford?" he greeted the desk sergeant, and then pushed his way through the double doors that led back to the section of the building that housed the narcotics division. He passed through the rows of desks and stopped at the one in the far right corner. There a man who held a phone between his shoulder and his ear was huddled over an open drawer of files.

"Yeah, yeah, I'm lookin' for it now," the man said.

Detective Kirkland took a seat in the chair next to the desk. He waited as Detective Sanchez argued with the person on the phone and flipped through the files. Phones rang in the background and officers shuffled throughout the office. Kirk told himself not to become impatient, and shortly after, "If you'd get your head out your ass you'da read it when I sent it the first time," Sanchez yelled into the receiver once more before slamming it back into its cradle.

"Sometimes, Kirk, these fuckin' people get on my fuckin' nerves," Sanchez said.

"Tell me about it, Gene," Kirk said.

"Sometimes I think this whole city is just circling the drain," Sanchez added.

"So I guess I don't have to ask how it's goin'."

"Fucked up, that's how it's going. It's fucked up, but you don't want to hear that shit. You came here for a reason, and it ain't to hear my shit, so what can I do for you?" Sanchez asked graciously.

"Mike Black," Kirk said.

"I kinda figured that's what you were here for," Sanchez admitted.

"I talked to one of his people yesterday, Nick Simmons. I asked him if he had any idea who killed Black's wife, of course he said no. But I just got the feeling there was something he wasn't telling me," Kirk said.

"Word on the street is that Birdie had a personal beef with Shy and that's why she was killed."

"You believe that?" Kirk asked.

"I don't think he did it himself. Not his style, but there's definitely something going on, two of Birdie's men were killed at a red light yesterday afternoon," Sanchez said.

"Capped them in broad daylight, huh?" Kirk asked.

"Last night there was a shooting at Cuisine. I don't know who was involved, the manager said it was probably just some kids riding by. But I don't buy that, not after Birdie's men were capped. I think we've got a full-scale war going," Sanchez added.

"So where does this leave us, and the investigation regarding Black?"

"You tell me, Kirk." Sanchez shrugged. "All I know is the shit is about to start 'cause if these guys are going to war, it's gonna get interesting around here."

"Yeah, body bags are gonna start filling up quicker than we can zip 'em." Kirk leaned back and started thinking about the evidence he'd uncovered since he began investigating Shy's murder.

"So you don't think it's this Birdie character's style?"

"Nah, he and his partner Albert wanna try and play it like they're businessmen, so they wanna stay away from all that shoot-'em-up bang, bang stuff."

"What about the two guys killed at the red light?"

"Those two are a different story, those two I could see having something to do with it. If Birdie was gonna have somebody killed, those would be the guys he'd send," Sanchez said.

"You got any idea what this beef was about?"

Sanchez shook his head. "Nope, no idea."

"Maybe it's time I had a talk with this Birdie. Where can I find him?"

Sanchez went through his files and looked at his computer. He quickly hit a couple of keys, then wrote down an address for Kirk.

"So lemme ask you something, Kirk, you think Black did it?"

They stood as Sanchez held the paper out for him.

"Honestly, I'm starting to have my doubts," Kirk said as he looked at the address, then turned to leave.

"Any particular reason why?" Sanchez asked.

Kirk turned and looked at him, then said, "A lot of little things, a lot of inconsistencies in the way the story goes. But it's obvious his crew doesn't think he killed her, they think this Birdie guy was behind it."

"So what's next?"

"I'll keep you posted," he said before he walked toward the double doors that led to the hallway. Instead of leaving the building, Kirk decided to stop by the homicide division and ask a few questions. He checked in with the desk sergeant first. "Ford, how's it going?" he asked the pudgy man seated behind his desk.

"Can't complain. What can I do for you?"

"Who caught the case, involving the double in broad daylight?"

"Smith and Petrocelli," Ford said, motioning across the way and toward the back where two empty desks were.

"Smith is out, but Petrocelli's in the captain's office. Wanna wait around or want me to have him call you?"

Kirk used to work with Detective Smith, but he hadn't talked to him in years. He looked toward the back of the room. "I'll wait on Petrocelli."

Just then, the phone on Ford's desk rang. Kirk took that as his cue to move on. By the time he arrived at the two desks, he could hear Petrocelli's voice. He was laughing when he burst through the door. Ford covered the phone, and motioned toward the back where Kirk sat waiting on Petrocelli. Their eyes met and Kirk stood as the man approached the desk.

"What's going on, Detective?" Petrocelli asked.

"Just a quick question about that double in broad daylight, you know at the red light," Kirk said.

"Yeah, that kind of shit don't happen every day," Petrocelli confirmed.

"I know, I know, but I was wondering, were there any witnesses?"

Petrocelli was a tall and stocky Italian, with thick wavy hair that Kirk and others suspected he had dyed monthly. He used his beefy hands to comb through his thick mane then said, "Sure, there was one, but he wears glasses and can't identify anybody. He works at the newsstand across the street from where it happened. Says he saw a guy walk up and shoot both of 'em, but he can't ID anyone, he wears big, thick lens glasses. Only thing he could tell for sure, was that the shooter was black."

"Oh, that's a great ID there," Kirk said sarcastically.

Kirk left the precinct and began his search for Birdie. His first stop was the Spot. Sanchez had told him that Birdie had taken over D-Train's club. When he pulled up in front of the place he had a sinking feeling in the middle of his stomach. It was early in the day and parking was available right up front. He knew not to expect a crowd, but he had no idea how deserted the place would be. Kirk walked into the darkened building and noticed a few tables occupied, but for the most part the place was empty. He pulled a stool at the bar and slid onto it. When the bartender placed a napkin in front of him, he glanced around the empty place.

"I'm looking for Birdie," Kirk said.

"I can get you a nice little buzz, but that's about all I can do," the bartender said.

"Whoa, hold up a minute, I'm just looking for Birdie, you know if he's been here," Kirk said.

"I ain't seen him," the bartender snapped, and moved the napkin.

Kirk looked at the stack of napkins then at the towel the bartender picked up.

"That's all you know, huh?"

"That's it, ain't nobody else in here gonna be able to help you either," he tossed in.

With that, Kirk rose from the stool and pulled a card from his breast pocket. He made sure his badge was visible for the bartender to see.

"This is my number, when Birdie comes in, use it, and I won't have to come back here to see just what you really know about what goes on around here," he said.

The bartender looked at the card lying on the bar then back up at Kirk. Reluctantly, he picked it up and tucked it somewhere Kirk couldn't see. Kirk wandered around the place looking for nothing in particular, *but you never know*. It was more to be intimidating than anything else. Kirk walked back to the bar and waited for the bartender to come over. "You be sure to tell Birdie that I'm lookin' for him." Kirk turned to leave but stopped. "And I'm gonna keep coming back until I talk to him."

CHAPTER 29

"Kirk," the captain said as Kirk walked in and took a seat in front of his desk. "I heard you been a very busy man."

"That's what I wanna talk to you about, Captain."

"You know, Kirk, I knew when I told you about Black that you wouldn't be able to let it go. I thought about not tellin' you, but I knew you'd find out anyway, so I told you. I mean, what was I gonna do, swear the whole city to silence? Don't tell Kirk." The captain laughed and so did Kirk. "Then I figured, having you investigate Goodson and Harris's case wouldn't be a bad thing. Goodson and Harris aren't bad cops, they're just two racist pricks who are more than willing to cut corners to get a collar. And if that means taking what they see things at face value and not digging any deeper, then that's what has to get done. They close cases, period. How they do it may not always pass the sniff test." The captain got up from his desk and poured himself a cup of coffee, and one for Kirk.

"But not you, Kirk," the captain continued. "You're a

bulldog. As soon as I heard Black had got locked up for murder, I knew that we'd have to have a tight case against him, because all he's gonna do is hire a bunch of high-priced lawyers to make sure he doesn't serve a day for it. So what you got, Kirk, what'd you find out?"

"Let's start with the timeline," Kirk said. "Black was in Miami the day before, he came back to JFK the day of the murder. I confirmed that their flight arrived at nine-fifty. I checked what time they got out of the parking lot. Ten minutes after ten. Now I don't know about you, but it's an hour ride from Kennedy for most people. Black says he got there after eleven, because the news was on. The nine-one-one call came in at ten-fifty-five. Officer's report says they arrived at the scene at twelve minutes after. So from the time the nine-one-one call came in, the killer's got seventeen minutes to beat her and kill her."

"That's plenty of time, Kirk," the captain said.

"I would think so, too, but here's the thing, the nine-one-one call, I listened to that, too, but we'll get to that in a minute. I talked to the ME, he noticed some things, so he dug a little deeper."

"Like what?"

"First thing he noticed was that there were no defensive wounds on her arms. So he checked her nails and there was no skin under there, didn't scratch him, didn't do anything. That's when he noticed the small cuts on her wrists. He believes they were made by handcuffs."

"Handcuffs, Kirk?"

"That's what I said, Captain. He also noticed small cuts at the corners of her mouth. He thinks she was gagged. Handcuffed and gagged. And there's one more thing. ME said he found a very small trace of nitrous oxide in her system."

"What the fuck is that, Kirk?"

"Laughing gas."

"Slow down, Kirk. So you're saying that Black comes home, handcuffs her, beats her, gives her nitrous whatever then he kills her. Is that what you're telling me, Kirk?"

"I'm just telling you what the evidence says, Captain. The beating didn't take place in the kitchen, it took place in the living room. Reyes and I found traces of blood on a lamp shade and a chair in the living room. We think she was beaten while handcuffed to that chair."

"Okay, what about the nitrous stuff, where does that fit into this?"

"ME thinks he gave her the nitrous oxide so he could beat her longer."

"Why would Black do all of that?"

"That's not the question I asked, Captain. The question I asked was, what was Black doing at the crime scene after doing all of that. If Black's the murderer and he ripped the phone from the wall, he knows she called nine-one-one. What's he waiting around for? They didn't find the handcuffs or whatever he used to gag her, or anything he had to use to administer the nitrous oxide, so Black would have had to gotten rid of that evidence before the uniforms got there."

"That makes sense, Kirk, but maybe he had somebody take the stuff away from the crime scene."

"Why would he do that and leave the gun? I just got through talking to Sanchez, he says there's a war brewing between some character who calls himself Birdie and Black's crew. Sanchez tells me this Birdie had some kind of problem with Black's wife. Yesterday afternoon two of Birdie's men were killed at a red light, last night there was a drive-by at Black's supper club."

"It's obvious that they think this Birdie had something to do with it," the captain said. For a moment, neither Kirk nor the captain spoke.

"There was no way, if the timeline was correct and they knew for certain it was, that Black would've been able to kill his wife and sit there holding her body when the officers arrived. It just didn't make sense, not for a man like Black." When the captain shook his head, Kirk shrugged.

"The evidence is what it is, Captain. Like Black or not, that's what the evidence is saying here."

The captain believed Kirk may have a point, but wondered what he should do about it. Suddenly, the captain rubbed his palms over his face, and then he sighed, and shook his head again. He looked at Kirk. "Let's say you're right, what do we do with him?"

"Release him," Kirk said.

"And what then?"

"I don't follow you."

"We let him out, what do you think Black is gonna do the minute he gets out?" The captain paused for effect. "He's gonna go right out and kill everybody that he thinks has something to do with it."

"So what do we do?"

"Leave him right where the fuck he is. You find out who killed her and lock them up. Once we got the killer in custody then we'll let him out."

CHAPTER 30

"All I'm saying is, we need to find out for sure," Wanda said as she, Freeze, and Nick were seated at a table at the Famous Oyster Bar on Seventh Avenue and Fifty-fourth Street. Things at Cuisine had already returned to normal. Long gone were the signs that a shooting had taken place just a day ago. The regulars wasted no time in returning to their normal spot. And that meant business was back to normal at Mike Black's supper club. They needed to talk things over and talking there was out, so Wanda suggested one of her favorites places.

"What's there to find out? Those muthafuckas tried to take us out." Freeze pointed at his chest for emphasis. "Ain't no way in the world I'ma just sit here like a fuckin' target for them muthafuckas! 'Cause we all know they ain't gonna stop."

Wanda shook her head, "No one's talking about being targets. I'm just saying we need to find out for sure," she insisted.

Wanda looked at Nick and watched his eyes quickly look away. She felt herself get warm, as images of their lovemaking flashed through her mind. She'd give anything to be back in that moment, instead of at the table discussing going to war. She wondered if on some level he could feel it, too, that electric sensation she now got from looking at him. She swallowed hard and tried to focus on the discussion at hand.

"I'm well aware of that, but I'm just saying instead of fighting this battle now, we really need to do what we can for Mike. All of our efforts should go toward freeing him, not this foolishness." Wanda tried not to get too emotional. "I don't know how much longer he'll survive in there." She sucked her teeth.

"Can't believe that shit; Black on lockdown."

"He's in the hole more for his protection, than for punishment," Nick added.

"What's up with that punk-ass lawyer you hired?" Freeze asked out of nowhere. "I mean, isn't that the type of shit he's supposed to be working on?"

"Marcus Douglas is no punk."

The waitress appeared at the table with their food before Wanda could attempt to answer. Everyone stopped talking as she struggled to match each dish to its correct customer. "T-bone medium rare?" the waitress asked.

"That's me," Freeze raised his hand to signal her and she stretched over Wanda to place his plate in front of him. "Excuse me," she said.

All eyes were on the large steak.

"Grilled shrimp with steamed vegetables?" the waitress asked.

"That would be me," Wanda said, reluctantly pulling her stare away from Freeze's plate.

"Then that means the surf and turf must be yours." She leaned over to deliver Nick's plate.

The waitress stepped back to look at her work. "Okay, that's everything; can I get anything else for you guys?"

"No, I think we're good," Wanda said preparing to dig into her food, as the waitress turned to leave.

"Look, I say we do what we gotta do, take care of them niggas and get this shit over with a quickness," Freeze suggested. "I know you don't just expect us to roll over, is that what you're saying?"

Wanda shook her head. "If you two would just listen to me, just listen to what I'm trying to say," she tried unsuccessfully.

"I heard you then, I hear you now, and what I'm sayin' is it ain't happening. Them niggas tried to smoke us, and you want to investigate?" Freeze shook his head, then stuffed his mouth. "Ain't happening, Wanda," he said.

"All I'm trying to say is we should at least try to talk to Birdie first. Set up a meeting," she reasoned.

"Okay, so you set up a meeting with Birdie, we meet, shake hands, smile, then ask, Oh, by the way, did you send a few of your boyz over to shoot up Cuisine after I smoked your boyz?" Freeze said sarcastically. "I wish you could hear yourself. That ain't the way to do shit, Wanda. This ain't your perfect little world where people get together with a mediator and work their shit out. There's nothing else to do, but to hit them before they hit us," Freeze said.

Wanda searched Nick's face for some sign that he might remotely agree with her, that Freeze was just being Freeze. She wanted Nick to understand that she didn't want to risk what they had just discovered with each other, and that's what Freeze's threat meant to her. But when she looked at him, his attention was on his food.

"What do you think, Nick?"

"If we don't hit them they'll think we're weak and they come after us," Nick finally said. "I say we kill them."

Reluctantly, Wanda agreed, knowing they were going to do it whether she agreed or not.

CHAPTER 31

Detective Kirkland parked in front of Mike Black's house and got out of the car. After talking to his captain about the inconsistencies in the case, he had returned to the crime scene looking for a direction to go in next. Kirk realized that the captain was right, if they let Black out without a suspect in custody that Black would get out and go on a killing spree for the brutal murder of his wife.

While walking up the path to the house, Kirk thought about the fact that he was working hard to get somebody out of jail that he'd been trying to get in jail for years. Kirk stopped on the porch, thinking that Black had killed or been responsible for the death of so many people. *So he goes down for this, ain't that justice?*

Kirk let himself in and closed the door behind him. As he stood in the foyer, Kirk had to admit to himself that he liked Black. Despite their conflicting professions, Kirk had some respect for Black and the things he'd done to change his life. The answer to his question was no. If he didn't kill her then that's not justice.

After Kirk decided that he was only doing what any good cop would do, *find the killer,* he went toward the basement. On the way down the stairs, Kirk mused, *Besides, this case is proving to be much more interesting then anything else on my plate.*

There was a light knock at the front door before it opened and Kirk's partner walked in. "Morning, Kirk," Richards said. He had been on leave for the last few days, but Kirk called him the night before and brought Richards up to speed on what he'd been doing.

"Morning, Pat. How you doin'?"

"Wishin' I was still in the bed."

"Come on. I wanna walk through the house again. Maybe you'll find something we missed."

Now that the detectives were in the basement, Kirk walked to the back door and turned to face the room. It wasn't a huge basement, one large room with a couch, a chair and a big-screen TV. Mike's free weights, Bowflex, Total Gym, and a treadmill. "This guy takes his workout seriously," Richards commented as he wandered around the room.

"Tell me about it," Kirk replied. He glanced at the alarm keypad next to him. "I assumed that if the killer entered the house through the basement they would've had to disable the alarm. For that to happen, the killer would had to have disabled the alarm or cut the power and disable the phone."

"That's logical."

"I paid a visit to the security company that monitors the system. They said that they could report no interruption in the signal coming from this house."

"Any prints?"

"When the crime-scene technicians rechecked the house, they found no fingerprints on or around the keypad."

"Not surprising."

"I know. If this murder took place the way I think it did,

then there would be no prints. But despite the lack of evidence to support my theory, I'm convinced that the killer entered the house through that door."

After looking around the room for anything that might give them something to pursue, Kirk went into the bathroom and then into the laundry room. There wasn't much to see in there, nothing on the shelves, no detergent or bleach or fabric softener. "Doesn't seem like a lot of clothes got washed in there," Richards noted as he appeared at the door.

"They're probably fold-and-fluff people and take their clothes to the laundry," Kirk said and continued his search.

Kirk was about the leave the laundry room and go upstairs, when he noticed something on the floor by the dryer. "Hello." Kirk got down on his hands and knees to get a closer look.

"What you got?"

"It's a cigarette butt," Kirk said. "To my knowledge, neither Black nor Shy smoke cigarettes.

"This could be important."

"Run out to the car and get something to put this in," Kirk instructed his partner.

Richards quickly went out to the car and returned with tweezers and a plastic bag. Kirk knew that there would be DNA on the butt, however, without a suspect to match it to, it could prove useless. "Maybe we'll get lucky and there'll be a fingerprint on it," Kirk said as he collected the evidence he'd found and placed it in the bag.

"Maybe. But if the killer had on gloves that ain't happening."

"You're right, Pat. But how many times have you seen people take off the glove on their smoking hand before they light up."

Richards shrugged his shoulders. "Long shot, at best."

Once the evidence was collected, Detectives Kirkland and Richards made one more pass through the basement before going upstairs. Kirk went through the living room where the beating took place. "This is where the beating took place. I believe he cuffed her to this chair. We found blood splattered on the chair and that shade," Kirk said and pointed.

Richards leaned in and took a closer look. "That's it? I woulda thought if she was beaten as badly as you say, I would think there'd be more blood than just a few splatters."

"I thought about that, too. The spots are small, so I was thinking that either he used some type of cover or he cleaned up what he could and missed these."

Then they went to the kitchen and the killing floor and found nothing they could use. Kirk stood still and quiet in the kitchen and walked through the evidence and his theory of the crime again. "Killer enters the house through the basement and waits in the laundry room, smokes a cigarette before he comes upstairs. Why does he wait?"

"When we catch him I'll ask."

"Why not just go upstairs and kill her?" Kirk held up the plastic bag containing the cigarette butt. "You were waiting for something, and you waited so long that you had to have a cigarette." Kirk thought about the timeline. "This thing was planned, planned down to the second. So how does he know when to go upstairs?"

"Okay," Richards said. "Let's assume that you're right and this is a setup to frame Black for murdering his wife. He could have come in the house long before the murder and knew about what time Black would get here."

"Even if he knew that Black was out town and would be back that night, even if he knew what time his flight came in, how would he know that Black would come straight home?"

"Let's get outta here. There's nothing for us here. When we catch the prick we'll ask him," Richards said and headed for the door.

Kirk started to follow him out, but stopped in his tracks.

"What?" Richards asked.

"When the DEA was investigating Black, they installed a monitoring system in the house."

"Yeah, I remember. In every room."

"You think it's still active?"

"Doubtful," Richard said. "That was a year ago."

"But if it's still active we just may have a videotape of the murder."

"One way to find out," Richards said as they walked up the stairs.

The system was set up with a storage drive. This way the captured images could be viewed in real time as well as recorded for future use. The system was housed on the second level, under the stairs that lead to the attic. When they reached the spot, Kirk took out his pocketknife to remove the wood from the wall and see if the system was still in place. When he knelt down, Kirk noticed the small scratches on wood. "Take a look at this, Pat," Kirk said and Richards knelt down next to him.

"Those look fresh," Richards said and put on his gloves. Richards was able to easily pull the panel from the wall. In fact, it practically fell into his hands. "It's gone, Kirk."

"If those scratches are truly fresh—" Kirk started.

"Then the killer removed it," Richards finished. "Now how would the killer know the system was here? Even if the killer happened to see those little-bitty cameras, how would he know the system was here?"

"I don't know, Pat. But I can think of somebody who might know. Come on."

It wasn't too long after leaving the crime scene that Detectives Kirkland and Richards found themselves in the Manhattan offices of the DEA. Richards approached the receptionist. "Good morning," he said.

"Good morning," the receptionist responded. "How can I help you gentlemen?"

"Detectives Richards and Kirkland to see Agent DeFrancisco, please."

The receptionist gave the detectives a very uncomfortable look. "Agent DeFrancisco no longer works at this office, sir."

"Can you tell me what office he works at?" Kirk asked.

The receptionist looked at the detectives, who were making this harder than it had to be. "Mr. DeFrancisco is no longer employed by this agency," she told them.

"Really," Kirk said and thought about asking why, but he knew that even if she knew, she wouldn't tell him. The word would be *classified*. "Okay, well, how about Agent Vinnelli? Does he still work here?"

"Yes, sir, Agent Vinnelli does still work out of this office. If you gentlemen would have a seat, I'll see if he is available to speak with you."

"Thank you." Richards flirted with the receptionist. She smiled at the detective before returning to her duties.

Kirk left Richards at the desk and sat down. When Richards joined him he glanced in his partner's direction. "No longer employed by this agency," Kirk said.

"I take it you don't think he retired?"

"Do you?" Kirk asked louder than he needed to.

"My bet—he's in jail."

"At best they fired his ass. After the DEA shut down the operation against Black, I knew there were going to be some tough questions that he would have to answer."

"You know if DeFrancisco is in jail, this prick isn't gonna be all that happy to see us."

"You think I give a fuck?"

At that moment, a tall black man walked into the reception area and stood in front of the detectives. "Good morning, gentlemen, I'm Agent Masters." Kirk and Richards stood up and shook his hand. "Agent Vinnelli is just wrapping up a meeting and asked me to escort you to his office."

"You look familiar to me, and I never forget a face," Kirk said and looked the agent over carefully.

"Like they say, I just have that kind of face," Masters said.

Once they dispensed with the introductions, the agent escorted them to Vinnelli's office. "Have a seat, gentlemen, can I get you anything?"

"No, we're fine," Kirk said.

"If there's anything you need I'm just down the hall," Masters said and left the office wondering if Kirk really had seen him before.

It didn't take Agent Vinnelli long to get finished with his meeting. "This is a surprise."

Richards stood up and shook Vinnelli's hand, but Kirk kept his seat. "How you doin', Vinnelli?"

"Busy. Sorry to keep you guys waiting."

"How's things been going, Vinnelli?" Kirk asked as Vinnelli sat down.

"Not bad, Kirk, just wrapping up an investigation."

"Successful?" Richards asked.

"Extremely. Operation Twin Peaks, was what it was called. It was a multi-jurisdictional investigation that targeted Enrique Guzman and his drug-trafficking organization."

Kirk and Richards glanced at one another. "I'm not familiar with him," Richards felt embarrassed to admit.

"Not surprised, Guzman's a little above your pay grade, detectives," Vinnelli said smugly. "He operates a cocaine ring responsible for smuggling more than fifteen tons of cocaine per month from Colombia to here and Europe. The investigation has been going on for three years and over that time period there have been more than one hundred arrests and the seizure of fifty-two tons of cocaine, and nearly seventy million dollars in cash and assets."

"Pretty big deal there," Richards said.

"It really was, but I know you didn't come here for that, so, detectives, tell me what brings you two downtown?" Vinnelli asked and leaned back in his chair.

"Mike Black," Kirk said.

Agent Vinnelli sat up straight in his chair. The smug look that once covered his face was now gone. "What about him?"

"I was just wondering about the surveillance system that was installed in his house," Kirk said.

"What about it."

"I was just curious about what happened to it."

"What do you mean, what happened to it?" Vinnelli asked, trying to conceal his nervousness.

"I mean what happened to it? Is it still active? Is it still in the house? I want to know its status."

"To my knowledge, all of the surveillance equipment was removed from the house when the operation was scrubbed."

Kirk stood up. "That's all I needed to know."

Richards looked at his partner curiously, but he got up, too. "Thanks for your time, Vinnelli."

Vinnelli got up and came around the desk to show the

detectives out. He stopped in front of Kirk. "You came all the way down here for that?"

Kirk got in his face. "I like to ask questions face-to-face, Agent Vinnelli." Kirk took a step back and smiled. "But I'll catch you later."

Kirk and Richards walked a little behind Vinnelli as they made their way to the elevator. When they got there, Vinnelli turned to the detectives and extended his hand. "If there's anything else I can help you gentlemen with don't hesitate to drop in again," he said as the elevator door opened.

"There is one more thing that I was curious about, Agent Vinnelli," Kirk asked as he and Richards stepped on the elevator.

"What's that?" he asked.

"Agent DeFrancisco."

Vinnelli quickly reached out and prevented the door from closing. "What about him?"

"The receptionist said that he was no longer employed by this agency. What happened to him?" Kirk asked.

"Retired after his wife died." Vinnelli let go of the door.

The detectives rode to the first floor in silence and didn't speak until they were in their car and on their way back uptown. Finally Richards broke the ice. "I think this prick is involved in this thing," Richards said as he drove.

"Yeah."

"Did you notice the way his entire facial expression changed when you mentioned Black's name?"

"Yeah."

"And why didn't he ask why we wanted to know, unless he already knew. Yeah, this asshole is involved in this thing up to his fuckin' eyeballs."

"Yeah," Kirk replied, but he was deep in thought. He

agreed with Richards, Vinnelli definitely had some prior knowledge and that troubled him. But how deep was his involvement? Now Kirk wondered if maybe Vinnelli himself was the killer, but what motive would he have? "Find out what happened to DeFrancisco. If he's retired I wanna know where he's retired to. I wanna talk to him. And find out how his wife died."

When the detectives returned to the precinct, they immediately got started looking into DeFrancisco. It didn't take long for Richards to come up with the answers they were looking for. "I got it, Kirk."

"What you got, Pat?"

"DeFrancisco is retired, all right. He's serving time at the federal pen in Atlanta."

"What was the charge?"

"Conspiracy to distribute, income tax evasion, that type of shit," Richards said. "Buddy of mine is faxing a copy of the indictment now." Once Richards received the fax he read it to Kirk. "Kenneth Lawrence DeFrancisco did knowingly and intentionally combine, conspire, confederate and agree with each other and with other persons both known and unknown to the grand jury to import into the United States, from a place outside thereof, a controlled substance, in violation of Title twenty-one, United States Code, Section nine-fifty-two a, blah, blah, blah, where alleged that this violation involved five kilograms or more of a mixture and substance containing a detectable amount of cocaine. Motive?"

"Maybe. Knowing what we know about DeFrancisco and Black's history."

"Count two," Richards continued. "Kenneth Lawrence DeFrancisco did knowingly conduct financial transactions, affecting interstate and foreign commerce, which transactions involved the proceeds of some specified unlawful activity, with the intent to promote the carrying on of said specified unlawful activity, and knowing that the property involved in the financial transactions represented the proceeds of some form of unlawful activity," Richards said as the phone on Kirk's desk rang. Kirk answered and when he hung up he had the answer. "His wife committed suicide while the IRS agents raided their house."

"Wife, huh," Richards said. "I'd say we found our motive. That would give him a reason to want Black in jail and his wife dead."

CHAPTER 32

It was getting late in the evening and there was still no word on the whereabouts of Birdie and Albert. Freeze had everybody out looking for them, but it was as if they had dropped off the face of the earth, or at the very least, out of the city. Even their people didn't seem to know where to find them.

With nothing else to do, Freeze and Nick were sitting in the office at Impressions, when the phone rang. "This is Nick."

"Whatup, Nick. This Mylo. Freeze there?"

Nick handed the phone to Freeze.

"What's up?"

"This Mylo. Listen. I think I may know where Birdie and Albert been hidin'," he said.

When Freeze heard that, he sat straight up in his chair. "Where?"

"Atlantic City at Trump's."

"How'd you hear this?"

"I friend of mine is down in AC now. She said she saw

Albert in the casino playin' poker. I'm guessin' if he got his ass down there then Birdie can't be far away."

"And she's sure about this?"

"Yeah. What you want me to do?"

"Nothin'," Freeze said and checked his weapon. "I got this. Thanks, Mylo, I'll call you if I need you."

When Freeze stood up, Nick did, too. "Since you checkin' your gun, I figure we goin' somewhere."

"Atlantic City. Mylo said he got a tip that our friends are hidin' out at Trump's in Atlantic City."

Without another word passing between them, Nick and Freeze left the office. Once they were out of the building, Nick stopped at his car and took a bag out of his trunk. "What's that?" Freeze asked as they walked to his truck.

"My little bag of tricks," Nick replied.

When they got in Freeze's truck, he started it up and drove off. When Freeze turned on the CD and the music began, a smile came across his lips and he said the words slowly along with 2Pac. "This is what it sounds like when we ride on our enemies."

"What you say?" Nick asked.

"This is what it sounds like when we ride on our enemies. You never heard this?"

"I probably have, but you know me and hip-hop. I'm old school. I'm into the Brand New Heavies."

"Whatever, this us tonight. 'Cause niggas love to scream peace after they started this shit." By the time the song was over, both Freeze and Nick were nodding their heads to the music and screaming the words, "When we ride on our enemies!"

They proceeded across the bridge into New Jersey, before making their way to the Garden State Parkway, and finally to the Atlantic City Expressway. Once they arrived Nick and Freeze wasted no time in getting to the Trump Taj Mahal.

Freeze parked the truck in the parking lot, and they headed for the hotel. On the way, Freeze spotted Albert's car. "Nick," he said and Nick stopped. Freeze pointed at the car. "At least we know we're in the right place. There go Albert's car."

"Wait a minute," Nick said. "Watch the car, I'll be right back." When Nick returned, he had his little bag of tricks with him. While Freeze looked on, Nick went to work on Albert's car. When he was done, Nick returned his bag to the truck and they proceeded inside.

"What you do?"

"A little insurance. You think he's still in the casino?" Nick asked.

"If he's any kind of player he is," Freeze answered. After a quick stop at the nearest bar, they went into the casino. It wasn't long before they spotted Albert. "I got him," Nick said.

"Where?"

Nick discreetly pointed in the direction of the poker table. "Right, where Mylo said he would be."

Albert and his blond companion had been at the poker table for most of the night. He was holding his own, won a few big pots, but for him it wasn't the money, it was the game itself that fascinated Albert.

Freeze started walking toward Albert, but Nick grabbed his arm. "What you gonna do? Put a gun to his head and drag him out?"

"Sumthin' like that," Freeze said bluntly.

"Have another drink and relax. Watch some of these lovely and not so lovely ladies. You keep your eye on him. I'm gonna take a look around, do a little recon. See how many exits there are in this joint, if you see Birdie take him. But try to be discreet about it."

Freeze saluted the ex-soldier. "Cool. I'll try but I ain't

makin' no promises," and turned toward the bar to order another drink.

Once the bartender refreshed their drinks, Nick proceeded to check out the casino. Once he had satisfied himself with the layout of the room, Nick returned to Freeze at the bar.

"You see him?"

"No. I see our boy is still at it," Nick said.

"I say we take him now. Worry about Birdie later."

"You might be right. Mylo's girl didn't say she saw Birdie. But let's wait till he leaves the table. It'll cause less of a commotion."

"Damn!" Freeze said.

"What?"

"I hate fuckin' waitin'. You might be used to all this waitin' and reconnaissance shit from the army, but not me. I ain't like that."

"If you had waited before you killed them two muthafuckas, we wouldn't be here."

"Fuck you, Nick."

"Whatever," Nick said and ordered another drink.

At that moment, Birdie walked into the casino with a woman on each arm. Freeze nudged Nick. "What?"

"There he is. Can we take them now?"

"You take Birdie, I'll get Albert." Nick downed his drink and went after Albert, while Freeze made his way behind Birdie.

When he was right behind him, Freeze put his gun in Birdie's back. "Surprise, muthafuckas."

Birdie cursed when he felt the gun in his back.

"Get rid of the bitches," Freeze instructed.

"Ladies, would you two excuse me for a minute. I gotta talk to my man here."

Although they didn't seem happy about it, the ladies kissed Birdie on the cheek and walked away. "Good boy."

Albert looked up and saw Birdie, and then he noticed Freeze standing behind him. He looked around the room quickly and saw Nick coming at him. Albert quickly grabbed as many chips as he could carry and ran away from the table. Nick watched as Albert ran out of the casino, and headed for his car. Nick didn't chase him, he simply turned around and joined Freeze, who by this time had discreetly walked Birdie into the lobby.

"Albert get away?"

"He saw me comin' and ran."

"Like a bitch," Freeze said. "I told you we should have taken him when we had the chance."

"Don't worry. I got him," Nick said as they walked Birdie out to Freeze's truck. They put Birdie in the front seat and Nick covered until Freeze was in the driver seat. Nick got his bag out the back. While Freeze held a gun to Birdie's head, Nick put some double-cuff plastic restraints around Birdie's wrists and ankles. Then Nick used another longer piece to connect the two restraints. He made sure Birdie's seat belt was securely fastened, before getting in the back-seat behind him. "Let's go."

"Look, Freeze. We can work this out. I ain't have nothin' to do with Black's wife gettin' killed."

Nick laughed a little. "We know that."

"What?"

"I said we know you didn't have nothin' to do with it," Nick said, fighting back the laughter.

Birdie looked over at Freeze, who continued to drive in silence. "If y'all knew I ain't have nothin' to do wit it, then why you kill Smiley and Lonnie?"

"We didn't know it at the time. Did we, Freeze?"

Freeze didn't answer and continued driving out of the city.

"I think you owe Birdie an apology," Nick kidded Freeze.

"Fuck you, Nick."

"Well hold up then. If y'all know I didn't have nothing to do with it, then what are we doin' here?"

"You tried to kill us," Nick said matter-of-factly.

"But that was only 'cause y'all killed my people. I had to do somethin'."

"I understand that. But we're still gonna kill you."

"Come, man. We can work somethin out. I got money. How much you want? I'll get it. It don't matter how much, I'll get it and then I'll leave New York. Y'all will never see me again. Just please don't kill me," Birdie pleaded for his life.

"Too late for that now. But what I wanna know is since you didn't have nothin' to do with it, why didn't you come talk to us? Why you come hide out down here?"

"For real, that was Albert's idea. He thought if we waited a couple of days before we talked to you, it would improve our position on the street and we could expand."

"Damn, y'all some stupid muthafuckas," Freeze said.

"It was just business!" Birdie screamed.

"It was bad for business!" Nick yelled. He reached in his bag and pulled out a plastic bag and some duct tape. "Tryin' to kill us was bad for business, you dumb mutha-fuckas!" Nick put the plastic bag over Birdie's head and wrapped the duct tape around the edge so he couldn't get any air. With his wrist hooked up to his ankles, Birdie couldn't get his hands to his face to try to get the bag off his head.

"Die slow, muthafucka," Freeze said.

Birdie twisted and turned in his seat as he struggled

feverishly to breathe. It wasn't long before Birdie's movement slowed as the plastic bag got tighter around his head. Then his head dropped and Birdie stopped moving.

"I still think we should put two to his head," Freeze said.

"What you wanna do with the body?"

"Dump it. I mean it ain't like we can take him past the tollbooth cops and back to the parlor." Freeze drove across an overpass that covered a small river. He pulled over and he and Nick dragged Birdie's body to the river and threw him in.

Once they were back in the truck, Freeze turned to Nick, "What we gonna do about Albert?"

"I almost forgot," Nick said and reached in the backseat for his bag.

Confident that he had gotten away clean, Albert sped up the Atlantic City Expressway, on his way back to New York. He wondered how they found them.

Mylo.

That wasn't important now. The fact was that they did and by now Birdie was dead. Albert had no intention of suffering that same fate. He had some money stashed at a girlfriend's house in Brooklyn. His plan was to make it there, get the money, head for JFK and get on the first plane out.

Nick reached in his bag and pulled out a remote transmitter with a fifty-mile range. He raised the antenna and pushed the button.

Albert's car blew up.

CHAPTER 33

Freeze dropped Nick off at his car and he made his way to Impressions. Along the way he thought about Wanda and their beautiful night of passion. He marveled at how she'd wanted him, just as much as he wanted her. Nick wondered what would become of them and if they really had a chance. Deep down he hoped they did.

When Nick arrived at his destination he considered calling her, but thought better of it. He didn't want to appear pussy-whipped, even if he was. Calling Wanda now would only serve to confirm what, for now, was to remain his secret. Nick wanted her with every breath he took. When he walked toward the club, he felt a sense of relief, and he had no one other than Freeze to thank for that. After all, it was Freeze who had single-handedly assured them all that Black wouldn't do time for a crime he didn't commit. That's what Freeze getting rid of the gun meant.

As he walked up to Impressions, a stranger yelled from the line, which had wrapped around the corner. "Nick, whassup?"

Nick nodded, and blew him off as just another person trying to use his connection to beat the line. He stepped inside Impressions and walked past the dance floor and made his way into the sanctuary of his office. He unlocked the door and turned on the lights.

The minute the lights went on, Nick's eyes widened at the sight of the nine millimeter pointed right toward his head.

"Don't reach for your gun, just lock the door and keep coming, quietly," a voice ordered. "Keep your hands where I can see them while you're at it."

Nick complied with his demands and kept walking forward. "You want me to put my hands up, too?" Nick asked.

"Just keep coming."

"X, what the fuck are you doing here?" Nick asked calmly.

The man with the gun was Xavier Ashanti and Nick knew X well. They were in the same special operations unit in the army. He got discharged early because he was suddenly unable to pass the psychological test and said he wanted to kill his commanding officer. Since then, X had been working independently, doing the type of contract work that other people didn't want to do. Another life that Nick had happily left behind. He wasn't pleased to see Xavier, especially pointing a gun. If Xavier was pointing a gun at him, that meant he was there to kill him.

"I came to see you, naturally," Xavier answered. "Why else would I be sitting in your chair." He shrugged, with the gun still pointed at Nick. "I mean, this is your chair, right?"

"X, what the fuck are you doing here? I mean how did you even get in here? My office is locked, there's a security guard standing in front of a locked door. But here you are, with your pistola pointed at me," Nick said.

"That's the first thing we need to discuss, Nick."

"What's that, X?"

"Your sloppy-ass security. I mean, Nick, you been hangin' around these gangsters long enough, upgrade the security here."

"How'd you get in here, X?"

Xavier laughed a little. "A chick walks by with her skirt up her ass and the bum at the door is so busy watching her, he lets me walk right by him. If you wanna keep somebody out, get a better system."

Nick didn't flinch, he didn't panic, "We're friends, right?" he asked.

Xavier didn't answer.

"I take that as a yes, so why are you still pointing a gun at me?"

"Come on, Nick, you know what a cautious guy I am, nothing's changed. I mean you guys are *at war*, right?" Xavier laughed. "I mean, do these people even know what war is? But anyway, I just wanted to make sure one of your *soldiers*, didn't bust in behind you and shoot me," Xavier said and put the gun down. "So, how've you been, Nick?" he asked like he didn't just have a nine pointed at Nick's head. "Damn, it's good to see you, what's it been, five years?" Xavier continued.

"Yeah, it's been about that long, but what the fuck are you doing here?" Nick asked as he took a seat across from Xavier.

"Mind if I make a drink? This is a nice little deal you got here," Xavier said as he casually strolled over to the bar.

"Make it two," Nick said.

"Even if security sucks, you gangsters sure know how to live," Xavier teased. "You still drinking Johnny Black?"

"Make it a double."

"I heard about Jett, I'm real sorry." Xavier said about their old army buddy. "I hate to see a good soldier go down. But I hear Monika is doing better," he added as he poured liquor into two glasses. They were Nick's partners; Jett died and Monika barely survived when they went up against Chilly.

Xavier walked back to the desk, gave Nick his, then tilted his to the air. "For old times?" He motioned toward Nick.

"And fallen comrades," Nick added.

Nick and Xavier both drank their drinks in one swallow. "That's good stuff, I should've brought the bottle."

Nick stood and went and got the bottle. He always liked the way Johnny Black went down. He poured Xavier and himself another drink. This time there was no toast, just bottoms up.

"But you want to know what the fuck I'm doing here, right, Nick?" Xavier looked at his watch, "And I need to tell you because I got a late flight to catch. You got a problem and a big one at that," Xavier said casually.

"I know," Nick answered.

"Your boss is in jail, and his wife's dead."

"How do you know all of this, X, you been keeping tabs on me?"

"Well, yes and no, Nick," Xavier said and poured himself another drink. "Every once in a while your name comes up and I ask about you. It's a small community we operate in."

Nick shook his head. "Oh, no, small community *you* operate in. I'm out."

"So you mean to tell me, you'd rather do this gangster shit, than what you used to do? I know you still get the itch. C'mon, Nick, you know, taking a guy out from two hundred feet away with a heavy crosswind."

"All in the past. I don't roll like that anymore. Like you said, us gangsters know how to live."

"Yeah, that's a nice Caddy you pushin'. What's it, a XLR?"

"That's how I'm rolling these days, but enough about me, what's up with you, and why don't you start by telling me about my problem, and what it's got to do with you?"

"It has absolutely nothing to do with me, Nick, I swear. Anyway, I just ran into this information by chance. As much as I'd like to say I did some amazing intel, I was just in the right place at the right time. And that place was Singapore."

"How's Lucy?" Nick asked.

"As good as ever," Xavier assured him. "But that's a story for another time." Xavier downed his drink. "I'm in this bar with these two guys, you might even know them. George Swanson and Kip Bartowski."

"Don't ring a bell," Nick said.

"Bart's a big sucker."

"And I'd know these guys how?" Nick asked.

"Oh, if you knew them, you'd remember, contract killers."

Nick straightened up in his chair. "What do contract killers have to do with Shy's murder?"

"Oh, by the way, I'm sorry about that. I heard she was a very fine woman. If something like this had come my way, I'da passed and tipped you before she—"

"I know, X."

"Anyway, I'm in this bar in Singapore and I'm drinking with these guys and they're telling me about this last job they did. And they're both drunk, loud and telling me about it, laughing all over each other. So when they get through, I asked who the woman was. He told me the name and said it was some gangster's woman. I knew he was talking about your guy. Black, Mike Black, the guy you always talked about."

"Whoa! Whoa, slow down, X. You're trying to tell me that two contract killers hit Shy? Why?"

"I have no idea, Nick. Didn't get around to asking all that, didn't think they'd tell me if I did. I might've died violently if I asked that," Xavier said.

"How'd it happen?" Nick asked.

"Two-man operation. One guy picks up Black at the airport, lets his partner know when he's leaving the airport, tells him how long he's got. You want the whole story in detail? 'Cause you know I remember."

"Yeah, the whole story in detail, word for word if you can give it to me."

Xavier glanced down at his watch again, "How 'bout I leave out the slurring and the laughing?"

"Just tell me what happened, X."

"Apparently they'd been following your boy for a while, getting his pattern down. They'd had him under surveillance, eyes and ears, for more than a minute. They picked up on the trip you and him took to Mexico and that was their opportunity. So they set up one at the airport, one at the house."

"How'd he get in the house, X? The alarm's always on when Shy's in the house by herself," Nick said.

"The alarm wasn't on. They broke in while Black was there, hid in the basement until he got the call to move. Once he got the call, he went upstairs, since she was on the couch watching TV, she didn't hear 'em coming. The job was that he was supposed to beat her, so they handcuffed her to the chair and they used some kind of drug on her to minimize the pain."

"How'd they give it to her?"

"Just a little bit on a handkerchief, they didn't give her a whole lot of it, just enough so she could take that beating without doing a whole lot of screaming and not pass out on them. And he beat her," Xaiver said easily. "He'd sit down, take a break, watch TV, then he'd hit her some more. Once he figured he'd beat her enough, her face was pretty messed up from what he said. He took the cuffs off and led her to the kitchen. He told her that he'd let her go if she could make it out the back door. Said it was funny watching her stumble to the floor over and over while she tried to make it to the back door. Then he shot her in the back."

"When did she call the police, then?" Nick asked, disgusted and a bit confused.

"She didn't," Xavier said. "Remember, my friend, they had eyes and ears on them. She liked to talk on the phone. They put together a tape recording of her voice. After he confirmed she was dead. He made it look like there'd been a fight in there, pulled the phone off the wall, cleans the living room, makes sure he doesn't leave any traces. Now the alarm is on, so he waits. Waits until Black comes in and turns off the alarm, he slips out the basement door. His guy was waiting outside for him. So I ask him, why would you go to so much trouble, why not just walk in, shoot her and leave?"

"What'd they say, X?"

"They said the client wanted them to set it up so that the husband would walk in just in time to find the body and get taken by the cops. They had the whole thing planned out, right down to the police responce times."

"Where are they now?"

"I don't know."

"How could I find them?"

"The usual way, Nick, you're no stranger to this, unless this gangster stuff has made you soft."

"I still got some contacts, but did they give you any idea about who hired them and why?"

"No Nick, and like I said, I didn't ask. Since I was coming back to the States, I scheduled a flight to New York on my way to Atlanta."

"What are you going to Atlanta for?"

Xavier got up to leave. "I'll find out when I get there."

CHAPTER 34

Detective Kirkland walked into his captain's office and tossed the thick file onto his desk. Captain Keys was busy on the phone. He looked up at Kirk and rolled his eyes and waved for Kirk to sit down, then jumped right back into his conversation. "I hear what you're saying," he said into the phone.

Kirk wondered how long the phone conversation would last, and then he started looking at pictures in the small office. There were two tacked to the wall right above the coffeemaker. One was a professionally done five-by-twelve of President Bush, thumbtacked to the wall, and the other was a similar sized picture of a woman with dart holes in the face, and a dart still lodged in her chest. It was a picture of his ex-wife. It too was hanging by a thumbtack. Finally, the captain hung up the phone. "What can I do for you now, Kirk?"

"Mike Black."

"What about him?"

"He should be released," Kirk said firmly.

The captain sighed and rubbed his face with the palm of his hands. "Not this again, Kirk. I thought we talked about this, I mean, I thought we agreed Black should stay exactly where he is until we find the real killer," Captain Keys said.

"That's why I'm here. I don't think we can ignore the facts or the evidence any longer. Mike Black didn't kill his wife and—" Kirk slammed his palm down on the over-stuffed folder. He paused for effect. "The information in this file here proves that we've got a bigger problem than Black."

The captain shook his head. He closed his eyes and then looked up at Kirk. "Damn, I don't need this right now," the captain hissed. The captain picked up the folder. "Well, I'm not about to go through all this shit. So let me ask you this, Kirk. You got your shit together in there?" The captain held up the folder. "I mean, really got your shit together. There has to be undisputable facts that clearly show that Mike Black did not kill his wife."

"It's all here, Cap. It's all here in black and white," Kirk assured his captain.

"Okay," the captain said reluctantly. "Show what you got."

Once Kirk finished explaining in nauseating detail what his investigation had uncovered, the captain sat back in his chair. "What did I say when you came to me the last time?"

Kirk didn't answer.

"What, you forgot? Well, let me refresh your memory. I said you find out who killed her and lock them up."

"I know that, Cap, but—" Kirk started.

"I believe I said, once we got the killer in custody then we'll let him out. I haven't heard or maybe you haven't got to the part where the killer is in custody." Captain Keys paused to see if Kirk was going to say anything. "Do you even have a suspect, Kirk?"

"Yes, sir. I do have a suspect."

"Then why aren't they in custody?"

"That's where it gets problematic," Kirk said and went on to tell the captain about the missing security system, about his visit to see DEA Agent Pete Vinnelli and the conclusions he'd drawn. "I think these guys put a contract out on Black and his wife in retaliation for DeFrancisco being in jail and his wife's suicide."

"Did you know three members of the Aryan brotherhood attacked Black in his cell?"

"No, I didn't know that."

"Yeah, it happened one night after lockdown."

"After lockdown?"

"That's what I said."

"That means a guard had to be involved. He was supposed to die in his cell," Kirk said slowly as the last piece fell into place for him.

"I called the DA after our last chat. We had a meeting about this already. Their fear is the same as mine, we'll be putting a killer back out on the streets and we could have a massacre on our hands. And if that happens, it's your ass on the line, Kirk, you hear me? It's your ass on the line!"

Kirk could see the veins throbbing at his boss's temple. He had turned a shade of crimson and was trembling as he delivered his threat.

"I can say with all certainty I believe Mike Black has killed before, but Captain, we do not have the evidence to prove that he killed his wife."

The captain shook his head, sighed, then looked at Kirk again. "Okay, Kirk, I'll make the call, but as God is my witness, if another pint of blood is shed in the streets of New York behind this shit, so help me you'll be on every shit detail there is and I'm talkin' about some really fucked-up shit that I'll think up just for you, Kirk."

Kirk put his hands up in mock surrender. "Captain, you can trust me on this one."

Captain Keys reached for the phone and said, "I sure hope so for your sake," then started punching numbers on the keypad.

"What do you want me to do about DeFrancisco?"

"Fuck him. He's already in jail, we can put our hands on him anytime we want him. He's not going anywhere." The captain stood up. "It's your case now, Kirk. You and Richards go after Vinnelli. Make a case that will stick and he'll hand us DeFrancisco."

CHAPTER 35

Approximately four hours after Captain Keys made the call, Mike Black stood at the cage of the property section in the jail. He was thumbing through the contents of the large manila envelope that held his personal belongings. "It's all here," he mumbled to no one in particular.

"And what were you gonna do if it wasn't?" Sergeant Adams asked.

Black gave her a menacing stare and then he smiled. "I'm gettin' out of here now, so I'm in a good mood." Black leaned forward and glanced at her name tag. "Sergeant Adams, is it?"

"That's correct."

Black nodded in recognition of who she was and what she represented to Freeze. He had no idea what she had done for him, but she was sure he would find out. "So let's just say you should be glad you don't have to find out," he said, gathered his things, then turned and strolled to the door. His proud swagger didn't give any indication about his feelings. With his head held high and his back straight he looked like his time on lockdown hadn't fazed him at all. But Black had mixed feelings as he walked down the corridor. Sure, he was more than excited about being free, but still devastated by having to go on without Cassandra. He had vowed to find her killer and kill them. *Slow.*

Now that he was free, Black thought about the hours he spent thinking of ways in which he'd kill. He wanted to avenge his wife's death with no heart and no mercy.

With his release papers held firmly in one hand, he used the other to push the glass door open. He didn't even flinch at the sunshine he hadn't seen in days. When he saw the black stretch limo waiting, he walked directly toward it. The driver hopped out before Black could reach for the handle. The man opened the door and allowed him to step into the back of the car. Black was so glad to see familiar faces smiling at him.

"Damn, it's good to see you, Black," Freeze said. They shook hands, and Wanda handed him a champagne flute. When Black looked at it strangely, Freeze quickly said, "That was her idea, Black," he offered, nodding toward Wanda.

"Thanks, Wanda," Mike said, thinking about the last time he and Shy shared a glass of champagne together. "But I'm gonna need something a bit stronger."

Freeze held up a bottle of Rémy Martin VSOP; they all laughed and quickly drained the fancy champagne flutes Wanda had brought along.

"So what's up?" Mike said as he eased back into the leather bucket seats. He was now on his second shot of Rémy.

The liquid burned a trail down his throat, but it kept his mind on the revenge he wanted to execute. It had been all he thought about for days. He wanted to look Shy's killer in the eyes right before he squeezed the last breath from his lungs with his bare hands. Black wanted him to know exactly why he was gonna die.

"You okay, Mike?" Wanda asked.

Her voice brought him back to the celebration going on in the back of the limo. He could tell they weren't sure exactly what to say to him. He may have been down for a minute, but he was back and ready for somebody to feel his pain.

"Oh, yeah, I'm cool, my mind was just somewhere else," he said. Mike looked at Freeze. "Hit me again."

Freeze poured another drink from the bottle.

"So much has been going on while you were gone," Wanda began. "We've been busy trying to hold it down but—" Wanda said and looked at Freeze.

"Yeah, but things got a little outta hand, Black," Freeze tossed in.

Black knew that meant that Freeze had killed somebody, but at that moment he just wanted to know if they had found out who had killed his wife, or at least had an idea.

While Wanda talked about everything but what he wanted to hear, Black zoned out as she updated him on what had been happening in his absence. He didn't give a fuck who Freeze had killed, he didn't give a fuck about anything other than finding who was responsible for her death.

Finally, Mike grew weary of Wanda's update and asked the only question he wanted an answer to. "You find out who killed Cassandra yet?"

Silence fell on the limo's interior. Wanda and Freeze exchanged glances. "Not really," Wanda answered.

"So what's the word on the street?" he asked. "Anybody heard who killed Cassandra?" he asked bluntly.

Black looked at Wanda and Freeze and wondered just

what the hell they'd been doing while he was on lockdown. "You mean to tell me ain't nobody talkin' about this shit?" He shook his head and took the glass to his lips again. Instead of taking another sip, he moved it away and said, "Somebody somewhere knows what the fuck happened to Cassandra. I would've thought y'all were on top of this from the minute they took me in." Black looked at Wanda and he shook his head.

Wanda looked at Freeze again, hoping that he would just tell him. "Freeze!" Mike said quickly.

"Huh?"

"The way Wanda keeps lookin' at you, I know you got somethin' to tell me. So let's hear it," Mike said to Freeze and Wanda dropped her head.

"The night before it happened, Shy got into it with Birdie at Cuisine."

"What do you mean, got into it?" Mike demanded to know.

"I mean, Shy and Birdie got into an argument."

"About what?"

"I don't know, but by the time I put my gun to Birdie's head, they up in each other's face and I heard her say that she don't know how he get any pussy, as ugly as his ass is," Freeze informed him.

"That sounds like her," Mike said and laughed a little.

"Birdie chilled out and left when I put my gun to his head. But he told Shy that she would see him again and she wouldn't like it."

"Okay, so you think Birdie killed her?"

"Tell him the rest of it," Wanda prodded.

"Me and Nick went lookin' for Birdie, let his boy Albert know we was lookin' for him and when he didn't come talk to us and I killed two of his boyz. Then they tried to hit me and Nick, but—" Freeze said, but Black cut him off.

"Did Birdie kill her?"

"No," Wanda finally said. "After Nick talked to Kirk, we figured that Birdie couldn't have put it together that quickly."

"What happened to Birdie and Albert?"

"Me and Nick took care of that last night."

"So while I was in jail, y'all niggas been fuckin' around fightin' a war with the wrong muthafuckas? Is that what the fuck you're tellin' me, Freeze?"

"Yeah," Freeze said and dropped his head.

Black turned to Wanda. "And you just sat around and let him do it?"

Wanda dropped her head. "Yes, sir."

"So the two of you have no fuckin' idea who killed Cassandra. Is that what the fuck you're tellin' me!"

Once again, there was complete silence in the limo.

"How'd you get them to release me anyway, Wanda?" Mike asked.

"I wish I could take the credit, but I can't. They called me and said that you were being released due to a lack of evidence." Wanda waited for Mike to comment. When he didn't, she continued. "My guess is that Kirk turned up something and they had to let you go."

"I need to know what Kirk knows," Black said.

"The only one he talked to was Nick," Wanda said.

"Where's Nick?"

Wanda looked at her watch. "Impressions."

By the time the limo pulled up in front of Impressions, they were just getting set up for the club to open. When Black stepped into the place with Wanda and Freeze on his trail, the room broke into applause. Black smiled and nodded a few times, but made his way up to Nick's office. He would have come in the limo to meet Black, but he had to get the club open. "Damn, Black, it good to see you," Nick said and got up.

"It's good to see you too, Nick." Black turned to Freeze and Wanda. "It's good to see y'all, too." He stood in front of Freeze. "And I appreciate what you did—even if it was the wrong guys. I never did like Birdie or Albert's bitch ass anyway."

Everybody laughed but Black, he was still all business. Black walked over to the bar, Wanda and Freeze took a seat.

"Wanda thinks Kirk is responsible for gettin' me out. You talked to him, Nick, what did he tell you?"

"You know Kirk, he didn't give up any info. But he did put me on to the fact that it couldn't have been Birdie. But I have it from a very reliable source that this was a setup from the start."

Black put down his glass, and turned his attention to Nick. "What you got?"

"Last night I came in here and found an old army buddy of mine waiting for me. We worked black ops together; he's still into it. We were pretty close back then, we've saved each other's life once or twice, so I told him about you, Black. All of you. Anyway, he tells me this story he heard while he was in Singapore. He said he was drinking with two contract killers. They were both drunk, laughing all over each other, telling him about the last job they did. When they got through, my guy asked who the woman was. He told them the name and said it was some gangster's woman. My guy knew he was talking about you, Black."

"Wait minute, so you're tryin' to tell me this was a hit on Cassandra? Why?" Black said in total disbelief.

Nick shrugged, "He didn't know, Black. Says he didn't ask all that 'cause he didn't think they'd tell him anyway. I asked him how it happened," Nick said, then paused.

Black swallowed dry and hard. He blinked a few times, then looked at Nick, "Go on."

"You sure you wanna hear this?" Nick asked. The piercing look Black gave told him to continue the story. "Two-man operation. One guy picked us up at the airport; let the other know when we were leaving."

Nick went on to explain how the killers followed Black until they had his pattern down. How they waited until he was home to break in and hid in the basement until he got the call to move. And how the killer handcuffed her to the chair and used some kind of drug on her to minimize the pain.

"Keep going," Black mumbled.

"After he beat her, he took off the cuffs, and led her to the kitchen. He told her if she could make it out the kitchen door he'd let her go. They thought it was funny watching her fallin' down, tryin' to get away. Then he shot her in the back."

Wanda started crying.

"After he established she was dead, he made it look like there'd been a fight in there. Then he waited, because the alarm was still on. He went back into the basement, until you got there and turned it off. When you did, he slipped out the basement door. His guy picked him up right outside. So my guy asked why they went through so much trouble."

"And?" Black asked.

"Apparently the client wanted it set it up so you'd take the fall," Nick confirmed.

Black nodded a few times, and then he finally said, "Where are they?"

CHAPTER 36

Two Weeks Later, Miami, Florida

It was just after 3:00 in the afternoon when Leon Copeland got off the American Airlines 35 jet at Miami International Airport, accompanied by his female associates Diamond and Pearl. They had caught the flight in from Jacksonville to do a very big favor for a very old friend.

Before Leon relocated to Jacksonville, he used to work for André. He and Black were good friends, they used to hang out together. So when Black took over from André and established the dead zone shit, Leon chose not to go to war with him like everybody else. "I took my business elsewhere."

"With his blessing and support, Leon. Don't forget that," Leon remembered Wanda reminding him the last time they talked. But he could honestly say that he was more than surprised to get a call from Wanda. He had taken advantage of Wanda's legal services not too long ago, when Nina Thomas, his cousin's girlfriend, was charged with murder.

Being old friends, naturally, Wanda didn't charge him to represent Nina during her appearance before the grand jury, but Wanda made it plain that Leon owed her a favor.

"Good morning, Leon. This is Wanda. How are you doing?"

"I'm doin' great, Wanda. What about you?" Leon asked knowing that Wanda didn't just call.

"I'm great, too. I know you don't know this but Mike was in jail recently."

"Black, in jail? Who'd he kill?"

"Somebody murdered his wife and tried to set him up for the murder."

"That's fucked up," Leon said, sure now that Wanda wanted something. "Does he know who killed her?"

"We have some ideas."

"Well, if there's anything I could do to help, you know all you gotta do is ask."

"If you're willing to help, there is something that you might be able to help us with," Wanda told him.

"Anything at all, Wanda. Just let me know."

"Are you busy now?"

"Not at all, why?"

"Mike's flight arrives in Jacksonville in about two hours. He'd appreciate it if you were there to meet him."

A little more than two hours later, Leon, Diamond, and Pearl met Black at the airport. Leon hadn't seen Black in years. When Black stepped into the baggage-claim area the first thing he noticed was Diamond and Pearl. Then he saw Leon standing in between them. Leon stepped away from the ladies and greeted him. "Mike Black," he said and shook his hand. "You look good for somebody that just got out the joint."

Black patted Leon on the stomach. "You look like life is treatin' you good."

"I've done all right for myself."

"So Wanda tells me," Black said as Diamond cleared her throat.

"Oh, yeah, Black, this is Diamond and this is Pearl."

Black laughed a little. "You're kiddin'."

"No, I'm serious. That's right, you're a Prince fan."

"Right." Black smiled and turned to the ladies. "Diamond, Pearl, it's a pleasure to meet you."

"Pleasure to meet you, too," they both said almost in unison. "Leon talks about you all the time," Pearl added.

"I hope it all good," Black said.

Pearl ran her tongue over her lips. "It looks all good to me."

"Come on, Black. I got a car waiting," Leon said and started out the door. "You got any luggage?"

"No."

There was a good reason why he had no luggage. The day after he got out of jail, Black and Wanda went by his house. Black stood in the living room for a while, staring at the couch and the chair. Then he went into the kitchen. As Wanda looked on, Black knelt down at the very spot where he found Shy's body. Wanda really couldn't tell because his back was to her, but she knew that he was fighting back the tears. When he got up, Black told Wanda to get rid of everything and sell the house. He hadn't been back since.

The next day he attended Shy's funeral. It was the single hardest thing he had ever had to do. Standing there, holding Michelle. She stayed quiet while the reverend spoke, but as soon as he was done, Michelle began crying, screaming really. Black told Bobby that she knew what was going on and that was her way to say good-bye to her mother.

Once Black was released there was no more discussion about Michelle's future. She would be with her father.

Leon had rented a limousine for the trip to his house and made sure that he stopped by the store and picked up a bottle of Rémy Martin VSOP for Black. On the way to Leon's, the two friends talked and laughed about the old days. During the ride, Pearl, who sat next to Black, had slowly inched closer to him and at that point had looped her arm in his. Black felt a little apprehensive about it; her being so close to him. Although he found both Pearl and Diamond to be very attractive, he had just buried his wife two weeks ago. He just wasn't ready.

Two hours later, Leon and Black were sprawled out in the living room waiting for the Greek food to be delivered. Since Diamond and Pearl couldn't cook, they had to settle for delivery. By the time the food arrived, it was really late and the ladies had been yawning throughout Leon and Black's entire conversation. They didn't discuss anything too deep, but still, the yawns were becoming a distraction. Black didn't really like the idea of talking around the two women, even though he knew Leon trusted them like family. Other than a brief discussion about what happen to Shy, he purposely kept the conversation light.

Once they finished dinner, they sat back to enjoy drinks. After the third round, Diamond stretched, released a less than ladylike yawn and stood up. "That's it, I'm goin' to bed," she announced. She looked at Pearl who sat curled up on the nearby love seat, "You comin'?" she asked.

Pearl brought the glass from her still glossy lips and shook her head. "I ain't sleepy, you go ahead," she said and took another sip from the glass. This time she swallowed all that was left.

By this time Pearl's neck was bending. It was obvious she was going down for the count. When her chin finally touched her chest, Leon looked over and snapped, "Pearl, take your ass to bed!"

Pearl jumped up at the sound of her name, "I ain't sleepy," she whined.

"Nah, you right, you ain't sleepy, your ass is asleep. We don't wanna sit up here and listen to you snoring. Take your ass to bed," he demanded.

Reluctantly, Pearl got up and made her way to the staircase, sucking her teeth all the way. She looked over her shoulder one last time and mumbled, "See y'all in the mornin'." Then she sashayed up the stairs.

Black watched as she made it up the steps and stopped at the first door on her left. She hesitated a moment, then opened the door, walked in and slammed it shut. As soon as the door shut, Black turned to Leon. "Dude, you fuckin' both of 'em?"

"Yup," Leon answered easily. Black noticed his chest was sticking out just a little more.

Black shook his head, "You the man," he joked.

"Nah, Black, you the man. Right now, I'm just the man sittin' next to the man. But anyway, I know you didn't come all this way just to talk about old times. Tell me what I can do to help," Leon said.

"It's about Cassandra," Black said and swallowed hard. There were still times when he couldn't believe she was gone.

"You know who killed her?" Leon's eyebrow inched up.

"I do."

Leon sat back in his chair. He took a sip of his drink; he looked like he was pondering something, then stroked his mustache, hoping Black wasn't about to ask him to commit a murder for him. Yeah, they were mad cool, however, Leon considered himself a businessman.

Black was the killer.

"Tell me what you want me to do?" Leon asked.

"I need you to do something real important for me," Black said, looking straight in his eyes. "I'd get one of my people to do it, but they've had us under surveillance. This guy might recognize them. I can't take chances like that. So right now, you're the only one I trust enough to handle this."

"Tell me what you want me to do?" Leon asked again, nodding this time.

"Cassandra was killed by two contract killers. Through his contacts, Nick was able to find out that they're handled by a guy named Rosstein. What I need you to do is meet with Rosstein and arrange to have these guys at a certain place at a certain time."

Leon put his drink down and looked at Black, "That's it?" he asked, astonished.

"Yeah, Leon, that's all I want you to do," Black answered calmly.

"That's it!" Leon shook his head. "I ain't gotta kill nobody?" Leon looked shocked, but relieved.

"Nah, Leon, I know you ain't no killer," Black said. "You remember when we were at that club and that nigga Go-Go slapped the shit outta you over Nicole?"

Leon snapped his fingers. "Yeah, I remember that shit, I wanted to kill that nigga badder than a muthafucka. Kill him so bad I could taste it," Leon said, with his face all twisted up over the memory. "But I just couldn't do it, had the muthafucka on his knees, and I couldn't do it," he said sadly.

"So I killed him for you," Black said.

"Damn sure did," Leon admitted quietly.

"Whatever happened with you and Nicole anyway?"

Leon shrugged. "Last I heard, she got hooked up with a shooter who got her strung out on heroin. I ain't seen her in years."

"Whatever, Leon," Black laughed. "So look, tomorrow morning Nick will be here and he'll brief you on what you need to know to talk to this Rosstein guy." Black polished off his drink.

Through his contacts, Nick had arranged for Leon to meet Rosstein at Hilton Miami Airport Hotel, in the Coral Café. Leon was told to sit there and eat, and Rosstein would join him during the meal. Leon and the ladies ordered their food, and were in the middle of the meal when Rosstein walked up.

"Mr. Copeland?"

Leon looked up, and said, "Mr. Rosstein?"

Rosstein nodded; he looked at Diamond and Pearl. "I was under the impression that we would talk alone," he said, taking in the skimpy outfits the ladies were wearing. When he said that, Diamond and Pearl automatically knew it was their cue to leave.

Rosstein cleared his throat and sat down. He glanced around the restaurant and turned back to Leon when he noticed the ladies were comfortably seated at the bar. Diamond and Pearl winked and waved. "I have to compliment you on your taste in women," Rosstein said to Leon.

"I thought we were here to discuss business, Mr. Rosstein." Leon reached in his jacket and pulled out an envelope. He slid it in front of Rosstein. The envelope contained money and a picture. "That man will be coming out of Villa De La Reina Hotel in Madrid next Tuesday at ten o'clock at night. He'll be accompanied by two bodyguards. All three of them need to be eliminated."

Rosstein signaled for the waiter. He didn't speak as they waited for the waiter to come.

"Bourbon and water," he said to the young man.

While he waited for his drink he glanced at the picture in the envelope, at Leon, then at Diamond and Pearl.

"Since this is our first time doing business, I'm gonna let this go, but usually I don't like to do business like this," Rosstein said softly.

"This is how I've always handled business with Felix, straight to the point. None of this bullshittin' around," Leon said coolly.

"You used to deal with Felix, huh? Shame he retired," Rosstein tossed in.

Leon leaned forward. "What is this? Some kind of fuckin' test?" Leon paused. "Felix retired when somebody put a bullet in his brain."

The waiter returned with Rosstein's drink and he took a sip. "Can't be too careful these days," he said.

Leon stood up. "Just let me know when it's done," he said then walked to the bar.

CHAPTER 37

Madrid, Spain, Tuesday evening, 10 P.M.

George Swanson was laying in wait on the roof of a building that sat directly across the street from the Villa De La Reina Hotel, located on Gran Via, overlooking Plaza Cibeles, in the heart of Madrid. He couldn't get over how easy this would be; easy money. He sat poised and ready, he looked at his watch and lifted his rifle, looked in the scope and waited for his targets to appear.

Suddenly he felt a barrel at the back of his head.

"Put the gun down slowly, and stand up," Nick said.

At first, Swan, as he was called, didn't move or react.

"I'll put a hole the size of that scope right through your skull. I said put it down and back up," Nick warned.

Swan slowly turned around, Nick took the rifle from him and walked him away from the edge of the building and into the stairwell where Black and Freeze were waiting.

"Remember me?" Black asked and punched him in the face.

Swan could hardly believe his eyes. The way the plan was supposed to go, once he and Bart did their part, Black was supposed to be killed in jail. His presence on the rooftop meant that not only did that not occur, but he knew who they were, and how to find them. Swan began to think quickly of a way to get out of the situation. Nick had disarmed him and in the small stairwell there weren't that many options.

"Where do I find Kip Bartowski?" Black asked.

"Fuck you, nigger," George spat. "I don't know what the fuck you're talkin' about!"

"Freeze," Black called.

Freeze put his gun away and walked up to Swan. Nick held him while Freeze went to work on his face and gut. Freeze would hit him, and Black would ask the question. "Where do I find Kip Bartowski?"

Freeze hit him again.

"Where do I find Kip Bartowski?" Black demanded.

Freeze hit him again.

Swan spat blood, and took all of Freeze's blows, but he wouldn't talk. The beating continued until Black tapped Freeze on the shoulder. "Take him outside."

By this time, Swan wasn't able to walk too well, so Nick and Freeze dragged him outside, and Black followed behind them. Once they got Swan back outside, Black said, "Let him go." Nick and Freeze let him go and his beaten body fell to the rooftop. Black stopped, crouched down next to him. "Where do I find Kip Bartowski?"

"What you gonna do, kill me? If I tell you you're gonna kill me any fuckin' way, so what difference does it make, go on and do it! Get it over with, nigger."

Freeze kicked him in the face. "I got your nigga!" he shouted, then he kicked him again.

"I wasn't gonna kill you," Black lied. He wanted everybody involved dead. "I never had planned on killing you. I know you wasn't the one who killed my wife. Bart killed her. But now I'm thinkin' maybe you do need to die," Black said. He looked at him and eased back up. "Throw him over," he ordered.

The plan was to beat Swan until he gave up Bartowski, and then get Rosstein to tell them who hired him. Now, George Swanson was dead and they still didn't know where they could find Bartowski. Black put in a call to Leon. He explained to Leon what had happened and told him it was time to implement plan B.

Leon smiled and said, "You got it."

Once he hung up the phone from Black, Leon called Rosstein. "Mr. Rosstein?" Leon said into the phone.

"Yes, Mr. Copeland?"

"Has the work been completed?"

"I'm waiting for confirmation now," Rosstein said.

"Well, if your man is as good as I've heard he is, you should receive your confirmation very soon and we can relax and celebrate like gentlemen."

"Exactly!" Rosstein said, smiling, hoping that celebration would include Diamond and Pearl.

"Are you still at the Hilton?" Leon confirmed.

"Yes I am, I'm in room four-eleven. Bring the rest of the money," Rosstein said.

"I'll be there tomorrow afternoon," Leon said. "Hopefully you'll have confirmation by then."

"Right, you just bring the money."

The following afternoon, Rosstein paced back and forth in his room. He still hadn't heard from Swan and he knew that Copeland was on his way. He was becoming concerned when he heard a knock at the door. Rosstein went to the door and looked through the peephole and was pleasantly surprised to see Diamond and Pearl carrying a brief-case.

Rosstein swung the door open, Diamond smiled and be-fore he could do or say another word, Diamond reached from behind her back and hit Rosstein with a long blast with a Taser gun. It shocked him but didn't put him down, so Diamond hit him again. His body dropped to the floor, and Leon dragged him inside.

When Rosstein came to, he was stripped down to his boxers, and handcuffed to the bed. Diamond and Pearl were sitting on either side of him.

"Leon, he's waking up," Pearl said.

Leon came into the room and put a chair in front of the bed. He sat down and said, "Rosstein."

Rosstein lifted his head. "What the fuck is this, Cope-land! What's going on?"

"You're gonna tell me who put the contract out on Mike Black and his wife and you're gonna tell me where to find Kip Bartowski."

Rosstein laid his head back down. "Fuck you! How long do you think I'll stay in business if I tell you that?"

At that point, Pearl zapped him with the Taser gun and then passed it back to Diamond. Leon asked again, he re-fused to answer. Diamond zapped him again.

After a while Diamond noticed the bump in Rosstein's shorts. She pointed toward his crotch. "Pearl, his lil' thing gettin' hard. You think he likes it?"

"Zap him again, Diamond, see if he cums," Pearl gig-gled.

Leon stood up and shook his head at them. "Y'all two somethin' else. Y'all do what y'all gon' do," he said and left the room.

Leon had no idea what was going on in the room, all he heard was Rosstein screaming and Diamond and Pearl giggling. Soon, the door opened and Pearl was standing there with a devilish grin across her face. "He ready to talk now," she announced. Leon came back in the room and looked at Rosstein, who was struggling to breathe. "You had enough? Looks like these two could go all night."

Diamond moved the Taser gun toward Rosstein again.

"All right!" Rosstein yelled. He took a deep breath and tried to compose himself. He glanced in Diamond's direction. She smiled and held up the Taser. "Kip Bartowski. Day after tomorrow, he'll be in Italy, in Palermo."

"What's he doin' there?"

"What do you think he's there for?" Diamond motioned toward Rosstein. "He's there to kill Pietro Brusca."

"Who the fuck is that?" Leon barked.

"Underboss for the Luigi family, in New York. He had a beef with—" Rosstein started.

"I don't wanna know anything about that. Just tell me where he is."

"He's hidin' out in Palermo, at Giovanni Falcone's house, it's his cousin or some shit."

"How do I find it?"

"The address, it's in my briefcase."

"Now," Leon said. "Who hired you?"

"Look, I gave you Bart. I'm gonna assume the reason I didn't hear from Swan is because he's already dead. I can't give you anything else. You don't know how these guys are. They'll kill me."

"What you think I'm about to do if you don't tell me what I wanna know?" Leon lied.

"I know, but they won't stop at me, they'll kill my wife and kids. Of course, it will all look like an accident," Rosstein pleaded. "But they won't stop there. Once they're through with me, they'll take my brother's farm. They'll do all kinds of stuff, they'll ruin my whole family. Please," he begged.

"Diamond."

Diamond zapped him again. But this time Diamond got a little carried away. Rosstein, who was already weak from the session with the ladies, screamed out. Diamond didn't let up as his back arched, his eyes widened in horror and he suddenly stopped moving.

"Oh shit! I think Diamond done killed him," Pearl said.

"Great!" Leon said.

"I'm sorry." Diamond shrugged innocently.

Leon snatched the Taser from Diamond. "Pearl!" Leon said, shaking his head in disgust.

"Yes, sir," Pearl said quickly.

Leon grabbed Rosstein's briefcase. "Get the handcuffs and let's go. Diamond, you wipe this place down. No fuckin' prints."

CHAPTER 38

Palermo, Italy, Friday Morning, 2:45 a.m.

Kip Bartowski sat dressed in all black, in his vantage point in the hills across from the house of Giovanni Falcone, and waited for the appropriate time to move. He took another bite of his tuna fish sandwich and looked at his watch. "Won't be long now," Bart said and picked up his binoculars. He had been there for the last three hours, getting a feel for the property. "Glad there are no search-lights."

By that time, Bart knew how often Falcone's men swept the grounds and in what time intervals. Based on the location and angle of the security cameras, he had figured where the blind spots were. Bart had identified the control room, or what passed for one, where the security system was housed. It was a small shack, about twenty meters west of the main house. His first objective would be to make it there without being seen. If things happened the way he planned them, "And they usually do," he should be able to make it to the house without being detected.

Bart finished his sandwich and washed it down with a bottle of water. He stood up and began to gather his gear and policed the area, so there'd be no trace of him ever being there. With that task complete, he picked up his binoculars and turned his attention to the ten-foot wall that surrounded the house. "Right about now," he said as almost on cue, two men with AK-47's and dogs walked by. They were followed by a Jeep with two more armed men, cruising slowly behind them.

Once they passed, Bart put on his night-vision goggles and began an all-out sprint on the wall. He moved very well for a man his size and had made it down the hill and to the wall in under a minute. He stood motionless with his back pressed against the wall and waited for any evidence that his move to the wall had been noticed. Confident that he had not been detected, he took off his backpack. He took out a rope with a grappling hook attached to it and preceded to scale the wall.

Now that Bart was on the grounds, he checked his position against the angle of the cameras before moving toward the house. He stayed low to the ground and began his approach to the house. Once Bart made it to the house, he heard somebody coming. He quickly ducked into the shadows. As the man passed, he stepped out of the shadows. *"Ha preso una luce?"* Bart said in Italian.

"Sicuro, nessuno problema," the man replied. He reached into his pocket for a lighter and turned around. When he looked up, Bart shot him.

Bart dragged the body behind some bushes. He looked at the lighter the man had. It was nice so he kept it. He could use a cigarette right about now, but he knew that he didn't have time for a smoke break.

Bart stood outside the window of the control shack and peeked inside. There were two men seated in front of a console. One was playing solitaire, while the other fought sleep. He made his way around to the front of the building. Once he was in position in front of the door, Bart kicked it in. He stepped inside quickly and fired two shots. He moved toward the two men and fired again, this time it was two to the head to make sure they were dead.

Bart sat down at the console and looked at the monitors, which appeared to cover all the halls and access points in the house. He shut down all the alarm systems that he could find and as quickly as he could, Bart made a five-second repeating loop of all the monitored areas, so all the monitors displayed the same five seconds. This way anyone looking at the monitor would see nothing. He looked at his watch; he had fifteen minutes to complete his task before Falcone's men came to the control shack to check in.

Now that the security was disabled and with no cameras to worry about, Bart moved quickly through the house, up the stair's and to the room of his victim, Pietro Brusca, who was currently being entertained by a dark-skinned Italian beauty. He opened the door quietly and slipped inside. The lovers were so engaged in what they were doing that they didn't notice Bart standing there watching them, watching the woman ride Pietro Brusca. The woman was breathtaking, with her long legs and large breasts. He stood looking at her for a second when suddenly the woman's eye sprang open. *"Oh il mio dio!"* she shouted. Brusca pushed the woman off of him and rolled out of the bed, as the woman tried to cover herself.

Bart let out a little laugh and raised his gun. He shot

Pietro Brusca twice in the head and then turn the gun on the woman and shot her, too. With his task complete, he resisted his necrophilia tendencies and got out of the house. Once he was off the ground, Bart made his way to his car, which he had parked two kilometers down the road.

When he got to the spot where his car was parked, Bart found that all four tires had been flattened. "Shit!" Bart raised his weapon and scanned the area for movement. He didn't see or hear anybody, so he stooped down next to his car to assess the damage. He thought that he heard a noise behind him. He was just about to turn when he felt a pin prick in the back of his neck. All of a sudden, Bart felt woozy, he tried to stand up, but he fell flat on his face.

When Bart came to, he found himself alone in a room with a small desk lamp. His mouth was gagged with duct tape and his hands were cuffed behind his back.

"He's comin' out of it," Nick said and approached Bart.

Freeze stood up. "About fuckin' time."

Bart could hear their voices, but couldn't see anybody. His head still wasn't clear. He tugged on the cuffs. Bart was strong, but not strong to bust handcuffs. Bart looked around the room and tried to get a sense of where he was and how he was going to get himself out of this one.

"Do you know why you're here?" Black asked quietly and put on his gloves.

Bart didn't answer.

Black hit him. "Do you know why you're here?"

Once again, he didn't answer.

"Maybe this will help," Black said and punched Bart again before ripping the duct tape from his mouth. "Now, do you know why you're here?"

"I don't know who the fuck you are, but you better kill

me now, 'cause if I get free I'm gonna cut your fuckin' heart out!" Bart yelled, but he still couldn't see anybody. All he could see was Black's hands coming at him.

Black hit him again.

"That's the one thing you can be sure of. I am going to kill you," Black said and punched Bart in the face again. He started to walk away, but turned right back and hit him again. "You know, the whole time I was in jail I thought about how I was gonna kill you. I thought about you, on your knees, me lookin' in your eyes."

"Say good-bye," Freeze said.

Black turned and looked at Freeze, seemingly annoyed by the interruption, then turned back and hit Bart again. "But then I thought, why shoot you quick like that? That's not the way you would do it, is it Bart?"

"Do whatever you want. Just get it over if you got the balls. Come on!" Bart yelled. "Leastways I don't have to listen to you." For the first time, Bart began to realize that this wasn't about Pietro Brusca, and he hadn't been grabbed by somebody working for the Italians.

"You won't have to listen to the sound of my voice for too much longer. I promise not to say a word while I kill you. But I'm gonna do it slow. I'm gonna kill you the way you killed her. I'm gonna beat you until you pass out. Then I'm gonna have Nick here give you a shot of adrenaline, then I'm gonna beat you until you pass out again. I'm gonna beat you until my hands hurt and I run outta shit to hit you with and then I'll shoot you in the back. How does that sound to you—Bart?"

In the dimly lit room, Bart struggled to get loose. The look that covered his face was one of bewilderment.

"Look at him," Black said. "He's all curious and bothered now. He's wondering what the fuck did he do to piss off somebody that much that they'd wanna kill him like that."

"Why don't you tell him, Black? You know you want to."

"Thank you, Nick. I was just about to get to that," Black said and hit Bart again. "You have no idea what this is about, do you?"

"No, I don't. So why don't you tell me so we can get this over with," Bart spat out.

"Don't be in such a rush." Black looked at his watch. "My flight to New York doesn't leave for another eighteen hours. But I really do need you to know why you're gonna die in this room tonight. You were in New York not too long ago, weren't you, Bart?"

Bart didn't answer, but the look on his face confirmed that he knew exactly what this was about.

"Did you catch a show while you were there? I guess not; you had work to do, didn't you, Bart? You were in town to kill my wife. You beat her and then you shot her in the back."

"That was just business. I was just doin' the job I was paid to do," Bart said although he knew it wouldn't change anything.

"I know, 'cause you're a professional, right? It was all just business, I understand, but it was very personal to me." Black hit him. Then hit him again. "She was my wife!" Black shouted as loud as he could and continued to hit Bart in the face. "She was my wife! And you took her from me." Black turned and walked away from Bart. "Gag him and blindfold him," he said to Nick.

Nick stepped up and immediately put duct tape over Bart's mouth. Once he had the duct tape on, Nick put plugs in Bart's ears and blindfolded him to deprive Bart of the sensory stimulation, of sound, light, and sense of time. Nick then ripped the sleeves off Bart's shirt. Nick took out his knife and made long cuts on his arms to get him bleeding. Nick stepped out of the way and Black began.

The rest of the time went pretty much as Black said it would, with one exception. When Black's hands began to hurt and he had hit Bart in the head with a phone until it was in pieces, and a wooden chair. It broke on the first swing, but Black used the pieces to beat him, and then Freeze took over.

Freeze had Nick help to stand Bart up. They walked him into the bathroom, where Freeze hooked the handcuff up on the shower head. "What do you think this is, *Scarface* or some shit?" Nick asked as Freeze stepped back and went to work on Bart's face and stomach. When he got tired of hitting him, Freeze turned to Nick. "You want some of this?"

"Nah, kid. I know how much you been lookin' forward to this. Have fun."

Bart was one tough muthafucka. He took the vicious beating that Black and Freeze dealt him and never did pass out. It was as if Bart wanted to prove to Black that even though he was going to die for what he had done, that he wasn't going to give Black the satisfaction of breaking him.

Four hours into the beating, both Black and Freeze had grown tired of beating Bart and were ready to kill him. "You ladies had enough yet?" Nick asked.

Neither Black nor Freeze said anything.

"Y'all don't know how to torture nobody."

"And you could do better?" Freeze said.

"Yes."

"What would you do?"

Nick smiled at Freeze. "Son, I forgot more forms of torture than you'll ever know."

"He's probably right, Freeze. You know nobody better at torture than good old Uncle Sam," Black commented.

"Like what, Nick? Give us a little demonstration," Freeze suggested.

"Okay," Nick said and stepped up to Bart. He hit him a

couple of times and then he said, "This is called blunt trauma, punching, kicking, slapping, whipping, or beating him with wires or any object," Nick said as he demonstrated. "Then there's positional torture, like what we did in the bathroom. Using suspension, stretching limbs apart, prolonged constraint of movement, forced positioning." Nick took the pack of cigarettes out of Bart's knapsack. He lit one. "Then there's burning him with cigarettes." Nick pressed the cigarette against Bart's skin. He recoiled from the pain. "Heated instruments, scalding liquid or acid."

"That used to be one of your favorites, Nick. Even before you joined the army," Black commented.

"Then there's electric shock, asphyxiation, smashing fingers, chemical exposures to salt, chili pepper or gasoline in wounds or body cavities, amputation of digits or limbs, surgical removal of organs. I could go on and on," Nick said and continued to hit Bart. "There's psychological techniques to break him down. Exposure to ambiguous situations or contradictory messages."

"Enough!" Black said and stood up. "Take the cuffs off him and stand him up."

Freeze took off the handcuffs and he and Nick stood Bart up. Once he was on his feet, a beaten and bloody mass, who was unable to lift his arms, Black stood behind and took out his gun. He closed his eyes and raised his weapon. With his eyes closed he could see Shy's face. "Rest in peace, Cassandra. I love you," he said softly and shot Bart four times in the back.

CHAPTER 39

DEA Headquarters, New York City
Monday Morning, 9:12 A.M.

Detective Kirkland, along with his partner Detective Richards, sat patiently in the lobby of the DEA offices. Kirk had come there that morning to ask a question that he already knew the answer to, but was determined to ask anyway. They had been there for over an hour when Agent Pete Vinnelli came into the area. "Detectives," Vinnelli said and extended his hand. "You two keep showing up down here, I'm gonna start thinking that you want to come to work with us."

Richards laughed and accepted Vinnelli's hand. Kirk shook his hand, too, but didn't laugh. "I just got one or two questions that I need to ask you, Agent Vinnelli. I won't take up a lot of your time, we both got bad guys to catch," Kirk said.

"Ain't that the truth and they're gettin' badder every day," Vinnelli commented.

"Tell me about it," Richards said.

"Can we talk in your office, Agent?"

"Sure, follow me," Vinnelli said and led the detectives back to his office. Once everybody was seated, Vinnelli asked, "So tell me what I can help you gentlemen with today?"

"You know we've been investigating the murder of Cassandra Black. You know, Mike Black's wife."

"Yes, how's that going?"

"We had run into a brick wall and it had us confused for a while. But we got some information this morning that put all in its proper prospective. Anyway, I had planned on getting down here last week to ask you about it but, shit, there just ain't enough hours in the day."

"Tell me about it. If only we didn't have to sleep," Vinnelli commented smugly.

"You probably don't know this, unless you've been keeping up for some reason, but we had originally arrested Black for the murder."

"Yes, I heard that."

"Yeah, but we had to let him go. All of the evidence pointed to a contract killer."

"You're kiddin' me. A contract killer, huh? Now that's something," Vinnelli joked.

"Yeah, something, huh?" Richards said, barely able to hide his contempt for Vinnelli.

"It seems that it was set up to look like Black had come home, beat his wife and shot her in the back. Most cops would have taken the case at face value: bloody perp, found at the scene of the crime, with the murder weapon. Ballistics matched up," Kirk said.

"Sounds like it. What led you to believe otherwise?"

"ME found evidence that suggested that it didn't happen that way. Make a long story short, we found a cigarette butt in the house and we were able to pull a partial print off of it. But what we got back kind of threw us for a loop."

"How so?" Vinnelli asked.

"The print we pulled came back as a match to this man." Kirk reached in the folder he was carrying and handed Vinnelli the report. "His name is Kip Bartowski. United States Army, Special Forces. Killed in a training accident, October twenty-seventh, 1998. Helicopter went down, body was never recovered." Kirk took a second to observe the look on Vinnelli's face as he stared at Bart's picture. "At first we were wondering how a dead man could smoke a cigarette at a crime scene."

"This sort of thing happens all the time, Kirk. These black-ops guys are ghosts, and the government treats them like they don't exist."

"So I've been hearing. I also heard that you guys sometimes hire guys like this to do the dirty, off the reservation kinda stuff."

Vinnelli sat down in his chair and laughed. "You've got us confused with the CIA."

"I'm sure," Richards said.

"I can assure you that this agency doesn't sanction those types of operations," Vinnelli said firmly.

"So you wouldn't know how one would even begin to look for one of these ghosts?" Kirk asked.

"Sorry, Detective. That's not something that I could help you with."

Richards leaned forward. "You sure?"

Vinnelli shot him a look, but didn't bother to comment.

Kirk stood up. "Once again, we've wasted enough of your time. Bad guys to catch, right?"

"Right." Vinnelli got up and escorted the detectives to the elevator.

"Well, thanks for taking the time to see us, Agent Vinnelli," Kirk said, extending his hand.

Vinnelli shook it. "Anytime, Kirk. Drop by anytime you have questions." The elevator door opened and the detectives started to get on. "One more thing."

"What's that?" Kirk asked.

"You said you got some information this morning that put your case in its proper perspective. What was that?"

"We got a call from the Italian police in Palermo. They found the body of a man that had been severally beaten and shot four times in the back and the prints matched our guy. Only problem is, since he's dead, I'll never know who hired him."

"So I guess that closes your case?"

"For the time being. But you know what, Agent Vinnelli, you know as well as I do that these guys always slip up. And when they do, I'll be there," Kirk said, staring directly into Vinnelli's eyes. "'Cause I never quit." As the elevator door closed, Kirk said, "Catch you later, Agent Vinnelli."

CHAPTER 40

Mike Black

"Black."

"Huh?"

"Black," Nick said and shook my arm. "Wake up, Black."

"What?" I said and opened my eyes.

"We're getting ready to land. You gotta fasten your seat belt."

"How long was I asleep?"

Nick shrugged. "Not long, half hour, maybe."

We had just flown in from Todos Santos. It's an island off the coast of Mexico. While we were on the island I closed the door on some unfinished business. You see, a year ago, Diego Estabon masterminded the kidnapping of my wife, Cassandra. For that he had to die.

When Nick dropped me off I headed to the house. I was glad to be home. It was getting to the point that I didn't wanna go anywhere that I couldn't take Cassandra and Michelle. They were everything to me. And if that's really the case, I need to start thinking about getting them away from all this. I know I tried that once, but this time I won't go somewhere that will make Cassandra feel isolated. Some place close enough to the city; the island or maybe even Jersey. I knew Cassandra was having fun playin' gangster, but we got a child to raise.

I unlocked the front door, and went to turn off the alarm, but it was already off. I got out my gun right then. This was exactly what I was talkin' about. It ain't safe for them here.

"Cassandra!"

But there was no answer.

I peeked into the living room, and noticed the news was on. The remote was on the couch, so I picked it up and turned the TV off. "Where the hell is she? Cassandra!"

I went upstairs as quietly as I could on those creaky steps and went straight for our bedroom. The door was cracked open, so I pushed it a little and went in.

"Shhh," Cassandra said, rockin' Michelle. "She's almost asleep," she said and then noticed the gun.

I put my gun down on the dresser, walked over to her and kissed her on the cheek. "When you didn't answer, I thought something was wrong," I whispered and looked at my beautiful baby girl. "Hi, Michelle. Daddy's back."

"Be quiet. You'll wake her up," Cassandra said and put Michelle in her crib. She turned and started coming toward me. I could see the terror come across her face. "Michael, look out! Behind you!"

My eyes sprang open when I jerked myself out of the dream. I looked down at Michelle. She was sound asleep; I was glad I didn't wake her. I had that dream all the time, sometimes I save them, sometimes, like that one—I usually jerk myself outta it. One time after she put Michelle down, Cassandra told me that she had to go now. When I asked her why she had to go, she said "Because Father's here to take me home." Then she pointed and when I turned, there was her father, Chicago.

Weird, right?

But I don't think I need a psychiatrist.

Right?

I have no idea what I'm gonna do now. I mean, I never gave much thought to what I would do if Cassandra died suddenly. When I look at Michelle I know that I can't just go back to doin' what I was doin'.

Since I got back from Italy, I'd been hidin' out at Bobby's house in Rockland County. It's nice out here, quiet. Too fuckin' quiet sometimes and it's so damn suburban. The only place I've been was to the grocery store, and that's because there's nowhere else to go. I go there with Michelle and buy Pampers, milk, and baby food, that type of stuff. Some woman always stops me and tells me how nice it is to see a black man spending time with his daughter. And when I tell them that I'm a single father they just about lose their minds, but I feel like Michelle is safe here. And that's the only thing that's important. I promised my mother I would come to Freeport for a while so she could get to know her granddaughter. Naturally I've thought about going down there and staying. Put all this behind me, for good this time. Look at what it's cost me. I got up and put Michelle in her crib. Look at what it's cost us.

There's a part of me that knows I can't quit, not without knowing who it was that hired Bart and Swan. When Leon told me that Diamond shocked Rosstein into a heart attack I almost fell out laughing. Even though it meant that I'd never know who hired them, it was still funny as hell.

Kirk knows something, he may not know who hired them, otherwise they'd be in jail, but he knows something. I believe it was that something that got me out of jail. But when I tried to talk to Kirk about it, he said it was police business. Like I give fuck about what's police business. Somebody knows who hired them muthafuckas, and I'll find them, somehow.

Once I was sure that Michelle wouldn't wake up, I went downstairs to the basement, which Bobby had claimed as his own private space. He was sitting in his chair, half asleep and the Yankees and the Detroit Tigers were watching him. I turned on the baby monitor and sat down.

"Why didn't you make us a drink before you sat down," Bobby said without opening his eyes.

"I thought you were sleepin'."

"What does that have to do with anything? I'm awake now," Bobby said and got up to make the drinks.

I watched him as he poured. "Is this it, Bobby?"

"What do you mean?"

"I mean look at us. We're livin' out here in suburbia." I picked up the baby monitor. "Me sittin' here guardin' this baby monitor like my life depended on it. You playin' Mr. Mom and tryin' to nurse Pam back to health."

"One, I'm startin' to think Pam is fine and she's just milkin' that shit now. She was her old self the whole time we were on vacation. Pam didn't start gettin' depressed until I started talkin' about goin' to Italy." Bobby handed me my drink and sat down. "And two, if you any kind of man you'll be protecting Michelle for the rest of your life, because her life depends on it."

"I understand your point, but let me ask you a question."

"What's that?"

"Are you armed?"

"No."

"Neither am I. What if somebody came to kill us?"

"Ain't nobody comin', Mike. And even if somebody came out here lookin' for us, you know as well as I do that they'd miss the turn at Wildginger Run," Bobby laughed.

I laughed because it's true. I miss that fuckin' turn every time. "They'll be lost forever after that."

"Okay, so this ain't how I thought it would be. I thought we'd be around forever. But you been lookin' for an excuse to get out for a long time. Well, she upstairs sleeping. All you gotta do is decide to do it."

"Havin' kids didn't stop you."

"It's different, I had Pam. All Michelle has is you. You need to decide whether you're gonna step up or not. It's your choice. The game will go on with or without you and the money will keep on comin'." Bobby looked at his watch and jumped up. "Oh shit, I gotta pick up Bonita and Brenda from ballet," he said and started for the door.

"Pick up some Similac for me on the way back."

"You want me to get some baby food, too? She really didn't like that beet shit you was tryin' to shove in her mouth last night."

"I didn't think she could move her little head that fast. I was gettin' tired just tryin' to feed it to her." I laughed and it felt good. "But go ahead and pick some up."

"You got enough Pampers? You know how she runs through them."

"Pick up some of them, too. It ain't like they'll go to waste."

"You got it," Bobby said and left.

And so it ends, I heard somebody say once.

Not with a bang, but a whimper.

Mylo

It's funny how quick shit can turn around on you. It wasn't too long ago the Black was in jail, Albert had a great plan and Birdie was havin' delusions of grandeur about him being the next kingpin. That was then; now, Black's a free man and Birdie and Albert are dead.

Of course that means for the time being, I'm out of the drug business, and maybe that's for the best. These niggas claim to want to coexist peacefully with drug dealers, but the proof says that these muthafuckas delight in killin' drug dealers. I heard about what Black did when he found out that somebody was dealin' in one of his spots. So I just figured that the way to avoid gettin' found out, 'cause I hear Black is psychic about that shit, was to not deal in his stops. Common sense, right? But Black got these niggas so scared that nobody was willin' to try it. Dead zone my ass, niggas in the so-called dead zone was so hungry that they ate the product alive. I was makin' mad cash, so much cash that I couldn't come in, at least not yet.

Sooner or later I would have to, but before I do, I wanna have enough money to retire on. I wanna have enough money to live the way these assholes do, and for that I need a little more time and a whole lot more money.

What I didn't want was to get caught out here dirty the way I am. Another rogue DEA agent, but that's what I am and I've been that way so long I don't even know if I can come in.

My name is Clint Harris and I've been working deep-cover assignments for the last five years. I'd work my way into the target's organization, get as much information as I can, then bring the whole thing down. That's been my life, until my handler didn't show up for our weekly conversation. During those meets, I'd turn over whatever evidence I had, drugs, money, documents, recordings, what have you. So I sold the drugs and kept the money, but I would show up every week. This went on for months, until one day about a year ago, I'm arrested. But nobody can tell me what I'm being arrested for. "Just come with us, sir, and it will all be explained to you."

My first thought, somebody realized that I was out there and they were bringing me in, so I didn't ask any more questions. I began to worry when federal marshalls took me to the airport and flew me to North Carolina. Then we drove for hours before they deposited me in some small-town jail. After three weeks in that cell, I wake up one morning to find Agent DeFrancisco standing in front of my cell.

He told me that he knows what I've been doin' and shows me picture to prove it. DeFrancisco gave me a choice, turn over all the evidence to him or I was going to jail for a very long time. Then he flips, starts tellin' me that men like me are a very valuable asset, and I immediately knew where that was goin'. "You work for me now," DeFrancisco said.

"What do I have to do?" I asked.

"Exactly what you do. I put you in position, you make contact and work your way in, and report to me."

"No problem," I answered, knowing that it couldn't be that simple.

"There's only one minor difference. You're not there looking for evidence of a drug conspiracy, you're there to create one."

That's when he put me in touch with Albert and it's been on ever since. But then DeFrancisco went to jail and I'm left out here again, making crazy money and no handler.

One thing that I don't understand was how easy it was for me to get inside, but now after I told him where to find Birdie and Albert, I'll be able to get close to Freeze.

But sellin' drugs around these niggas ain't the way to get rich. They're gamblers, that's how they make their money; numbers, bookmakin', gambling houses. What I gotta do is figure out how to make that pay for me.

The End of *Outlaw*
Mike Black returns in
IN A COLD SWEAT
February 2008

THE WRONG MAN
BY
roy glenn

Part I

It was almost 11:00 at night and I was getting tired of surfing the Web. Tired of reading information to sound interesting at parties, but wasn't really useful in everyday life. So I turned off the computer and began to wander aimlessly through the house, picking up this and straightening up that. When I started to dust, I knew it was time for me to get a life.

It had been almost three years since Dennis, my husband of ten years, decided that he needed more out of life.

"More out of life?" I asked him.

"Things I just can't do here, Carla," he said.

Things he couldn't do being married to me, was what he meant. The next day he left for California, leaving me with our two children. Sure he sends money and he calls every blue moon, but that doesn't replace the children growing up with their father, or me having a husband. So I've become both mother and father, and that's become my whole life. But this summer, much to my surprise, shock would be a better word for it, Dennis called and said he wanted the children for the summer. So I let them go, and for the first time in ten years, I am alone.

I poured myself a glass of wine and went out on the deck. It had been a very humid summer in Atlanta and this night was no exception. As I sat there, I listened to the neighbor's music, which they always played too loud for my taste. Not that I have anything against rap music, I just don't understand it anymore. I'll just say it's come a long way from Kurtis Blow and Run-DMC and leave it at that. I can't even say what the name of the song was, but this particular song, for reasons I can't explain, got to me. I started tapping my foot and before I knew it, my head was rocking. It started me thinking about the old days, when I had a life. Me and my girls, Meka and Shika, we were the happy hour queens. I loved to dance. We'd hang out all night and go to work the next morning looking like hags, but we didn't care, we always had the best times. But that was before I met Dennis, got married and had the children. Don't get me wrong, I love my children and I love being their mother. But sometimes I wish there were some semblance of my former life associated with it.

I finished my wine and got up to pour myself another. When I got to the refrigerator I said, "Hold it. Why not go out? It's Friday night and the kids are gone."

Why not?

But where?

All of my old hangout spots have long since closed their doors. I opened the refrigerator and poured another glass, marveling at how easily I talked myself out of it. I returned to my chair on the deck. I remembered hearing some of the gossip girls at work talking about a place they went to in Buckhead that played a tight mix of old school music. But I couldn't remember the name of the place. "Bell Bottoms!"

I took a big swallow of liquid courage and went inside to change into something more appropriate for the big event. "Big event?" Damn right, my return to the club after a ten-year absence was a big event.

I stood in front of my closet for what seemed like an eternity in a state of brain lock, trying to decide what to wear. I wanted to look sexy, but not hoochie. I had gained a few well-placed pounds since my club days, (read, a big butt and the gift pouch I got from the children) so the outfits that I wanted to wear just didn't look right. I finally settled on a pieced-together black outfit. The top from one outfit, which I couldn't wiggle all this big butt into the pants, and the skirt I had bought years ago that Dennis would never let me wear. It was a little tight and I was showing plenty of thigh, but it was on. I tried a few steps to see if I could dance in it. I checked my hair and makeup and I was on my way.

Part 2

After standing in line for what seemed like a long time, but was more like ten minutes, I was in. The club was crowded but not packed, and the music was pumpin'. I scanned the crowd, which was predominately black with a smattering of whites, mostly female. It always has amazed me how some of my brothers will jump over a sister to get to those three or four white girls with jungle fever. Anyway, most everyone was dressed comfortably, but stylish, so I didn't feel overdressed or out of place, as most of them seemed to be in my age group.

I took the long way to the bar and walked around the dance floor to get a feel of the place. The DJ mixed in "The Men All Paused," which I felt was appropriate since I had turned a head or two as I walked around the room. It made me feel good that me, a woman in her mid-thirties and mother of two, still rated a double take.

Once I reached the bar, I stood behind a man and woman who seemed to be in deep conversation and tried in vain to get the bartender's attention. When the man noticed me, he immediately got up and offered me his seat. "Thank you!" I said over the music and sat down. Once I was seated the woman glanced in my direction and rolled her eyes. I thought she didn't appreciate him giving up his seat for me. Until she quickly turned back and leaned toward me, "Girl, thank you," she said.

"Excuse me?" I said.

"Thank you for showin' up and standing behind him like you did."

I looked at her like I didn't understand what she was talking about, which I didn't. Then she looked around and leaned toward me again. "I told that guy when he sat down that I was waiting for somebody, but he didn't care, he sat down anyway and started layin' down his mack. He had just trampled on my last nerve when you walked up and stood behind him. So I told him that we were together. I hope you don't mind?"

"No," I laughed. "Sistah gotta do what she gotta do sometimes to get rid of a pest."

"No, girl. I don't think you understand me," she said.

I gave her that same, I don't understand look, because I didn't.

"I told him that we were, you know, together, together."

I thought my eyes were going to pop out my head. "You told him we were—" and stated laughing.

"Yup. It was all I could think of. Nothing else was working. But when I told him that, he frowned up at me like I had some kind of disease, looked at you, and jumped up."

I laughed, "Well, like I said, sometimes you gotta do what you gotta do."

The bartender finally arrived to see what I was drinking. "Vodka collins."

"You ready for another?" the bartender asked my new friend.

"Bring me another Henny and Coke and put her drink on my check."

"That's all right."

"No, I insist. It's the least I can do for you, after you did so much for me."

"You're right. She gets the check," I said to the bartender and sent him to do his business.

She looked around and leaned toward me again. "Look at him," pointing with her eyes at him. He was standing at the other end of the bar talking to some guys. "He's probably over there right now tellin' his boys not to bother with us cause we're gay." Then she looked strangely at me. "Oh. You're not, are you?"

"No. Are you?"

"Chile, no. I'm very strictly dickly," she said casually and picked up her glass. "I hope I didn't ruin both our evenings."

"Let's hope. You know how stuff like that gets around."

"Yeah. After a while, they'll be talking about it in the men's room," she mused as the bartender returned with our drinks. She paid the check and raised her glass. "Here's to men. Still the only game in town for me."

I raised my glass in complete agreement and we drank to it. "Well, here's hoping, 'cause I did come here to dance at the very least." I laughed.

"I did, too. But I haven't seen anybody I want to dance with, much less anything else."

I scanned the room quickly and was about to agree. That's when I saw him. "But I feel confident that some self-assured black man will step up to the task."

"I'll drink to that." She raised her glass again.

"To black men." And I had just picked out the one I wanted. He was a handsome man, but not pretty, if you know what I mean. I looked him up and down from head to toe. But I did it on the low, 'cause my new friend had vulture written all over her face, so I knew better then to point him out. He was dressed in a black single-breasted suit with a black T-shirt under the jacket. Kind of California casual, for lack of a better term. He was at least six feet tall, which I love. Even though I'm only five-five, I love a tall man. And I like a man to have some meat on his bones, without being fat, which this man definitely wasn't. His hair was cut very short, but not bald, with just a shadow of a beard and his lips were full. He looked at me. He had the most engaging eyes. I tried to look away but I couldn't. He had me.

The DJ played "When Doves Cry" and I was startled when somebody asked me to dance. I love Prince and "Doves Cry" especially. I looked at him and he looked at me as if he were giving his consent for me to go on and dance, so I did.

After "Doves Cry," the DJ broke into "777-9311" then "Don't Stop 'Til You Get Enough," all of which I loved back then. So, I stayed on the floor, fending off my dance partner's dancing advances, scanning the club for him the whole time. But I lost him. Once Michael Jr. had had enough, I thanked him very much for the dance. Then I very politely refused his offer to buy me a drink and returned to my seat at the bar. But it was occupied.

IT WAS HIM.

And the vulture was all up in his face.

"I knew it," I mumbled.

As soon as he saw me, he stood up. "I thought you were never gonna come off the floor," he said in a voice so deep that it made my whole body quiver.

"Well—I," I babbled, as if I were some Nervous Nellie, who hadn't had a man show any interest in her in years. Probably because it was the truth. This was the first man who'd shown any interest in me in years, and I had no idea what to do next. The club scene sure has changed. But I knew it was me who had changed.

"Why didn't you tell me you were really waiting for somebody?" the vulture said, eyeing this man like she wanted to eat him alive. Which I could understand, since I wanted him, too.

"Well—I," I babbled again.

"I hope you saved a little bit for me?" he said, reaching for my hand. I nervously accepted.

He led me back onto the dance floor, holding my hand the entire time. Holding it like we had known each other for years. I started to resist, but my hand, not to mention the rest of my body, felt comfortable in his hand.

Once we found, or should I say, made some space for ourselves on the floor, he let go of my hand and he began to dance. Naturally, I followed suit, because after all, we were on the dance floor. I did a simple two-step, moving from side to side with the beat of the music as I watched him move. Which he did, effortlessly and gracefully. All without breaking eye contact with me. I looked away from time to time, but I felt drawn to his eyes like a bee to honey or a moth to a flame. It was as if his eyes had connected to mine and he was downloading a program into my brain.

When the DJ played LL Cool J's "Mama Said Knock You Out," it was like something kicked in and took over both of us. From that point on, we no longer danced politely like two people who hadn't actually been introduced. We were immediately transformed into two people, who had known and danced together for years. Each step, every move I pulled out of my dancing memory bank, he matched. Then I turned around and he quickly introduced himself to this big butt I was carrying. At first I resisted, tried to dance away, but he wasn't havin' any parts of that. He placed his hands gently on my hips and held me in place. Once I felt his body against mine, I knew that my halfhearted resistance was futile. Suddenly I felt comfortable with his body resting gently, yet suggestively against mine. I began to warm to the occasion and put my body in it.

We danced in this manner for who knows how long or for how many songs. It didn't matter. I was having more fun than I'd had in years. Then we both got completely off the chain and just got plain nasty with it. I began to feel him, and believe me when I say, I was very impressed with what I felt.

By the time we returned to the bar, the vulture was gone and somebody else had taken my seat. "I guess this would be a good time for introductions. My name is Xavier Assante," he said with his hand extended, and with a bit of an accent. "But everybody calls me Zavier."

"Carla Edwards," I replied, accepting his hand.

"Do you want to go somewhere," he said very sexually, "and find a seat?"

"Sure. But I'm goin' to get a drink first. You danced my throat dry."

"What are you drinking?"

"Vodka collins."

He leaned close to me, our bodies touched. "Why don't you find us a seat and I'll get the drinks," he said in my ear with that voice. My body shuttered and I felt my knees getting weak. I grabbed his arm to steady myself. "How will you find me?"

"The club isn't that big. And if I need help finding you, I'll just ask where the most beautiful woman in the club is sitting. That will lead me straight to you."

With that, I walked away. It was a line and I knew it, but it still made me smile. After years of being known as Dennis's wife and the children's mother, it was flattering to be thought of as a beautiful woman. "The most beautiful woman in the club, is what he said," I said out loud to no one in particular as I wandered around the club looking in vain for a place for us to sit. I settled on a spot against the wall and waited. Some time had passed before I looked up and saw him talking to some guy. The guy looked around then he pointed in my direction. "No, he didn't."

He maneuvered his way through the crowd, drinks in hand, seemingly oblivious to the glances he was getting from the sea of women he parted. He handed me my drink. "What did you say to that man?"

"I asked him which way the most beautiful woman in the club went."

"No, you didn't."

"You see he pointed me straight to you."

I was smiling so hard I thought my cheekbones were going to break through my skin.

For the next couple of hours, we alternated between dancing, drinking, and talking. I talked mostly about missing the kids, my job, you know, nothing intense. But mostly we danced. He listened well and spoke intelligently when he did speak, but I got the impression that he had actually come there to dance and not to find someone to sleep with. As the evening drew to an end and the club began to empty out, we filed out with the crowd. I had definitely drank more than I should have and was feeling no pain. But I wasn't drunk.

He walked me to my car and said good night, then we talked about this and that for the next half hour. He said good night again. "Can I give you a ride to your car?" I asked curiously, and a little put out that he hadn't even asked for my phone number.

"I'm not driving," he answered. "I took a cab here."

"A cab?"

"Yes, a cab, I'm staying at the Ritz Carlton. I'm only in town for the night. I have to catch a plane first thing in the morning."

"Oh," I said, "That's it."

"I guess you were wondering why I hadn't asked for your phone number."

"The thought had crossed my mind."

"I thought about asking you for it but I don't know if or when I'll be in town again, and that wouldn't be fair to either of us."

"Thank you for being considerate. So you travel a lot?"

"On business. More than I like to sometimes."

"Why is that?"

"'Cause if I were more stable, maybe I'd have time to get to know somebody. Somebody like you."

Once again I was at a loss for words. But this time I didn't start babbling like a fool.

"Are you going to be all right to drive yourself home?"

"I'm not that drunk that I can't drive myself home," I said to him partly to reassure myself. "In fact, I was going to offer you a ride to your hotel. You know it's not easy for a black man, even a professional black man such as yourself, to get a cab."

"I usually do all right getting cabs to pick me up."

"You catch a lot of cabs?"

"Like I said, I travel a lot."

"You never did say what you do."

"No, I didn't."

"Well?" I said.

"Well what?" he replied.

"What do you do?"

He smiled. "I do contract work for large corporations."

"What type of work?"

"You ask a lot of questions, don't you?"

"Of course I do. I'm a woman."

"I noticed that very early in the evening."

"But you haven't done much about it since then."

"No, I guess I haven't, have I?"

"No, you haven't. But that's not true. You have made me feel like a woman for the first time in years."

"A very beautiful woman, one who is to be spoiled and sought after. Appreciated for her beauty."

"And I've felt all those things coming from you. All that and so much more. So I really should be thanking you."

"For what?"

"For making me feel things I haven't felt in years."

"Well, you are very welcome," he said, and kissed my hand.

"Now about that ride." I stepped closer, "Do you want to catch a cab," and closer still. "Or do you want me?" I didn't mean for it to come out that way. I meant to say do you wanna ride with me. But whether I meant to or not, I had just offered myself to this man. I don't know how he took it, but there was definitely a part of me that wanted him.

"Well, since you put it that way, I accept," he said walking around to the passenger side of my car. Once we were both in the car with our seat belts on, he said, "By the way, I'm gong to assume that you meant to offer me a ride and not yourself."

"Thank you, that was what I meant to say." Just that quickly he let me off the hook. But I was more than ready to stand by my words. It had been 943 days since I felt a man inside me, so the words more than ready took on a whole new meaning.

Part 3

The Buckhead Ritz Carlton wasn't far from Bell Bottoms, so there wasn't much time for uncomfortable small talk about what was going to happen once we reached the hotel. But somehow I couldn't see this man being uncomfortable in any situation. I glanced over at him as I drove. He did comment on the fact that he hadn't seen any cabs and how glad he was to have accepted my offer for a ride.

My offer. Do you want me? If I wanted to be honest with myself I was offering myself to him and I was feeling very apprehensive about it. Do you want me? Was all that just talk about me being a beautiful woman?

"Beautiful, yes, but not desirable," I imagined him saying.

But no, he would let me down gently. "It wouldn't be fair if we were to get involved," is more what he'd say.

Forget fair, I wanna get fucked.

I felt cheap.

I wasn't "that" type of woman. I'd prided myself that during my fast and free days, I'd never had a one-night stand or even slept with a man on the first date. But here I was, a thirty-six-year-old divorced mother of two, perfectly willing to do just that. Sleep with a man I had just met at the club. A man who told me that he was catching a flight first thing in the morning. But the more I looked at him, the more I listened to that voice reverberating inside my head, the more I wanted him.

"Hoochie!" I called myself and smiled at the word I had used many times, but never in reference to myself. Now that I'd come to grips with what I was, the only question that remained was whether I was going to wait to be asked up to his room, or was I going to invite myself.

I pulled up in front of the Ritz, I felt it was only proper to let him take the lead, but I was ready to jump in at any point if he drifted away from my objective. "Well, here we are," he said.

"It seems that way," I said.

"It wasn't that far at all."

"No, it wasn't."

He smiled and unlocked his door. "I was going to ask you if you wanted to come up for a drink."

"Were you?" I was excited, but wouldn't show it.

"Yes, as a matter of fact I was, then I thought, why should I. Why should I say that?" I started to jump in but wanted to see where he was going with this. "When the truth of the matter is that I don't want to drink with you. What I really want to do is ask you up so I can make love to you."

"I was going to say that I usually don't do things like this; in fact, I've never done anything like this. But that's not what I wanna say."

"What do you want to say?"

"That I would very much like to come up so you could make love to me."

He got out of the car and signaled for the valet to come park my car. He then came around and opened my door. He reached for my hand; loving a gentleman I gladly accepted it. We walked hand in hand to the elevator in silence. Words no longer seemed necessary. I was too nervous to speak anyway.

In the elevator I did give some thought to my safety. Suppose he was Jack the Ripper? Or the Boston Strangler? I rationalized my fears by thinking that people like that don't stay at the Ritz Carlton. I was glad that the valet saw me, as did a few other employees in the lobby. But at that point I would be dead, and it wouldn't matter to me anymore. I've always trusted my instincts, and I follow them implicitly, so I was pretty sure he wasn't the wrong man.

We entered his dimly lit room and closed the door behind us. "Even though I said I didn't want to drink with you, would you like a drink?"

"Thank you." I accepted, thinking that it might help me relax as I sat down on the bed.

I watched as he unlocked the minibar and removed a bottle of Absolut vodka and Perrier water. "They don't have any lemon juice, so I can't make you a vodka collins."

"Vodka and Perrier will be fine."

He fixed my drink and poured himself a glass of Hennessy.

He sat down on the bed very close to me and sipped his drink, looking at me out of the corner of his eyes, watching as I sipped my drink. "Would you mind if I turned on some music?" he asked.

"That would be nice."

He put his drink down and walked around to the other side of the bed where he tuned the radio on to a jazz station. The melodic sounds of saxophone filled the room. I took another sip that was more a swallow than a sip. I put the glass down as he stood before me. "Do you mind if I take a shower?"

"Do you mind if I join you?" I can't believe I said that.

"Only if you let me bathe you."

"Only if you let me bathe you." *Who are you?*

"Deal," he said and extended his hand, which I accepted, unable to fathom just how nervous I was. Still coming to grips with what I was doing. No more time to rationalize, I stood up and my hand shook a little. He took both my hands in his and gently raised them to his lips. I guess he could tell how nervous I was. "You don't have to do this if you don't want to," he said and kissed my hands.

"I want to."

He took a step closer and once again our bodies touched. He slowly tilted my head back. I closed my eyes in breathless anticipation of the fullness of his lips against mine. Maybe it was the alcohol, but his kiss, long and passionate, made my head spin. He released my hands and soon I felt his strong hands in the small of my back, drawing me close into his embrace.

I reached up, touched his shoulders, and glided my hands slowly down his back, finally resting them around his waist. He touched my hands, removing them from his waist. He stepped away causing our lips to part. He led me by the hand into the bathroom. Once he turned the shower on, he reached out for me and kissed my lips a little more forcefully this time. He grabbed the nape of my neck and pulled me closer. He kissed my neck over and over again. My head drifted back. I was in ecstasy as he slowly and me-thodically worked the first of my weak spots. I reached be-hind my back and pulled down the zipper on my skirt. I began to wiggle my way out of it. He unbuttoned my blouse, slid it off my shoulders, and then used my neck as a gate to my cleavage; gliding his tongue along the lacy edges as I moaned.

I allowed my skirt to drop to the floor with my hands free to explore his body. I decided to see what kind of night I was going to have. I reached for his crotch, thinking what a shame it would be if he had me this hot from foreplay and didn't have the tools to back it up. I grabbed it, gently of course. My eyes opened wide, he smiled and unhooked my bra with one hand. He quickly returned to my chest, moving my bra out of the way with his teeth. Then his tongue slid across my erect nipples.

My knees went weak.

I squeezed him, felt the firm length of his erection. Even though I felt him while we danced, it was completely different feeling him in my hand. I became more excited. Like a greedy crack fiend, I quickly unbuckled his belt, unsnapped his pants, reached inside his briefs, felt its warmth, then glided my hands up and down his shaft. Distracted only by my bra sliding down my arms and dangling from my wrists.

We broke contact suddenly. He led me by the hand into the shower, picked up a bar of soap: Lever 2000, and not the hotel-issued soap. He began rubbing the soap between his hands until both were lathered heavily. I occupied myself by rubbing his rather large and very hard erection between my hands.

With the soap in one hand, he began to lather my body, sliding his hands delicately over what felt like every inch of my body. Once again, my eyes drifted shut and my head drifted back as I continued to massage his erection. I always have been just a little dick happy, you know . . . excited to the point of smiling from ear to ear at the sight of one, and the feel of it in my hand. Soft and silky to the touch yet hard and firm. "Oooh, my goodness!"

I forced myself to pull away from him. I quickly washed the remaining soap from his body and pulled him out of the shower. We toweled each other dry and I led him to the bed. On the way I gave some more thought to what I was doing here. The answer was simple. I glanced at him out of the corner of my eye. At his face, then at his erection. "I'm fucking you tonight," I said under my breath.

"Did you say something?" he said as we arrived at the bed.

"Yes, lay down."

He quickly complied with my request. He laid spread-eagle across the bed and I crawled across the bed to him. I looked at it again, gawked at it actually. I straddled his torso. I grabbed hold of it and glided him inside me.

I was tight or he was big.

More like a combination of the two.

He smiled and placed his hands on my ass. As my hands dropped to his chest, he spread my cheeks and slowly moved me up and down, inching deeper and deeper inside me. The deeper he got, the wetter I got. Soon I was sliding up and down on him effortlessly. He didn't move at first, he seemed very content to allow me to work at my own pace. My pace was slow and steady. There was a true rhythm to my movement, almost musical. I closed my eyes, enjoying the feeling of his stiffness inside me.

The thickness of him filled me, the warmth of him inside me, long and stiff, excited me. My hips shook. I began to quiver from the inside. I stopped moving, tried to slow my roll, but I couldn't. My entire body was quivering uncontrollably. For a second, maybe two or three, I felt like I was outside of myself. My excitement only proved to intensify the motion of my hips. He held me tighter; began to move with me. When I felt him throbbing inside me, I was no longer able to control myself. My voice returned. "Yes, oh yes!" I screamed as we thrust our bodies against one another. I could hear him moaning quietly, his face twisted and contorted. He throbbed and I felt him expand. My fingers dug into his chest. His body became rigid; I pumped harder. His mouth was open, his eyes were locked in mine now. I knew, now I had him.

Part 4

The annoying intrusion of the telephone ringing inter-rupted the bliss that was my morning. I reached out for the phone angrily, only to find that it wasn't where it was supposed to be. I opened my eyes and quickly realized that it wasn't just the phone that was out of place. I was, too. "Hello," I said shyly.

A female voice crept into my ear, "Will you be checking out this morning or will you be staying another night with us?" Like a cold slap in the face, I was suddenly very aware of where I was, how I got here and most of all, what I had done when I got here. "Mr. Assante has made arrange-ments in the event you wish to stay."

"No, I'll be checking out."

"Are you sure? You have complete access to the hotel. That includes use of our exercise facilities, our spa, all of our restaurants and bars, and our gift shop," the now bub-bly female said.

"No, thank you," I said, thinking about the spa. "I'll be checking out within the hour."

"Okay," she chirped. "But if you change your mind, you can simply charge any of our services to the room."

"Thank you," I said in the same singsongy way, and hung up the phone. I wasn't quite sure how I should take what I'd just heard. I already had some issues with what I had allowed myself to do last night. I believe *hoochie* is the word I used to describe myself. Now I feel used and cheap. Was this his way of paying me for services rendered, like some cheap hooker? "Excuse me . . . high-priced hooker," I said, and rolled out of bed. As I paddled my way to the shower, I thought that maybe he was just being a gentleman. Maybe this was how he would have treated me if he were able to stay. "Maybe," I said and turned on the shower. I looked at my naked body in the mirror. I shook my head and placed my hands on my pouch—my children's gift to me. I didn't think I looked bad for a mother of two. Apparently, he didn't either.

I stepped into the shower and slowly washed his scent from my body. The movie projector in my mind replayed for me the finer, more memorable moments of this morning's lovemaking, which we did repeatedly until I saw the sun coming up. I had never met a man with that much stamina, not to mention staying power. When we were done, my body felt limp, but wonderfully and thoroughly satisfied. The last thing I remember before I passed out was him getting out of bed and heading for the bathroom.

As I drove home, a conflict raged within me. My morals and my sexuality were having a no-holds-barred, knock-down, drag-out fight about this morning's behavior. My morals were, as they have been of late, dominating. My sexuality's only defense against this breach of moral code was it's been damn near three years, gimme a break. And I had to agree. But my morals would have none of that. I was a hoochie, but a well-fucked hoochie. So I told my morals to kiss any part of my ass that Zavier may have missed.

I went to work Monday morning to begin what I thought was going to be another dull workweek, and was caught off guard when I was met by a dozen long-stem red roses on my desk. The card read:

Thank you for a wonderful evening and the sensational morning!
Sorry that I had to leave so early, but I'd like to make it up to you.
I'll be back in Atlanta on Friday.
Maybe I could see you again.
Zavier

Once I finished reading the card, the office exploded in applause. Everybody knew I hadn't been out since my divorce, so the arrival of roses to them signaled the end of my dry spell. The workweek was still dull and seemed to drag on even more than usual. The difference was me. Now I was filled with excitement and anticipation of the weekend. Each morning my arrival at work was met with flowers and questions. Questions, questions, every day more questions. Who is he? What does he do? Where's he from? All questions that I wouldn't answer, mainly because I couldn't. As much as we talked about me, he was very elusive about everything about himself. At first, it didn't bother me, but day by day, those questions floated endlessly around in my mind. Who is he? What does he do? Where's he from?

On Friday morning I was surprised to see an e-mail from xassante@yahoo.com. Surprised because I had never given him my e-mail address. I did, however, tell him where I worked, so it wouldn't be too big a leap to figure it out. I eagerly opened it and found that he had forwarded me his travel itinerary. He was scheduled to arrive at Hartsfield-Jackson at 7:15 that evening. The e-mail contained no other information, so I assumed that he forwarded it to me so I could meet him.

I arrived at the airport in time to see him looking around as he walked slowly toward the baggage claim area. He smiled when he saw me, as I did when I saw him. "Hello, Carla," he said and kissed me gently on the cheek. "I guess you got my e-mail?"

"I sure did." I was only a little put out by the cheap peck on the cheek, but I tried not to let it show. "I wasn't sure if it meant that you wanted me to meet you or not. So I decided to take a chance and come on down."

"I'm glad that you did, Carla."

We made our way out of the terminal and I started to walk toward the parking deck. "I'm parked in the parking deck. It's not far."

"Well, like I said, I wasn't sure if you were goin' to meet me so I made other arrangements."

"Oh." I know he could hear the disappointment in my voice. And this time I made no attempt to hide it.

"Don't sound like that, Carla. All my arrangements this weekend are built around you. I hope you don't mind, but I've got a plan in progress for the weekend. Come on, your car will be all right in the parking lot for the weekend," he said and took my hand. As we walked hand in hand down the sidewalk, he continued to look around like he was looking for somebody. Suddenly, a black limousine came screeching to a halt in front of us. When the driver jumped out, I saw that easy smile return to his face.

"Zavier! Sorry I'm late. Traffic was a mess coming through downtown," the driver said as he took the bag from Zavier and placed it in the trunk. "Braves game."

"Who they playin'?"

"Mets," the driver replied as he held open the door.

"Damn, sure wish I knew that. I could have gotten here earlier and we could have gone to the game. Do you like baseball, Carla?" he asked once we were in the car.

"It's okay. I mean, I like it, but I just can't watch it on television. Too slow and too much talk. So, you're a Mets fan, huh?"

"Yankee fan, actually."

"Are you from New York?" I asked as my mission to find out something, anything about him, began.

"No."

"Where are you from?"

"From parts unknown." He smiled. "I always wanted to say that. When I was a kid I used to watch a lot of wresting and the masked guys were always from parts unknown."

"Oooo-kay." Angry at his unbelievable evasion.

"I did spend a lot of time in New York growing up, but I'm from Antigua."

"So that's where that sexy accent comes from." Satisfied that I now knew something about him. It wasn't much, but it seemed to make my apprehensiveness subside for the time being. But I knew I had plenty more questions.

We'd been riding for a while when I noticed that we had driven through downtown Atlanta and were heading north on Georgia 400. My apprehension kicked in again. "Where are we goin'?"

"Oh, I'm sorry, Carla. Do you like the mountains?"

"Yes, I love the mountains. Why?"

"I made reservations at a resort in the mountains for the weekend."

"Did you really?"

"Yes, really. I know I should have told you, but I wanted

to surprise you. You know, make up for slipping out on you at the crack of dawn. I hope you don't mind?"

"That's right, you do have a lot to make up for. And no, I don't mind, but that is a little presumptive of you, don't you think? I mean, I could've had plans for the weekend," I said, knowing that I had nothing to do and no place to go. Just another weekend of watching movies I'd rented and eating popcorn.

"When you put it that way, yeah, I guess it was quite presumptive of me. So, let's start over. Carla?"

"Yes, Zavier."

"If you don't have any plans, I'd like to take you away for the weekend."

"No, Zavier," I replied, smiling all over myself, but trying to sound as formal as possible. "I don't have anything in particular planned for the weekend. I think I would enjoy spending the weekend with you." I knew that once we got where we were going that I would call Shika and let her know where I was. She already knew I would be with Zavier. I had to laugh at myself, because this is exactly how it went last weekend. Me hoping that somebody saw me with this man. I had never been one to jump and run off with a man at the drop of a dime, even in my wildest days. I thought that you got more conservative with age, but just the opposite was happening with me. The list of chances I have taken with this man, a man I hardly know, was growing. And I seemed powerless to stop it. And if I choose to be honest with myself, I really didn't want to stop myself.

The weekend was wonderful. Our cabin had a mini-kitchen, which consisted of a small refrigerator and a microwave. It had a cozy little living room with a gaslit fireplace, which, even though it was ninety degrees outside, I felt compelled to light, and a big bedroom with a Jacuzzi. The bedroom had French doors that covered most of the wall and led to a deck that faced the woods. I couldn't have asked for a more romantic setting. When we arrived in the cabin, we opened the doors in the bedroom and we made love. No music, no lights, just the sounds of the great outdoors and the sounds of our passion.

I felt myself drifting off to a place where women go after they've been made love to and satisfied, when I felt Zavier roll out of bed. I lifted my head to ask him where he was going, but my head drifted slowly back to the pillow. I heard water running and shortly after, Zavier returned to the bed. He laid down next to me and put his arms around me. I snuggled closer to him and buried my head in his chest. "I'm goin' to get in the Jacuzzi for a while."

"Wake me up when it's full and maybe I'll join you."

Sometime after that, I couldn't tell you how long, Zavier called me, "Carla!"

I opened my eyes to the sight of him sitting up in the Jacuzzi. He had lit candles all around the tub and had a bottle of wine and two glasses. "When did you have time to do all this?"

"You've been sleeping for almost an hour, Carla."

"And what a good sleep it was," I said and rolled out of the bed. I started to pull the sheet off the bed to cover myself. Part of me still clinging to my inhibitions. But then I thought about the fact that I had just spent hours doing things with and to this man, so there wasn't much point in me covering myself up to walk less than ten feet, only to uncover myself to get into the Jacuzzi with him naked. Still, the sheet got wrapped around me.

"Are you cold?"

"No, just a little shy."

"You want me to cover my eyes?"

"No, just don't laugh."

"At what?"

"My fat," I said and shed the sheet and got into the Jacuzzi. Zavier handed me a glass of wine.

"What fat? Carla, you're beautiful."

"I'm fat," I said, wanting to hear him convince me that I wasn't. And to hear him tell me that I was beautiful again. Which he did.

"You're not fat, Carla. You are the most beautiful woman I've ever met."

I took a sip of my wine. "Stop it. You're making me blush."

"Smile for me, Carla. You have such a beautiful smile. I think I could spend a lifetime looking at you smile."

I smiled. "Thank you," was all the response I could muster.

We spent the rest of the night talking. Both in and out of the Jacuzzi. When the water got cold we refilled it once. The second time we talked the water cold, and got out. We dried ourselves off and I started to get back in the bed, but Zavier walked outside and sat down in one of the chairs on the deck. Naked. This time there was no hesitation, the sheet was wrapped around me like a toga.

We spent over an hour out there talking, and when I said I was cold, we came back inside and laid across the bed and we talked some more. Zavier was the most fascinating man I had ever met. He had done things and been places that I had only dreamt about. He seemed to be able to speak intelligently about anything. He had a philosophy about life that gave me reason to question my world and my very existence. He said, "Life is about risk, Carla. Some people choose to look at the risk in every opportunity, I choose to look at the opportunity in every risk. Remember, you will never steal second base, if you never take your foot off first base. You have to step out there."

Until now, I have always chosen to play it safe. Take the same road that everyone else was taking, instead of the road less traveled. Just like he said, I am one of the people who agonize over the risk in every situation, instead of looking at the opportunity and the gain that may come from it. I silently vowed not to let that happen again.

Late Sunday night, the limo drove us back to the airport. We said our good-byes and then sadly, Zavier was gone. The workweek was the same as the last. Every morning my arrival was met by flowers. The only difference was I gave Zavier my work number, my home number, and my cell phone number. I even gave him Shika's phone number, and felt stupid after I did it. He also gave me his number, which by the way, he never answered, but always managed to call me right back. We talked every day while I was at work and every night, well into the morning hours. One night we even had phone sex. I came so hard to the sound of his voice. On Thursday night, he told me that he would be in town again that weekend, but he would be working and didn't know if he would have very much time to spend with me. I told him not to worry. "The quality, not the quantity of the time was what was important."

Part 5

I got off from work early Friday afternoon. It had been a particularly frustrating week and I just wasn't feelin' bein' there, so I went home. I changed into something more comfortable: big shirt and sweats, and relaxed. As soon as I got comfortable the doorbell rang.

Zavier! was my first thought and I swung the door open. Imagine my disappointment when two white men in cheap suits stood before me. "We are looking for Carla Edwards," one said. He was fat, balding, and spoke with just a bit of an accent. The other one was tall with a thin mustache.

"I'm Carla Edwards."

"We are the police," he said, and both of them quickly held up their wallets. "Can we come in?"

"What's this about?" I asked, scared shitless.

"Do you know this man?" he said, holding up a picture of Zavier.

My first instinct was to say no, I never seen that man in my life and close the door in his face. "Yes."

"Do you know where we can find him?"

"No."

"When was the last time you saw him?"

"Sunday."

"Do you plan to see him anytime soon?"

"What's this about?" I asked.

"He's a very dangerous man, Ms. Edwards. We need to find him. Do you know where he is or where he lives?"

"No. Like I said, I haven't seen him since Sunday."

He handed me a card, "If you should see him again, please call me. Your life and freedom may depend on it." And with that, they turned and walked anyway.

I closed the door as they walked. I leaned against the door to catch my breath. How could I have been so stupid, so naive, so trusting. What had I gotten myself into? Who have I gotten myself involved with? I didn't even know this man and now the police were at my house, telling me that my life and freedom may depend on it.

I finally caught my breath and was able to walk into the living room and sit down on the couch. I didn't sit there long. I needed a drink. And not no damn glass of wine. There was a bottle of Absolut vodka in the refrigerator and that's where I was heading. I got a glass out of the cabinet and went to get some ice. I opened the freezer and the cold air made my head spin as those questions swirled around in my mind. *What had I gotten myself into? Who have I gotten myself involved with? Was he really the wrong man?*

Even though we talked just about the entire weekend at the cabin and every day this week, I still hadn't gotten around to asking any of the questions I had about Zavier. Little things like, who he was, where he lived, what did he do for a living? How about, do you have a criminal record? "Yeah, Carla, why didn't you ask that?" I poured the vodka then searched in vain for something to mix it with. I decided to drink it straight. I made my way back to the couch.

I can't tell you how long I had sat there when the doorbell rang again.

They're back.

"What now?" I said to nobody and went to open the door. I swung the door open. "I told you I don't know anything!" I shouted.

"Anything about what, Carla?" It was Zavier.

I fell into his arms. "Zavier." Then I quickly pushed myself away. "Who are you? What have you gotten me involved in?"

"Hold up a minute, Carla. Slow down," he said calmly. "Can I come in?"

I stepped away from the door and allowed Zavier to come in. I don't know why. I went back to the couch thinking that I should have slammed the door in his face and yelled that I never wanted to see him again. Then I should call the police and tell them that he was just here. After all, my life and freedom depended on it. I turned around to tell him to get out. I looked into Zavier's peaceful eyes.

"What's the matter, Carla?" I heard the soothing sound of his voice. Suddenly I began to think that even if I didn't know him, he did deserve the benefit of doubt. A chance to explain himself. Maybe it was just a misunderstanding and the police, being the assholes that they sometimes are, were just trying to scare me. Which they did.

"Sit down, Carla. Tell me what's wrong."

"The police were just here."

"What did they want?"

"You."

"Me?" Zavier said, his face a contorted mask of disbelief. "What would the police be doing here, looking for me?"

"I don't know, Zavier. I was hoping you would tell me why my life and freedom may depend on me calling them if I saw you."

"Did they really say that?" He smiled playfully.

"Yes. And in case you haven't noticed, this is not funny to me." His nonchalant attitude was starting to get on my nerves. And they were already bad at this point.

"I'm sorry, Carla, but you gotta admit, that does sound a little funny."

If I chose at this point to be honest, it did sound like something out of a movie. "You still haven't answered my question. What have you gotten me involved in?"

"Carla, I swear, I don't know why the police would come here looking for me."

That's when I saw the blood on his jacket. "You're bleeding."

"It's nothing. Just a flesh wound."

"Have you been shot?"

"I told you it's nothing."

"Take off that jacket, let me see." I anxiously began pulling on his jacket.

"Ouch. Take it easy."

"Sorry." Once I got the jacket off, I could see the left side of his shirt was red. He had wrapped his tie around it to stop the bleeding.

"See, it's nothing."

"Nothing!" I said, much louder than I needed to. "Zavier, you've been shot. You have to go to the hospital and get that taken care of."

"No. I'll be all right."

I picked up the phone and began to dial a number.

"Who are you calling?"

"My girlfriend Toshika, she's a nurse."

"No, Carla. I'll be all right. I just came here to clean up a little and then I have to go."

"No, Zavier. I'm going to call Toshika and you're going to get that looked at. And then you're going to tell me what this is all about. And don't give me that shit about you not knowing what this is about." I received no further protest from Zavier.

After asking fifty questions that I couldn't and wouldn't answer, especially not over the phone, *it may have been bugged*, you never know, Toshika came over and dressed Zavier's wound. While she was there, she didn't ask a single question, like how he got shot. She simply cleaned and dressed his wound. Laughing and talking with Zavier as if they were the best of friends. I busied myself by washing the blood out of Zavier's shirt. When she left she tried to reassure me by saying, "It's just a flesh wound, Carla. The bullet just broke the flesh and bounced off his rib cage. He's lost some blood and should rest for a while." Then she turned to Zavier. "You may have some pain for the next day or two, but you should be fine. It was nice meeting you."

"It was nice meeting you, too, Toshika. I know we'll see each other again soon."

When I walked Shika to the door, her entire demeanor changed. "Call me, girl," she whispered.

I returned to the living room just as Zavier was coming toward me putting on his shirt. "I like her. She seems nice."

"Yeah, yeah, she's a wonderful person and a good friend. Now, where do you think you're going?"

"I've imposed on you enough for one day, but there is one more thing you can do for me."

"Not so fast. You need to tell me what is going on."

"Okay, Carla," Zavier said and reclaimed his spot on the couch. "What do you want to know?"

"I don't know, Zavier. Zavier, is that even your real name?"

"That's not fair, Carla. I may not have told you anything about me, but I never lied to you."

"My bad. But under the circumstances I'm sure you'll allow me a little understanding here. So, let me rephrase the question. What do you do when you're traveling, Zavier?"

"I told you, Carla, I do contract work for large corporations."

"Yeah, but what does that mean?"

"You want the truth?"

"Yes."

"The whole story?"

"Yes."

"Nothing but the facts?"

"Yes," I said and started to giggle. "Tell me!"

"I'm the type of guy you call when you want something done that isn't quite legal and maybe just a little dangerous."

"Yeah, but what does that mean? Are you a hit man or something?"

"No. Nothing like that."

"Do you have a gun?"

"In my jacket pocket."

"Have you ever killed anybody?" I asked, surprised at how all this was making me feel. "Never mind, I really don't want to know. Just tell me what you do?"

"I'm more like an industrial spy, for lack of a better word, but I do more than that. In this particular case I was just the go-between. I was supposed to exchange some money for a CD."

"But something went wrong, didn't it?"

"You could say that. After we made the exchange another guy came out of nowhere. I should have been more careful, brought along somebody to back me up. It was supposed to be an easy exchange. Clean and simple. But I was distracted, thinking about seeing you again."

"Me?"

"Yes, you." Zavier smiled. "They shot me and took the CD. I guess they thought I was dead. I got lucky."

"You call being shot and left for dead lucky?"

"Yes, considering that they could have emptied the clip in me to make sure I was dead."

"What are you going to do now?"

"I gotta get that CD back."

"How are you going to do that?"

"Find the guys that stole it."

"Toshika says that you lost some blood and that you need to rest."

Zavier got up and put on his jacket. "I'm fine, really."

"You said there was something I could do for you?"

"I need a car." *OH HELL TO THE NO!* "Would you drive me to the airport so I can rent one?" Zavier said and had to steady himself.

I felt relieved, "You're in no condition to drive yourself." Then suddenly I went stupid. "I could drive you where you need to go."

"No, Carla, I'm going to look for the men who shot me. I don't want you involved in this anymore than you already are."

"No, Zavier. It's the least I could do. Since you say it was my fault you got careless."

"I can't let you do this. It's too dangerous."

"What was that you said? Life is about risk. Some people choose to look at the risk in every opportunity; I choose to look at the opportunity in every risk. So, I think there's a certain logic in me taking you where you need to go."

"There's no logic in that at all. I get paid to take the risk. There is absolutely no reason for you to do this."

"Except one."

"What's that?"

"You need me. So let's stop wasting time and let's go." I got no more argument from Zavier.

Part 6

"Where are we goin'?" I asked Zavier as we got in my car and left my house.

"Take I-twenty to Gresham Road and go south."

So now here I am, driving down I-20 taking this man who knows where, to get deeper involved in who knows what. And I had to ask myself why? Forget that line I gave him about there being a certain logic in what I was doing. Zavier was right, there was no logic in it at all. Then why? Why was I doing it? If I choose to be honest with myself, if not Zavier, there may not have been any logic, but it was definitely a certain degree of excitement in effect in what I was doing. You know, the mysterious man with a gun in his pocket. Shika having to rush over to tend to his gunshot wound. And now, we were on our way to find his attackers. Definitely more exciting than the evening I was planning, and maybe . . . just maybe, I was little turned on by the whole thing. Think about it. Me, Miss Play-It-Safe Carla, driving this very sexy man, who has made such passionate love to me; a spy. I felt like a Bond girl in one of the 007 movies. Wow! That's all I could say is, "Wow!"

"Did you say something, Carla?"

"No, just thinking out loud."

"If you had good sense, you'd be thinking about driving me to the airport to rent a car and going home. Not driving me to the Libra Ballroom."

"Libra Ballroom. Is that where we're going?"

"Yes. You know the place?"

"Yes. Back in the day, we used to hang out there."

We pulled into the parking lot at the Libra. I remember this being some other club back then. The parking lot was full. Security walked up to the car waving a flashlight. "Sorry miss, there's no place else to park, you have to park across the street," he said.

"You don't have a parking space for me, Ben?"

"Zavier!" he yelled at the top of his lungs. "Park in the handicapped space. Bull's already gone for the night."

"Thanks, Ben."

I backed up and parked as instructed, in the handicapped space. "I take it you come here often?"

"Once or twice, maybe."

"You never did say why we were coming here?"

"Maybe I just needed a drink."

"Is everything a secret with you?"

"There's somebody here I need to talk to. Besides, I need a drink. Come on."

We went inside the club and Zavier got the same reception. One of the waitresses hugged Zavier, and rolled her eyes at me. No respect, the bitch.

Then, "Zavier!" another man yelled over the music.

"Till!" Zavier yelled just as loud. The two men embraced as men do now days. "Till, this is my very good friend Carla Edwards. Carla, this is Gary Tilly."

"How you doing," he said very formally. "Come here, Zavier. Let me holla at ya a minute."

"Excuse me, Carla. I'll be right back." Zavier threw his arm around him and they walked away.

I was walking around the club checking things out, when a man said, "Are you enjoying yourself?"

"I just got here."

"This your first time here?"

"Yes, it is. I'm here with a friend."

"Well, if you need anything or you have a problem, just let me know. Enjoy your evening."

"I'll be sure to do that." I turned to say thank you, but when I did he was gone.

Not too long after that, Zavier walked up behind me. "Sorry about that."

"That's okay. I don't think your friend likes me."

"Who—Tilly?" Zavier frowned. "Don't let that bother you, Tilly loves women, he just doesn't trust them. Some of y'all got too much game for his taste. He believes that is one of life's traps. He's good people, though. One of the best I know. He's my—"

"Zavier!" another man yelled over the music. It was starting to get old.

"Keys!" the man walked up to us. It was the same man that I was just talking to. "How you doin'. Got a good crowd tonight."

"Yeah, they're coming on in," Keys, *I guess that's his name*, said and looked over at the bar. "Now they need to start drinkin'."

"We need to talk," Zavier said to him. He led us to a table in the back of the club and we sat down.

The waitress with the rolling eyes came up to the table and placed a drink in front of Zavier. "Can I get you something?" She didn't say it, but I heard *bitch* loud and clear.

"Vodka collins." I didn't say it, but *bitch* came through

loud and clear. As she went to get my drink, both men looked at one another and smiled.

"Dwight, this is Carla Edwards. Carla, this is my brother, Dwight Keys."

He extended his hand. "Call me Keys. You know, like door keys," he laughed. "Well, it's very nice to meet you, Carla. Like I said, if you need anything, or you have a problem, just let me know. Food, drink, anything in the house is yours, and your money is no good here." Then he kissed my hand.

"Well, thank you."

"Like I said," returning his kiss with a smile, as the waitress returned with my drink, "I'll be sure to do that."

"Enough of this already," Zavier said. "I need to talk to you."

"Don't hate," Keys replied.

"I got shot today." Zavier had his attention now.

"The Lithuanians you were meeting?" That raised an eyebrow. The accent?

"Yeah. I made the exchange with fat boy, then the quiet man shot me. They took the package and the money, and left me for dead."

"I told you to let me come back you up. I'll get my gun."

"No. You got a club to run."

"Tilly can run things."

"No, Dwight. I got this."

"You got this. That's how you got yourself shot. I'm coming with you."

"No. I just need you to put the word out that I'm looking for them."

"What they look like?"

"Two white men. Fat boy had a blue suit, white shirt, and a tie that looked like it was a holdover from the seventies.

The quiet man was dressed the same only his suit was black."

"Zavier," I said, and both men looked at me like they were shocked that I could talk. "That sounds like the men that came to my house looking for you." Zavier looked at me strangely. "The police."

"Those weren't cops," Zavier said.

"Hold up," Keys said. "That doesn't make any sense. Why would they come to her house if they already had the package and the money?"

"I don't know."

"You tell Cindy yet?"

"No. I was going to talk to her next. There's something that she's not telling me."

"I never did quite trust her," Keys said.

"Neither do I, but she pays good, up front and in cash. I might need you and Tilly to back me up later."

"Now you're talking like you got some sense."

Zavier got up and drained his glass. I finished mine quickly as I could and followed Zavier out the door. Once we got to my car Zavier turned to me. "Maybe you should stay here, Carla."

"No," was all I said and got in the car.

"Up till now I thought you had good sense."

I had to smile. "Up till now, I thought so, too."

Zavier had me drive him downtown to one of the many new condos they had built not far from Centennial Olympic Park. "So that's your brother?"

"Him and Tilly both."

"Was papa a rolling stone?"

"Huh?" I could tell he was distracted.

"None of you have the same last name."

"Life made us brothers, not birthright. There's a bond between the three of us that will never be broken. Blood is thicker than water, but life's bonds are stronger than both of them."

"So, who is this Cindy?"

"She's my contact." He didn't offer any other explanation. I had never seen him look so serious. Gone was that easy smile that I've come to know. I parked the car and Zavier got out. He walked fast and I followed behind him. When we got to what I guess was her apartment, Zavier knocked on the door but there was no answer. He tried the doorknob, it wasn't locked. "Wait here." Zavier took the gun out of his pocket. I felt my heart pounding in my chest. He pushed the door open with the barrel of his gun and went inside slowly.

After a while, my curiosity got the better of me and I went in. The place looked like it had been hit by a tornado. As I walked further into the apartment, I saw Zavier crouched behind the couch. "Is she here?" I asked as I walked closer to him.

"Not anymore."

"Oh my God!"

"Shhh, be quiet." Zavier was kneeling beside her body. He reached down and closed her eyes. There was blood everywhere. Her neck was slit from ear to ear. I felt my stomach and my knees getting weak. I reached out to steady myself. "Don't touch anything," he said quietly and grabbed my hand. "Let's get out of here. She's not gonna be any help to us now. Rest in peace, Cindy."

We walked quickly out of the apartment. Zavier wiped the doorknob and closed the door. Once we were in the car and away, Zavier said, "This doesn't make any sense. If they got the money and the CD, why would they be looking for me and why would they kill her and search her apartment?"

"I have no clue," I replied. Because I didn't. Seeing Cindy's body let me know that I was in way over my head.

Zavier was silent for a while and then he said, "Her body was still warm, they couldn't have been gone long. Take me to the Ritz. Fast."

I drove as fast as I could to the Ritz Carlton in Buckhead. We went to the same room that he had taken me to that very first night. "Wait here. I mean it this time, Carla." Once again Zavier removed his gun and went in. I peeked in behind him. The room appeared to be empty, but it was obvious that the Lithuanians had been there and searched the room.

"Damn!" I heard Zavier say. "You can come in now, Carla." I came inside to find Zavier holding up a suit with the sleeves torn out of it. "I really liked this suit."

"What are you going to do now?" I asked.

"I don't know. They're looking for something or they'd be gone by now," he said and threw the suit down. "Shit!" then he turned to me. "Come on. I'm taking you home. I want you to get some things together and go stay with a friend or something. I'll figure out what to do once you're safe."

This time he got no argument from me. I was starting to get a little scared. It's funny how fear brings back your common sense with a quickness.

As we walked through the hotel lobby, I glanced at the bar and there they were. They were sitting at the bar having a drink and talking. "Zavier, that's them."

"Who?"

"The men that came to my house."

"What?"

"The Lithuanians!" I said, louder than I needed to.

"Where?"

"Over there in the bar," I said and pointed them out to him.

Zavier said nothing. His eyes narrowed and he went in the bar. I followed him in. Why, I don't know. He walked right up to the table and without a word took out his gun and shot both of them twice in the head.

There were people running and screaming everywhere.

"Call security!" I heard somebody say.

"Call the police!" I heard a woman yell as she ran past me. I got to Zavier as he was going through the pockets of the two dead Lithuanians. He pulled what looked like a CD out of the fat one's pocket. There was a metal briefcase under the table, Zavier picked it up and turned around.

"Take this," he said handing me the case.

"What's in it?"

"Half a million dollars."

"Whaat?"

"Take it and get out of here, now."

"What about you?"

"Don't worry about me. You just get out of here. I'll get with you later. Now go."

"But—"

"GO!"

I walked out of the bar as fast as I could, and once I was out I began to run with the rest of the crowd. I got to my car and I began to cry. My heart was once again pounding in my chest and my hands were shaking, but I made it home in one piece. I ran inside and locked the door behind me. I went in the dining room and got a chair. Clutching the briefcase under my arm, I dragged a chair into the bedroom. The Lithuanians were dead, and even though I was pretty sure that nobody would be coming after me, I locked the bedroom door and hooked the chair under the knob. I sat there in darkness for hours with the case in front of me.

Still crying, still shaking like a leaf, until I cried myself to sleep.

When I woke up the next morning, I turned on the television and turned to the morning news. I expected there to be news about a shooting at the Ritz, but there was nothing. I logged on to ajc.com, the Internet site for our local paper. Nothing.

I looked at the case still on my bed. I sat down and looked at it for who knows how long. Later that night I finally got up the courage to open it. I flipped the latches slowly and carefully, halfway expecting it to explode or gas to escape from it. But nothing happened. I opened it slowly. "Oh my, God."

I had never seen a half a million dollars in cash before, so I counted it. There were fifty bundles of ten thousand dollars each. I thought about what Zavier said about risk and opportunity. "Life is about risk, Carla. Some people choose to look at the risk in every opportunity; I choose to look at the opportunity in every risk."

I don't know if Zavier was alive or dead, in jail or on the run for murder. I looked at the briefcase again, stared at it, opened it up and looked at the money. This is what he meant by opportunity in every risk. I had taken a risk big-time by going with him. Now I was sitting alone on my bed with half a million dollars in front of me.

Now I had to ask myself the question, one more time.

Was Xavier Assante the wrong man?

I had half a million reasons to believe that he wasn't.